SALINA PUBLIC LIBRARY
1701 9100 376 438 1

D1156875

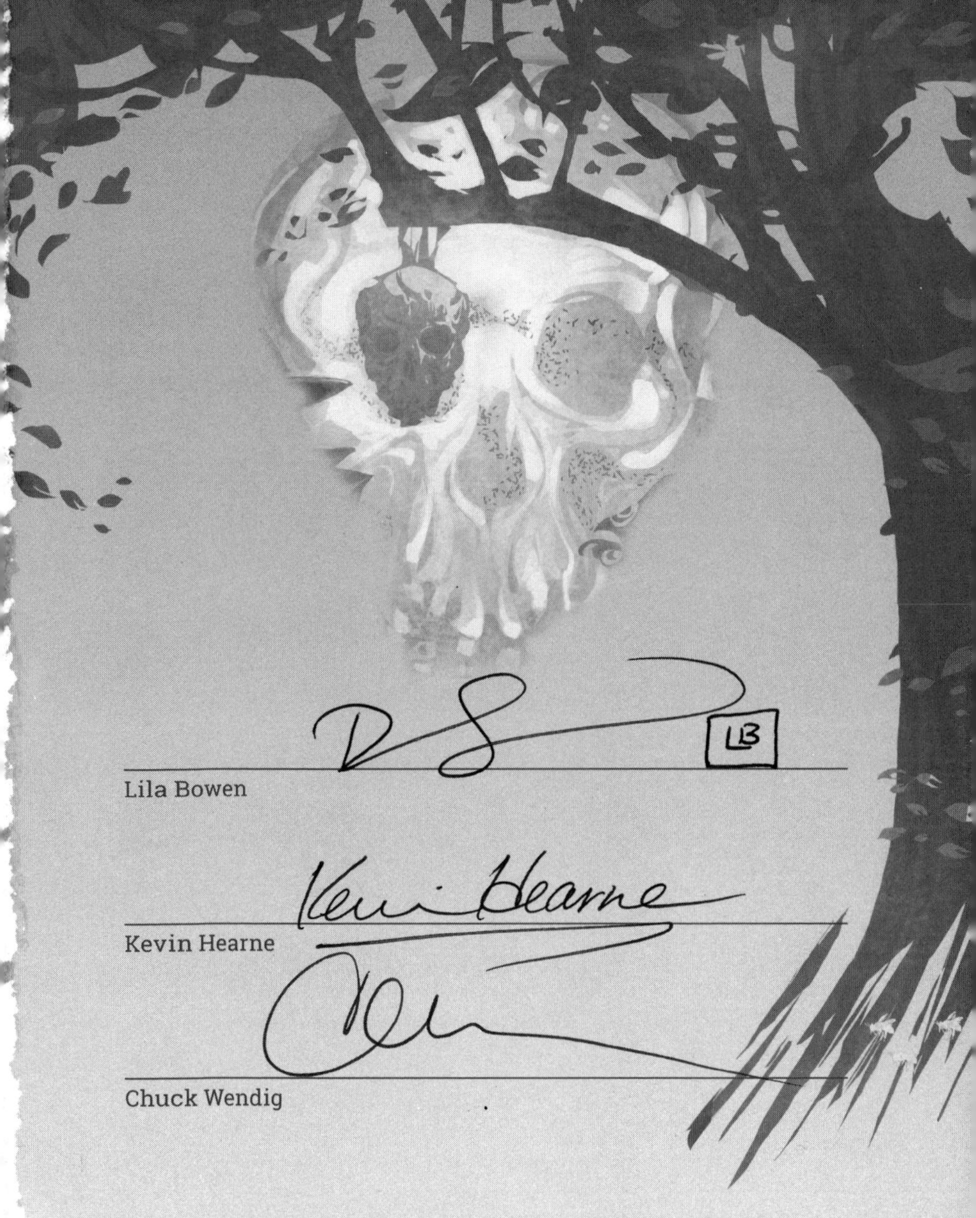

Lila Bowen

Kevin Hearne

Chuck Wendig

This special signed edition is limited to
1500 numbered copies and 52 lettered copies.

This is copy 1335.

# DEATH & HONEY

**Kevin Hearne**
**Lila Bowen**
**Chuck Wendig**

Subterranean Press 2019

**First Edition**

**ISBN**
978-1-59606-914-5

Subterranean Press
PO Box 190106
Burton, MI 48519

**subterraneanpress.com**

Manufactured in the United States of America

# CONTENTS

# THE BUZZ KILL

AN OBERON'S MEATY MYSTERY

Kevin Hearne

## CHAPTER 1:

# BEE ALERT

The true danger of trotting around Tasmania with a Druid is that there are so many interesting animals to bark at. It's difficult to stay focused, honestly, because in the course of chasing a wombat, for example, you might startle a tiger quoll or a barred bandicoot. Or you might run into a bunch of wallabies and they're loads of fun. Nothing on the island is really ready for me and Starbuck, however, and Atticus said it's not fair, so we don't hunt them seriously. It's all just exercise for me and my Boston terrier buddy.

Atticus has been healing Tasmanian devils every day for like five trillion days, I don't know, but it seems like a long time and it's not very interesting even if it's super important, so Starbuck and I have to entertain ourselves somehow since we don't have cable in the wild and can't watch cooking shows anymore. Atticus says we can play around as we like while he's busy healing as long as we follow the rules:

1) Stay in mental shouting range

2) Don't kill anything

3) Don't dump on anyone's lawn but go ahead on golf courses because they're not technically lawns and maybe a rich guy will step in it

4) Stay away from people and cars

Sometimes that last one is tough when we are near a city. Right now we're near one called Launceston, and you never know when you'll run into hikers who immediately cluck their tongues and loudly condemn Atticus for letting us run around off the leash. Not that they know him. They just say things like "Some idiot's dogs are loose," or "I wish people would take better care of their pets," or "Bloody hell, that's a big dog!"

Comments like that get my hackles up sometimes and I get tempted to go bark at them and tell them their socks are stupid or something else really damaging to human psyches, but Atticus said they might have pepper spray or cauliflower or other horrible weapons that could hurt us and we should just stay away no matter what they say—especially if they offer us food. "That's going to be a trap every time," he warned us.

Ha! He didn't need to tell *me*. I'm no puppy meeting his first cat! Besides, they usually offer things like dry dog biscuits and I have no interest in those. Atticus feeds us really well and someone would need to produce a saucier capable of whipping up some kind of hipster gravy before I'd even consider coming over for a look. And a sniff!

Mmm. *Rosemary sausage gravy.* That's the stuff. Uh...what was I talking about?

Oh yeah! The danger of chasing things in Tasmania. Once Atticus found a den of devils to heal outside of Launceston, he let us go explore and we soon found a butterfly called a Tasmanian hairstreak, a brown-and-yellow fellow we'd seen before, and we followed him for a bit and snapped in the air beneath his wings. Chasing butterflies is kind of like playing with a balloon, except you never know where they're going to land. But they have a thing for flowers the way we hounds have a thing for asses. They can smell things other creatures can't.

<Hey! Flying noise thing!> Starbuck said, distracting me from the hairstreak.

<What noise? Where?> I hoped it wasn't a mean old wasp. But as soon as I asked, I had my answer as the buzz of wings reached my ears and I found the source: It was a honeybee, flitting among the white-petaled flowers of a leatherwood tree.

<That's a bee,> I told Starbuck, who was much better now with his language but still needed plenty of help. <That sound it makes is a buzz.>

<Bee is food?> he asked.

<No, but they make food. Their vomit is called honey and it's very sweet. Humans love it. They put it in their tea and on their toast and all kinds of stuff.>

<Vomit is food?>

<Not usually. Bee vomit is the exception to the rule. It is without doubt the best-selling vomit in the world. There's also a market for whale vomit, which humans call ambergris, but it's not as popular as honey.>

<Where is honey?>

<Almost everywhere. You can find it in almost any store.>

<No. This bee. Honey from this bee.>

<Oh! Well, all the honey is going to be in the beehive where she lives. They take the nectar from these flowers back to the hive and then they convert it into honeycomb.>

<I want to see hive,> Starbuck said. <Can we follow bee?>

<Sure.>

It was nice to have a purpose to the day's wanderings. I had learned all about bees from a nature documentary plus some additional things Atticus told me, and I was happy to tell Starbuck all about them as we waited for the honeybee to load up on nectar before heading back to the hive.

Eventually, her legs were weighted down with a payload of vomit catalysts, and we followed her, crashing through underbrush for probably half a mile or something. I'm not sure, honestly, but I called out mentally to my Druid to make sure we weren't breaking rule #1.

<Hey, Atticus, can you still hear me?>

*Sure can, buddy,* his voice replied in my head, and I was still getting used to the fact that it had an Irish accent now. He'd been depressed for a while when we got here and then kinda snapped out of it when he realized that he no longer had to pretend to be anything but himself, that he could just serve Gaia from now on as the Irish lad he was. No gods were after him and he didn't owe anyone any favors after this big fight he called Ragnarok. He had lost his right arm in that fight and said he was lucky that was all he lost, and the considerable upside was that he was free for the first time in eons, or epochs, or something like that. *What are you up to?* he asked.

<We are following a bee because Starbuck wants to see a hive.>

*Okay, but try not to disturb it. It might be a commercial hive. Launceston is one of the hubs of the Tasmanian honey industry.*

<Oh yeah. Well, no matter. It'll be a hive and I'll warn him to keep his distance.>

We kept following the bee and came to an abrupt halt when she flew up a tree where a feral hive was wedged between the trunk and a lower branch. I only noted that briefly, however, as something else grabbed our attention.

<Bad smell,> Starbuck noted.

<Bad news,> I added. At the base of the bee's tree, sprawled on the ground face up, was a dead human white man. His face was swollen and red with bee stings, and he hadn't been dead all that long. I'm not one of those fancy doctors they bring in on all the crime shows to talk about morbidity and body temperature and DNA evidence, but I'm a hound who can smell blood. That man had been bleeding quite a bit. There was a pool of it underneath him.

His hands and forearms had pale, waxy skin and his hair was thick, dark, and styled somewhat wavy and poufy. He had been fond of product, I suppose. He had a rugby shirt on, blue jeans, and some chunky tan-colored hiking boots, all of which made it difficult to see where he'd been injured, but my guess was it had been in the back and somehow he wound up falling on top of it.

So, he'd been perforated by bullets or ventilated with a knife and then the bees stung him. Or maybe the bees stung him first and then someone ventilated him for making the bees mad. Whatever it was, he had been bleeding and stung at nearly the same time. Hard to tell which killed him, but the bees ultimately didn't matter. All that blood meant someone had murdered the dude, because bee stings don't cause people to bleed out.

<Hey Atticus, we haven't fought crime in a while. Want to catch some bad guys?>

*Well, uh, is this a hypothetical question in which you're suggesting we search for a crime scene and try to help the police?*

<No need to search for a crime scene. We've already found one.>

*Oh, bollocks. I was afraid you were going to say that. What's the crime?*

<We have ourselves a hot 'n' fresh murder! We can smell the mineral content of the dude's blood. And the load he dumped in his underwear.>

*Wait, so the murderer might still be nearby? Oberon, be careful!*

We heard some rustling in the bushes off to our left. Starbuck turned his head, his bat-like ears on alert, and growled.

<Something is coming,> he said.

I gave a warning woof but the rustling only grew louder. Whatever was causing it wasn't easily scared off.

<You might want to get over here, Atticus.>

*Start barking now and don't stop until I get there,* he said.

## CHAPTER 2:

# NOW I'M A BEE LEAVER

**The** thing making all the noise turned out to be a woman. She sounded like a happy person and probably was one until she came out of the bushes and saw us. She heard us barking and said, "Is that a puppy?"

I am not a puppy and neither is Starbuck. She realized her error when she emerged from the undergrowth and laid eyes on us. She was a middle-aged white lady with yellow hair underneath a wide bonnet thing wrapped in flowers and feathers. She had khaki pants tucked into knee-high brown leather boots that looked and smelled new. The rest of her smelled like she'd sprayed most of a perfume bottle on herself before she went outside. Her right hand carried a cell phone and her left carried a water bottle, and she had a backpack on that looked full of stuff.

Her pleasant smile melted away and her eyes widened in shock when she focused on me. "Gah! You're bloody huge!" Her gaze then shifted to the dead guy underneath the leatherwood tree, and her jaw dropped open and a small whine leaked out as she processed what she was seeing. Then she took a deep breath and belted out an impressive scream, supporting well from the diaphragm like a trained singer. She held it for three years or so before turning and diving back into the bushes.

We were still barking like Atticus told us to but he heard the scream too.

*Oberon, who is that?*

<Some lady, Atticus! She didn't give us her name. She saw us standing here near the body and all the bees and then she just screamed and left in a hurry. Didn't ask us to explain ourselves or even tell us that we are very good boys, which is a pretty huge oversight. She must be really upset.>

*Well, the good news is that she'll probably call the police. The bad news is she'll probably call the police.*

<Yeah, she had a cell phone. Why is it bad news? Don't we need police for justice? And beef?>

*Police occasionally serve justice, yes. But sometimes what they do is an injustice.*

<Doing anything without serving beef is an injustice.>

*If you're trying to be subtle about being fed soon, you're failing.*

<If you feed me, though, wouldn't that be succeeding?>

*Not at being subtle.*

<Irish wolfhounds are not built for subtlety, Atticus. If you wanted a subtle hound, you should have gotten a pug. They are not hounds so much as mobile loaves of snoring bread with a soft fur coat.>

We heard Atticus coming a few weeks before he arrived.

*Okay, you can stop barking,* he said in our heads. Then he saw the dead guy and said, "Oh, shit," out loud.

<See? Look at all that blood. We need the police.>

"Yes, the police need to get involved. But I don't want to get involved, and now I don't have a choice."

<Why not?>

"Because that woman saw you. She will describe an Irish wolfhound and a Boston terrier standing next to the body. The police will trace you to me and then I'll be a suspect—or at least questioned as to why I didn't report the murder. So, now I have to report it."

He pulled out his cell phone and dialed 000, which is easier to remember than 90210 or whatever the emergency number is in the US. "And they're going to be asking questions and my current passport is American, so I have to return to that accent now." He grimaced as a tinny voice picked up the phone and asked him what his emergency was.

"Yes, hello? I need to report a murder."

<Oh, that's perfect, Atticus! Cue the opening titles and theme music! Another episode of *Oberon's Meaty Mysteries* begins!>

He switched back to mental conversation with me as he spoke out loud into his phone.

*Give me a minute here, Oberon.* He gave his name as Connor Molloy, his best guess at the location, and no, he hadn't touched the body, and yes, he'd wait nearby until officers arrived. Once he hung up and pocketed his phone, he looked at the body again.

"Did you go anywhere near him? Sniff him up close, step in any of that blood?"

<No.>

"Starbuck? What about you?"

<No squirrel!> Starbuck replied.

"Good. I need you both to stay away from him. However, before the police arrive, I think it would be wise to see if we can figure out how he got here. Which way did the woman come from?"

I lifted a paw and pointed across from us. <From over there. She left the same way.>

"She was alone?"

<Yes. She had a water bottle and a phone.>

"Any blood on her?"

<No. She kinda smelled like chemical flowers. Sneezy perfume.>

"Okay. Without getting closer to the body, and trying not to disturb the ground at all, can the two of you use your noses and pick up his path to that tree? If you find it, then I want you to carefully follow it backwards, looking down to make sure you do not put your paws in any blood or footprints that might help the police."

<We can do that!>

<Yes food!> Starbuck added. We put our noses to the ground and started snuffling but maybe holding back just a little bit. Starbuck found the trail before I did.

<Blood here!> he said. <Goes this way.>

<Careful not to step in it,> I reminded him. I picked up the scent soon afterward and we carefully followed it back about thirty thousand foot-yards, or meters, or whatever, until there was no more. <Blood ends here. Or starts here,> I said.

Atticus caught up and looked down at the earth, covered in grasses in between the bushes and mashed flat by the dead guy's passage. There was a small collection of blood droplets.

"Weird. That looks like he was shot rather than stabbed."

<How do you know?>

"If he'd been stabbed, there would have been more blood in a kind of streaky pattern, dropping from the blade as the knife was yanked out. But this is a tight cluster, just drips from a puncture wound."

<People get shot all the time in the United States, though. Are you saying it's weird because people in Tasmania never shoot other people?>

"No, it's weird because this happened recently and we should have heard the gunshot. Except we didn't." Atticus squatted down on his haunches to have a closer look at the blood, and as he did, something whistled overhead and thunked into a tree. It was an arrow, planted right behind where he'd been standing.

*Back the way we came!* Atticus shouted in our heads as he rolled and scrambled to his feet, keeping low. Starbuck and I scampered back the five hundred kilo-furlongs or whatever to where the body was.

"The police are on their way!" Atticus shouted behind us. "I've already called them!"

<Call him a name, Atticus,> I said. <We need some hard-boiled grit.>

*How do you know it's a* he, *Oberon? Did you smell something?*

<No, it's just more likely. Because of those math things. Pixie sticks.>

*Statistics?*

<Right, that's what I said. Come on, call him a name.>

"You murdering bastard!" Atticus shouted.

<Oh, that was great! You deserve a snack.> Starbuck got inspired to join in.

<Cat person!> He barked and quivered with rage. <Super bad cat person!> He looked over at me, tongue hanging out and smiling. <Good yell? Snack for me too?>

<Oh, yes, you definitely deserve a snack. And so do I. We are very good boys.>

<Yes food!>

*Quiet now. See if you can hear him or her moving out there. Keep some tree trunks between you and that direction.*

Starbuck's ears perked up and pointed the way we came. His hearing was a little bit better than mine; his breed was supposed to be able to hear mice and voles and small critters patter around.

<Soft leaf crunch sounds,> he said. <Human foots. Feets? Boots.>

*Which way are they moving? Can you tell?* Atticus asked.

<Fast boot sounds now. Going away.>

*You're sure?*

<Yes. Gone now.>

Atticus let out a breath he'd been holding. *Good. I don't suppose either of you caught a whiff of whoever that might have been?*

<I only smelled the dead guy on the trail,> I said, and looked back toward the body. <But hey, Atticus, if that guy got shot in the back with an arrow, why'd he fall on it? Wouldn't it be poking up through his chest or something if he had?>

*Maybe. Or the shaft broke off and is trapped underneath him. Or…somebody pulled it out. That would explain the huge pool of blood underneath him. The barbs would have torn through quite a bit of tissue as the arrow was removed, and if that's what happened, I'm sure it wasn't removed gently.*

If someone had pulled out the arrow…it was probably right near that tree. So, somewhere around it we should pick up somebody's scent besides the dead guy's.

<Atticus, I know we can't get too close, but what if we keep our distance and go around the guy, sniffing for other people?>

*That would be fine.* Starbuck went clockwise, which means he circled around to the right, and I went counterclockwise, which is around to the left, because we have to counter this narrative that clocks are wise. People say they tell time, but they've never given me the time of day.

I found a different human scent than the dead guy's after the length of about six stretched-out wombats.

<Hey, Atticus. I think I found something. Starbuck, come over here—but go around, we can't go near that body. See if you smell what I smell. Body odor, sweaty leather, cigarette smoke, maybe some terrible vegetables.>

The Boston circled around and snuffled at the grass where I indicated.

<Yes food. Man smell.>

*Can you tell if it goes toward the body? Or comes from it, I guess?*

I followed the scent a few short steps toward the body. <It does.>

*All right, can you follow it away from here?*

I turned around with Starbuck and we followed the scent away and found where it turned to cross our own path. We'd missed it earlier because we were chasing the bee and not sniffing around.

<Yeah, we got it,> I said. Starbuck froze and turned his head to look behind us, his ears pointed up.

<Noises. People come.>

*That's probably the police. Okay, we'll track that scent later. While the police are here, I need you to respond to my verbal commands exactly. Come on over here and sit down next to me and don't move unless I say.*

"Mr. Molloy?" a woman's voice called.

"Over here," Atticus responded, and there was some back-and-forth like that until two police officers emerged from the undergrowth near where the perfumed lady had been. They had their guns drawn, though they were pointed down, and Atticus raised his single hand.

"Hello. I am friendly and unarmed," he said. "Same with my dogs."

The officers looked a bit different from the ones I'm used to seeing in the United States. They had dark ball caps on with a little checkerboard pattern running along the base of it. Where a team logo would be, they had a badge: a shiny circle with a golden lion in it and on top of that, a red crown.

They wore bulky yellow-ish vests over their shirts with a bunch of lumpy pockets full of stuff and things, but I knew they wouldn't have any meats in those pockets, so I didn't pay close attention.

One of them was a slim but fit woman with cool brown skin and lips a bit darker than the rest. She wore a thingy under her cap that covered up her ears and hair and her neck as well, disappearing underneath her shirt. I think Atticus mentioned one time that humans who did that practiced a certain faith and it was a sign of devotion to their god. Anyway, she was the boss. On her vest she had a little vertical banner in the center with three chevrons, and I knew what that meant from movies: she was a sergeant.

"That's good to hear," she said. "Constable Fosse is going to confirm that, if you don't mind. Please remain still and allow him to pat you down."

"Sure. You'll find all my stuff in my left pocket, since I have only the one arm," Atticus said.

"Sir, will your dogs remain still while I approach?" This was from Constable Fosse, who holstered his gun and shot a glance at me, uncertain if he could take me or not. Probably not, unless I was napping. He was a sizeable white man, much taller than the sergeant, and while my eyes are not the best at identifying reds, I think his skin must have been pretty pink or flushed or something since it appeared in those kinds of grays in my vision. He had enough muscles that I think he could qualify as "swole," in the parlance of gym bros.

"They will," Atticus assured him.

"They should be on a leash."

"Ah. Are we still inside city limits here?"

"Yes. Just barely. The ordinance applies."

"Fair enough. Despite the absence of a leash, Constable, they won't bother you. They're very good dogs." Mentally, Atticus added to us, *Please don't move.*

<We won't. We are very good dogs. Who deserve a water buffalo for all this public service we're doing.>

Constable Fosse approached while the sergeant remained where she was, watching. I understood what this was: they had to make sure Atticus wasn't a threat before anything else. They were following procedure. The constable patted him down and found that he had three things in his left pocket.

"What's in your pocket, sir?"

"My cell phone, my passport, and a bag of snacks for the hounds." Atticus had the rest of his stuff in a pack he'd left by the Tasmanian devil den.

"Would you remind removing them, slowly?"

"Sure."

Atticus pulled them out and offered them to the constable, but he said to hold on to them while he continued. Once he was satisfied that Atticus wasn't carrying any weapons, he nodded to the sergeant and she put away her gun. She then strode forward.

"Thanks for your cooperation. I'm Sergeant Naseer. May I see your passport?"

Atticus handed it to her and she flipped it to the page with his picture on it, comparing the photo to his face. "American, eh? Is this address current?"

"It is." Atticus still technically owned his cabin in Oregon, even though he'd put it up for sale.

"How long have you been in Tasmania?"

"About six weeks." I didn't know if that was right, because I'm pretty bad with time, but she was flipping through stamps in his passport to confirm the date of entry. I wasn't worried because I knew Granuaile had gotten his passport prepped for him. She snuck in all invisible to the Melbourne airport where the customs officers were, stamped his passport like he'd flown in on an airplane, then returned it to Atticus so he'd have it for situations like this. The police would never figure out that he was there illegally unless they searched for his name on flight manifests and never found it.

"What's your business here?"

"I'm a biologist working on saving the Tasmanian devils." I was impressed. He was telling the truth except for leaving out that he was a Druid. He gestured with his hand behind us, and the bag of snacks rustled with a delicious noise. "I was working with a den back there when I heard a woman scream. I followed the noise and found him."

Constable Fosse stepped a bit toward the body, paying attention to it for the first time, but the sergeant kept her eyes on Atticus.

"You didn't find the woman?"

"No. I stopped here and called it in."

"So it's possible there's a woman out here in trouble?"

"It's possible. I haven't heard anything since the one scream, and that was before I made the call. I kind of assumed she would have called this in too."

"Have you touched the body? Or have your dogs?"

"No. But the dogs went that way, sniffing something—I think it was the trail of this guy—and somebody took a shot at us."

"A shot? What kind?"

"An arrow. We haven't confirmed it, but the arrow is probably still stuck in the tree. We ran back here and yelled that the police were on the way. Nobody chased us."

"Right. Constable Fosse, please call the inspector and the forensic team." She handed Atticus his passport back. He put that and his cell phone back in his pocket, but then used his teeth to open the bag of snacks and pulled out a couple for me and Starbuck. He tossed them in the air, we caught them neatly, and then he resealed the bag and put it back in his pocket. "Will you show me where this arrow is, Mr. Molloy?"

"Certainly." He turned to me and Starbuck and said, "On my heels, guys." We followed him as he led us back to where the arrow was embedded in the tree.

"These really are very good dogs," she remarked, and I wagged my tail for her.

"They are indeed. Here we are. I was examining that splotch of blood there—I think it might be where the victim was shot—and as I bent down, this arrow thudded into the trunk. Someone was out there. Maybe still is."

"Right." Sergeant Naseer pressed a thumb to her radio thingy and asked for more officers on scene to search for "the perp and a possible second victim."

I hadn't thought about that possibility. Whoever had shot at us might have easily shot at that screaming lady, too. After she ran away, we didn't hear her scream again. She might be lying dead in the forest, her bonnet all ruined, her face fixed in a permanent expression of horror. But we couldn't go look for her ourselves at the moment. We had to wait for the inspector to arrive and inspect things and ask Atticus a lot more questions.

"Let's head back and not give anyone another shot at you," the sergeant said, and Atticus did not tell her that Starbuck had heard someone running away out there. We were probably safe to stay, but he walked back toward the body.

"Any idea of how long you'll need me?"

"That's up to the inspector. She'll be by within thirty minutes, and I'm sure she'll have more questions for you."

I'm not sure if it was thirty minutes, but a whole lot more humans showed up after a while wearing those same uniforms and checkered ball caps with the lion badge. One of them was a woman with skin a bit darker brown than the sergeant's and she had a vertical bar on her vest with three of those lion badges on it. I figured three lions must have been more important than three chevrons, and I was right. After she spoke to the sergeant for a moment, she came over to Atticus and introduced herself. She had curly black hair underneath her cap and a broad nose, big eyes and tiny ears.

"Mr. Molloy? I understand you found the body?" Her voice was smooth but I think her Tasmanian accent might have been a bit more pronounced than the sergeant's.

"Yes," Atticus said.

"I'm Inspector Badgely."

<Did she say Inspector Gadget?>

*No, she said Inspector Badgely. Don't you dare sing—*

<Do do-doo do-doo, In-SPEC-tor BADGE-ly! Do do-doo do-doo doo doo, HOO HOO!>

*Damn it, Oberon, now it's in my head. That's a snack penalty right there.*

<Whaaa? Awww!>

CHAPTER 3:

# THE HONEY BADGELY DON'T CARE

I missed some of the humans' conversation while I worried about how severe the snack penalty would be and watched a line of constables take off into the woods in search of the shooter, but I returned to the conversation as the inspector tried to catch Atticus in a lie.

"Describe the woman you saw for me, please," she said, and Atticus blinked at her a few times before answering.

"I didn't see any woman. I just heard her scream. She was gone by the time I got here."

"Oh, pardon me." I knew what she was up to. She was going to ask Atticus things incorrectly to see if he'd answer with some information inconsistent with what he'd said earlier.

Atticus was too smart for that, though. "Was the scream more like a woman's, or perhaps it was shrill, like a young girl's?"

"Sounded like a grown woman to me," Atticus replied.

He walked her through finding the body and showed her the blood and the arrow in the tree trunk while forensics technicians took lots of pictures of the crime scene. Inspector Badgely asked Atticus a lot more about what he was doing in the woods outside of Launceston, the precise nature of his work with Tasmanian devils, where he was staying, things like that. She was very surprised to hear that he was staying outdoors.

"Aren't you afraid of face-eating spiders? Most Americans are."

"My dogs eat them."

<What? We do not!>

<No spiders!> Starbuck chimed in.

*It was a bullshit question, so I gave her a bullshit answer*, Atticus told us privately.

The inspector only smirked, so I guess she understood he wasn't being serious. That was good because I didn't want her to think I had spider breath. I've heard legends. It's pretty bad.

"So, you must have a campsite somewhere?" she asked.

"No, I haven't made camp for the day. Happy to show you the den I was working on, if you'd like."

"Sure. I'd like to do that in a few minutes, though. I want to find out more about the victim. You don't know him?"

"No, never seen him before."

"Know anybody at all in town?"

"No. But if I may, I've aided in police investigations before. You can check with Detective Gabriela Ibarra in Portland, Oregon, and ask her about me. I helped her clear a couple cases."

Inspector Badgely raised just one eyebrow, which is a trick that humans do since they can't move their ears around. "How did you do that?"

"My dogs are pretty good trackers."

Before the inspector could reply, Constable Fosse came over to tell her that forensics was ready to turn him over.

"All right." Her eyes flicked to Atticus and she said, "Stay here. I'll be right back." She walked away and Atticus waited about three months before he followed after her, quietly, to get a better view.

*Listen carefully to everything they say,* he told us. *You might pick up something I don't.*

<Got it,> I said.

<Big ears. Hear good!> Starbuck said.

The inspector paused to look up at the beehive buzzing above everyone's head. "Feral honey. I bet that stuff's amazing. Wouldn't mind a taste of that."

The other humans agreed with tiny laughs, but the inspector kept staring. The longing was real. I thought she was going to climb that tree and go after some, just go for it like a honey badger that doesn't care, but she blinked and looked down once she heard the snap of gloves on Sergeant Naseer's wrists and had to put on a pair of her own. The sergeant was very careful not to touch the tree and disturb the hive again. She slowly turned over the body, grunting a bit because the victim was a fairly tall and solid fella. Once we could see his back, the cause of death was pretty apparent: a broken arrow shaft protruded from just to the left of his spine, and the remainder of the shaft was pressed into the ground where he had lain.

"Huh," the sergeant said. "The tip must have lodged against a rib bone so it didn't punch through. The shaft had to break instead."

Inspector Badgely nodded. "So he's shot in the back some distance away, but it's not instantly fatal. He staggers into the tree and it disturbs the hive above us. The bees descend to attack, he whirls around and falls backward, and that's probably what finished him. The additional impact of hitting the ground had to tear him up inside, maybe opened up an artery, which is why we have so much blood underneath him and not more spray trailing from where he was first shot."

Somebody who must have been a medical person said they would confirm once they got the body back to the lab but that sounded reasonable.

The inspector reached into the man's back pocket. "Let's see who you are, sir," she said, and flipped open the wallet she fished out to check the ID. "William Robert Howe, age twenty-seven, Melbourne address." She pawed through the wallet further. "A credit card and a tenner inside and some retail rewards cards. Nothing in here worth killing for, obviously. No cell phone, though. If that was taken and not the wallet, that could be the key. Sergeant, will you check with Melbourne and see what records we can find on him? I'd like to know when he got here and why he came, at least, but wouldn't mind hearing a nice, clear reason why someone would want to shoot him in the back with a bow."

<I guess Big Bad Bill is Dead William now,> I said. <Ha ha! I deserve a snack for that. Because it was a song pun.>

*Except you're on snack penalty,* Atticus reminded me.

<But I just gave you a different song for your head instead of the Inspector one!>

*The problem is not the song but that you sang it when I told you not to.*

<Awww! I'm sorry, Atticus. How do I get off snack penalty?>

*The apology was good. You can also help me solve this crime.*

<Well, yeah, I was going to do that anyway! This was my idea! But I'm going to solve it even faster now. Is Melbourne far away?> I asked as the sergeant departed with the wallet.

*No. It's north of here, across the Bass Strait, about four or five hundred kilometers.*

<But isn't a hundred a lot? Like more than a million?>

*No, you're getting your numbers mixed up again. It's more than you can walk in a day, but it would be a short airplane flight.*

<What's it like there?>

*It's a beautiful big city with lots of poodles in it. You'd love it.*

"What kind of arrow is this, does anybody know?" the inspector asked before I could answer. "Would it have been from a bow or a crossbow?"

"A bow, I believe," Constable Fosse said. "You can tell by the length and the fletching. That's a regular sort of arrow, not a crossbow bolt."

<Shooting someone in the back with an arrow is kind of rare, isn't it, Atticus? I mean for regular people, not the ones you hang out with. Because most people use guns?> I noticed that the inspector looked up at Atticus at that moment, confirming that his right arm really was missing, and he nodded at her.

*Yes, it is rare. And the inspector is realizing right now that because I only have one arm, I can't have shot him. A crossbow might be able to be wielded with one hand, but not a regular bow.*

<She thought you did it?>

*It was a possibility. She had to eliminate me as a suspect. It doesn't mean I'm not an accomplice, but it does mean I'm probably not the murderer.*

<Dang, Atticus, when can we get to the business of finding the actual bad guy?>

*As soon as the inspector believes I'm not the bad guy. Right now, I'm the guy at the crime scene and I'm a weird person who lives in the bush, so that's two strikes against me. And she thinks I'm American, so that might be three.*

<Whatever. At least the murder weapon is strange. That could lead us to the killer if we find it.>

*I'm rather hoping that trail you and Starbuck smelled will lead us to the killer.*

<Oh yeah!> But we couldn't get to that until the inspector left the poor guy to the forensics folks and asked Atticus a bunch more questions. She wanted to know why an American was so concerned about saving Tasmanian devils that he'd traveled around the globe to do it and lived in the woods. Atticus had done a lot of preparation for this kind of encounter, though, since he needed a cover for his Druidry. Soon after we got here, he figured that Owen and Granuaile could use some cover too, and the young apprentices that Owen was training would be full Druids someday and they'd probably need a job, so Atticus had his lawyers create a charity called the Gaia Stewardship, all legal and everything. He printed up some

cards and just told anyone who asked that he worked for them. The Gaia Stewardship's mission statement covered all sorts of "global natural emergencies," and that statement was on a fancy-schmancy website and listed his alias, Connor Molloy, as a field operative. He let the inspector know all this and led her and Constable Fosse back to the den of devils he'd been healing. He didn't say he was healing them, though; he pretended he was surveying them, noting their location and condition and so on to help Tasmanian biologists do the important work of saving them.

"How do you find them?" she asked.

"My dogs," he said, though of course it was the elemental helping him find all the dens.

"So, you heard the woman scream from here?" Inspector Badgely asked.

"Yes."

She pulled out her radio. "Sergeant Naseer."

Her radio made a static click and then the tinny voice of the sergeant replied. "Yes, Inspector?"

"Warn everyone first, but I want you to scream as loud as you can to see if I can hear it from where I'm standing now. Apologies for any embarrassment; I'm just checking out Mr. Molloy's story."

There was a pause, and then, "Of course, Inspector. One moment."

While we waited, I asked Atticus what he would say if we didn't hear anything.

*I'll just say the woman screamed louder than the sergeant. It's not an issue that they can use to arrest me. She's just checking the plausibility of my story.*

A moment later, my ears pricked up along with Starbuck's as we heard the sergeant scream. It was clear to us, but I wasn't sure the humans heard it until the inspector nodded.

"Okay. Your story hangs together so far. I'll check up on this charity of yours and confirm your relationship with Detective Ibarra in the United States. I presume I can reach you on your phone?"

"Yes, anytime, provided it's charged." She tested his number and once she was satisfied that it rang, she ended the call and said thanks for reporting the crime, she'd be in touch if she needed him.

"Oh, one more thing: How long will you be in Tasmania?"

"Another couple of months at least."

Inspector Badgely finally let us go after that and walked away with Constable Fosse. Atticus watched them go and had a tiny grin on his face, but I wasn't sure why.

<Are you laughing at her?>

*No, admiring. She's very smart, very thorough. Good at her job.*

<Uh-oh. Are you getting smitten?>

*What? No. I just met her.*

<You have that competence kink, though. Smart people turn your crank.>

*Oberon.*

<Did I get the saying wrong? Is it *rev your rotor? Start your motor?* Or is this the expression that has something to do with chicken, where you're throwing it or choking it or something like that?>

*No, Oberon, that's definitely not it. Let's forget about Inspector Badgely, all right?*

<All right. Now can we follow that trail?> I asked.

*Yes, soon. We might have to go in under camouflage, though, to pick it up.*

<You can still do that?>

*Yes. I can't change my shape or shift planes anymore, but I can still cast camouflage and do most of what I used to.*

We snuck back toward the crime scene, and Atticus spoke his Old Irish bindings to camouflage us so that our pigments looked like our surroundings. It wasn't perfect invisibility, but it worked great when people weren't paying close attention, and the police were all staring at the body and worrying about upsetting the bees. Starbuck and I found the scent again and began to follow it out. Atticus kept his hand on my back so he didn't lose me, and we took it slow until we were safely out of sight of the police. Then Atticus dropped the camouflage and we moved faster.

The trail flanked around clockwise in a flat half-oval and it was really strong in one spot. We told Atticus and he said, "Hold on." He looked around behind us. "Yes. See through there? This is where he waited and watched. You can see the arrow embedded in the tree from here, so this is where he stood when he took a shot at me. Probably where he stood to shoot William Howe as well."

<He smells a bit like onions, if it makes you feel any better.>

"Not particularly. Where did he go from here?"

<This way!> Starbuck said, already snuffling ahead of me. I hurried to keep up and confirm, and Atticus trailed after us on his clunky human feet.

We threaded our way through eucalyptus trees and all kinds of bushes that basically shouted "Urine luck!" because so many animals had peed on them, but we kept our noses trained on the human scent we were tracking. It was fun to track a human, and easy too, when they weren't thinking about covering their trail.

The trail ended at a muddy roadside. There was a shoulder there where someone had parked; we could see the tire treads in the muck. I'm not good at stuff like that, but maybe it was a Jeep or some kind of truck tire. The tracks seemed wide.

<It ends here, Atticus. He got in his vehicle and drove away. But hey…wait.>

"What?"

<Starbuck, do you smell the other human?>

<Yes! Flowers! Stinky!>

"Stinky flowers?" Atticus said.

<Yeah, but they're artificial, and we smelled it before. It's that lady's perfume. The lady who screamed and ran away! Atticus, she was here. She was with the killer!>

Atticus snorted. "Well, I guess that would explain why she didn't call the police."

CHAPTER 4:

# BEE-WILDERED

**Something** didn't make sense—I mean besides cats. <But if that perfume lady was involved in all this…why did she scream when she saw the body?>

"That's an excellent question, Oberon. Let's speculate."

<Lady very hungry!> Starbuck said. <She try to say words, but so hungry she just scream!>

"Okay, that's one possibility," Atticus allowed.

<Poor hungry lady,> Starbuck muttered, his voice mournful.

<Maybe she knew the victim,> I said. <Maybe he wasn't *supposed* to be dead and she knew who the killer was! Because there was a love triangle! Big Dead Bill and Perfume Lady were having an affair and her jealous lover killed his rival!>

"Wow. You've watched a lot of soap operas, Oberon."

<So?>

"I think the key fact we need to establish first is whether she willingly joined the killer in his vehicle. That's going to take some scent sleuthing. Can you trace their scents individually and see if there is any point where they intersect, perhaps walk together for a distance? And it would be great if you could isolate her scent from the perfume. She might not always be wearing it."

That took some work, especially isolating her scent from the perfume. But we were able to follow it into the forest in a slightly different trajectory than the killer's. And their trails never crossed. Atticus asked me and Starbuck to stand where the scents of the two people ended and we wound up standing across from one another, side by side, except that there were truck tire marks in between us. I was following the lady's scent and I was closest to the road.

"All right, so Oberon, since you're over there, that means the lady was the passenger because cars in Australia have the driver's seat on the right side. I can tell by the treads which way the car was facing. Okay, now, starting there, I want to follow the scent trails away from that spot for a short distance. I just want to see how that works."

I moved from my spot directly forward for a few paces and then veered into the woods. Atticus stopped me there.

"Oberon, look at what Starbuck did."

My little Boston buddy was also at the edge of the woods, but he was behind Atticus, from my point of view. <What? I wasn't looking at him.>

"Starbuck, will you go back, please, and do that again?>

He returned to his starting point, and then where I went forward from my spot, he spun around behind, taking a few steps toward the street.

"Right there, Starbuck, is the scent stronger?" Atticus asked.

<Yes food!>

"Good. So you see, Oberon? The driver—the killer—went to the back of the vehicle and stood there for a bit. Why?"

<To get his bow from the cargo area! And put it back when he returned.>

"Exactly. So they parked here, went into the woods, the man killed William Howe—or Big Dead Bill—and then it gets really weird."

<Because we still don't know why she screamed.>

"Right. Either she is surprised by the death when she arrives and screams, or she had some other purpose—did she see you first or the body first?"

<Us first!> Starbuck said.

"Maybe when she saw you and Starbuck, she knew you had to belong to someone, so she screamed to bring me running?"

<Why?>

"Maybe she wanted the body found. Think about it, Oberon: If we hadn't been in the area, would anyone know right now that William Howe is dead? We're technically in city limits, as the constable pointed out, but really, this is a preserve. This is not a high-traffic area."

<But I mean, why would she want the body found if she's with the killer?>

"I don't know. Apart from their actual identities, their motivation for the killing is the big mystery here. Being with the killer doesn't mean the same thing as being allied with him; she was obviously outside of his direct control for a brief time."

<That's true. But she had a cell phone, Atticus. If she wanted the killer caught, she could have called it in right there and then just told the police where to find him. Or asked them to trace her phone.>

"That's a good point, Oberon. I'm not sure what to make of this lady. She was middle-aged, you say?"

<I think so? A few wrinkles here and there but she moved well. It's the hat that tells me she's got some years on her. I don't think humans wear hats like that until they're older. It's like they have to reach a certain threshold before they opt for daring headgear.>

"Hmm. And she was for some reason involved in the execution of a twenty-seven-year-old man from Melbourne. Strange indeed."

<What do now?> Starbuck asked, and then sneezed.

Atticus checked the position of the sun in the sky. "It looks like it's about lunchtime. The devils will all be asleep now, so what do you say we jog into town for something with gravy on it?"

<Yes food!> Starbuck said.

<I'm never gonna say no to gravy, Atticus, but shouldn't we figure out what to do next in the case of Big Dead Bill?>

"Oh, I already know what to do next."

<What?>

"We find an archery club and use their members as a list of suspects. That killer was accurate at distance. That takes practice."

## CHAPTER 5:

# A ROSE BY ANY OTHER NAME

Let me tell you an ill-kept secret: kangaroos are delicious. And they know it, too, which is why they're so ready to fight. They assume, whenever you show up, that you are there to eat them because they're super tasty, and they quite sensibly prefer not to be eaten. They taste like cows but much better. Leaner, richer, the meat a darker red. And Atticus will feed us some when he runs across a restaurant that serves it.

We had kangaroo steaks and chili fries with no mustard on them, and after that, I was ready for a nap.

"You can nap tonight while I'm working on the devils," Atticus said. "We need to get to an archery club and track this guy down if you ever want to work off your snack penalty."

I agreed that Atticus had his priorities straight there, and he asked around about archery clubs. He doesn't have a smartphone to look things up anymore; he just keeps a cheap basic phone for calls and texts.

The server was nice and looked up the only one in the area and wrote it down for him; there was another one down in Hobart and that was pretty much it.

"Look there, Oberon," he said, showing me the paper with loopy handwriting on it. "If the killer's local we should be able to get a solid lead on him there."

<Hey, Atticus, why are there two phone numbers on there?>

"Huh?" He looked at the paper again more closely and his eyebrows shot up in surprise. "Oh. The second one is…her number."

<She's smitten!>

"I guess so. Time to go."

<What? Don't you want to flirt a bit first? It's okay, Atticus, Starbuck and I will just wait, won't we?>

<Yes, wait!> Starbuck said, and yawned. He was ready for a nap too.

"No, no, we should go." He got up to leave and we trotted after him.

<Oh, I get it! You're thinking of Inspector Badgely.>

"I am not."

<What was wrong with the server? Was she not pretty or something? I can never tell with humans.>

"No, she was very pretty. That's not the issue."

<It's that competence kink you have, isn't it? Was she bad at her job?>

"No, Oberon, it's simply the fact that I can't get into a relationship now. We're constantly on the move healing the Tasmanian devils of their cancer, and I can't start something now and then continue to get ever farther away. The work must come first."

<Okay, yeah, work first, I get that this is a human idea that lots of humans think is a good one, but that doesn't mean work *only,* does it? You need some time to play, too. Didn't Jack Nicholson basically prove that in *The Shining?* I mean, you ask me, he laid out a pretty strong argument for getting some R&R once in a while, like a thousand typed pages of how badly he needed to stop working because it made him a dull boy, and incidentally a homicidal one. Maybe that's what's going on with our killer. He just works too much.>

"I take time to play with you and Starbuck every day, Oberon." We'd started jogging together toward this archery club. We do all our traveling that way now. "And I'll point out that the time I'm spending helping you solve this mystery is time that I'm not working."

<You're counting this as playing?>

"I'm counting it as not doing my job. And look, I know you're trying to get me to go out on a date. I appreciate that you care."

<I care too!> Starbuck said.

"I know, buddy. And I'm grateful to you both. You're the best of friends. But you don't need to worry about it. I have you and I have the work. Right now, that's perfect for me."

On the one paw, I trust Atticus about most things. On the other paw, he doesn't see himself like I do. He's been hurting ever since that Ragnarok business. It was really bad for a little while, but he *has* been getting better. On the third paw, there's only so much I can do. On the fourth paw, I gotta try.

We got to the Paringa Archery Club about seven centuries later. Atticus was going to do the camouflage thing and just steal whatever information he needed, but he had to "shitcan that plan," he said, because the police were there.

"We'd better play this like I don't have any abilities except a keen mind and a roguish grin."

<Is that the word for your face? Roguish?>

Atticus shrugged. "I can live with it. But I don't think I want a citation from Constable Fosse if he's in there. Much as I hate to do it, I think I'm going to need to put you two on a leash until we are through with this business. Otherwise, they're going to give me grief about it."

That required a backtrack and some lost time, but he bought a couple of cheap leashes and held the silly things in his hand as we walked into the lobby of the archery club. The police were still there but on their way out. We nearly ran smack into Inspector Badgely and Constable Fosse.

"Oh! Pardon me, Mr. Molloy. What are you doing here?"

"Afternoon, Inspector. Thought I might inquire about skilled archers in the area, since one of them took a shot at me and the late Mr. Howe."

She did that eyebrow thing again, raising just one of them. "You're investigating on your own?"

"Well, I felt personally attacked because an arrow did move at terminal velocity through the space my head was occupying only a moment before. Did you find out anything?"

She kept the eyebrow raised but added in an upturned corner of her mouth on the same side. She found Atticus amusing. Hey, maybe she liked him too! I was pretty sure he liked her. I can never tell for certain, though, until humans actually mash their faces together and breathe heavily. Once you get to the heavy breathing and face-mashing, it's a done deal, but up until that point, I maintain my belief that human mating habits are stupid.

"I can't comment on an ongoing investigation."

"Come on, Inspector, I'm not the press. I'm trying to help."

"I'm well aware. I was able to contact Detective Ibarra in Portland. She says you're annoyingly helpful and very good with dogs."

"Oh, well, it's not me that's good so much as the dogs who are good. These two guys are extraordinarily good boys."

"I've noticed. And you have them leashed now, which tells me you heed warnings when they're given. What are their names?"

Atticus introduced us and we wagged our tails for the inspector and she held out her hand for us to sniff. Humans do that because they think they're being polite, and it's okay, I guess, but if they'd just let us sniff their asses, we'd figure out things a whole lot faster.

Underneath the traces of cinnamon and teriyaki sauce and coffee that she'd no doubt consumed at some point during the day, Inspector Badgely smelled like she was a tiny bit stressed out and maybe excited about something. Perhaps she was excited about a new lead in the investigation. Or perhaps she was excited to see Atticus again. More likely she was excited to see us because she was definitely a dog person. She gave us a couple of scritches behind the ears each and I could tell she wanted to lean in and do more but she was in a formal work situation and couldn't do as she wished.

"Have Oberon and Starbuck found anything interesting?"

"I think so. How about you, Inspector? Find anything interesting here?"

"A short list of people capable of firing those shots from a very cooperative manager. What did your hounds find?"

"The scent trail of someone who was not the police leading from the body of William Howe to a space where he probably shot at both Mr. Howe and myself, and then back to the shoulder of a roadside where he got into a vehicle and drove away."

The inspector's face lost its faint amusement and became serious. "You're saying they know what the killer smells like."

"Yes. Not admissible in court, probably, so you'd need to find some other evidence to get a conviction, but they can accurately point the finger, as Detective Ibarra can confirm from our last case. If any of the archers on your list were in those woods, my hounds will be able to identify him."

"Where was this car parked?"

"I can show you."

"Will you show Constable Fosse instead? I need to track down this list of names."

"Of course. Will you let Oberon and Starbuck give those people a sniff?"

"I will. Thank you, Mr. Molloy. I should have given you my card earlier. That was an oversight. Here you go."

She pulled a white rectangle with some words on it out of her vest and offered it to Atticus. It was a bit awkward since he had only the one hand and that was already filled with the ends of our leashes, but he reached out and took it with his fingertips.

<What's it say, Atticus?> He answered me via our mental link.

*Inspector Rose Badgely. Her name is Rose.*

<I knew it! You're sweet on her! I can hear the longing in your voice!>

*Oh, stop it.*

<I'll stop pointing it out when you stop denying it.>

"Thanks very much, Inspector," Atticus said aloud.

"We'll talk soon," she said with a small grin, and politely said goodbye to me and Starbuck before leaving us there with Constable Fosse, who was still very pink and swole.

CHAPTER 6:

# BAD BEE-HAVIOR

Atticus pocketed the inspector's card and looked expectantly at the constable.

"Got room for all of us in your vehicle, Constable?" he asked.

"I think you'll all fit in the back," he said. We did, but it was not my favorite ride ever. Constable Fosse was into health food and vegetables, and his car smelled like balsamic vinegar and the ghosts of sad salads.

<Dead leaves,> Starbuck said, sneezing to get the smell out of his nose. Then, softly, in a tone of disgust: <No squirrel.>

Atticus gave some directions and then tried to get the constable to share what they had found out about Big Dead Bill, but the constable claimed not to know anything since it was Sergeant Naseer who'd been on that duty.

Starbuck and I stuck our heads out the window once Atticus convinced the constable to roll it down and we could take in some relieved breaths of air free of balsamic vinegar. Soon, we were back at the spot where the murderer had parked and the constable called out a forensic team while Atticus walked him through the scent path we found to the crime scene and where the villain had most likely stood to shoot William Howe in the back. He got a call from Inspector Badgely as we were returning to the car.

"Would you ask Mr. Molloy if he'd be willing to swing by someone's house and have his hounds give the resident a sniff to see if he's the guilty one?"

I heard that even though Constable Fosse had the phone up to his ear. When he relayed the request, Atticus wondered aloud why the resident wouldn't be at the station.

"He's refusing to come down, which is within his rights so long as we don't have a warrant. He might have a legitimate reason for refusing, but his refusal might also point to a bit of guilt. We just need to eliminate him as a suspect."

Atticus agreed and soon we were on the road again, crammed into the constable's sad saladmobile. We drove to an eastern suburb of Launceston called Ravenswood, and Atticus asked the constable about his fitness regimen. The constable happily described it in detail for the entire drive, and all Atticus had to do was grunt in approval at appropriate intervals.

We rolled up to a fairly modest home in a neighborhood of similar homes. It had a nice tree out front with some happy birds in it, but Atticus said we weren't allowed to pee on it. The constable waited in the car while Atticus took us to the door. He rang the bell and we sat down next to him, waiting.

The door opened a crack and a scowling white man answered, peering first at Atticus and then at us. "Yes?"

"Hi, Jude Fothergill?"

"Yes, who are you?"

"We haven't met. I'm Connor, a friend of a friend over at the archery club."

"I don't have any friends."

"Are you sure?" Atticus said, and while he was just stalling for time, Starbuck and I inched forward and took some big whiffs of the air coming out of the house. There were English muffins in there, somewhere, freshly toasted, and maybe Jude was annoyed that we had interrupted his tea time. Or maybe he was just a disagreeable sort. Regardless, we got what we needed.

<He's not the guy, Atticus.>

<No squirrel,> Starbuck agreed, disappointed.

"Yes, I'm sure," Jude was saying.

"Oh! Well, never mind, then," Atticus said. "Sorry to trouble you. We'll be off." We started walking away and the door opened a bit wider behind us.

"Hey! Wait a minute. Why are you here? How did you know my name?"

"It was a mistake! My apologies," Atticus called over his shoulder, and he didn't respond to Jude's repeated demands that he stop and explain himself.

<Unhappy man,> Starbuck noted. <Alone in house with no meat. Only bread.>

"Well, he might be a vegetarian," Atticus guessed.

<Unhappy man,> Starbuck repeated.

"I'd agree with that. But his diet may or may not be a part of it. I think he simply prefers privacy and is suspicious of the outside world, which are perfectly legitimate explanations for why he refused to come to the police station."

Constable Fosse informed us that the inspector had a lineup ready and waiting at the station, which included two archery experts from the list. We were to head down and give them a whiff. Atticus asked the constable about his nutrition next, so we had to listen him *talk* about salad as well as smell his old ghost salads. It seemed like a very long drive.

We got to the police station and Inspector Rose Badgely smiled when she saw us come in. I looked up at Atticus and he had gone a little goofy about the mouth. Yeah, he was twitterpated or hot to trot or whatever. But he would probably never mash faces with Inspector Badgely because he felt he had to work, and of course I didn't know Inspector Badgely well enough to figure out if she liked Atticus back. Even if she did, she probably felt she had to keep things formal and professional too.

"Thank you for coming, Mr. Molloy," she said, confirming that she was going to stick to the formality…for now.

"Glad to help."

"If you will follow me? We have four men in a room and I'd like to simply have you walk on in there with your dogs. Two of them are master archers named at the club who have agreed to come in. Two are random strangers. Hopefully, if one of them is the culprit, we'll see some kind of reaction. Your dogs won't bite anyone, will they?"

"No, they won't," Atticus said, and then added privately, *Please don't bite anyone or even bark if you find the right person. A small growl will be sufficient to signal your disapproval. Okay?*

<Okay,> I said.

<Yes food,> Starbuck acknowledged.

"We'll be watching. My understanding is that the killer took a shot at you and your dogs were in sight as well, correct?"

"That's right."

"So he should recognize you when you enter. We'll see."

She asked us to wait outside a door while she ducked into another one. <Is she going into one of those rooms where they have the one-way mirrors?>

*Presumably,* Atticus said.

<How do they make those things?>

*Science.*

<Oh! Did Bill Nye the Science Guy ever explain it in one of his episodes?>

*I'll have to check.*

Constable Fosse said we were clear and he opened the door. We walked in on leashes to smell four dudes. They all looked surprised, so I don't know how the inspector could tell one from the other.

Two of the men had darker skin tones and two were white guys. The closest man said, "What's all this, then?" and Constable Fosse said it was nothing to worry about, we were harmless dogs and were just going to give them a quick sniff.

"Look, droogs, I don't like dogs," the first man said. "Like, really, when I was a kid, there was this episode, and I still have some scars."

<Wag your tail, Starbuck! Let him know we're friendly!> I said. Because sometimes, very rarely, there are some bad boys out there who bite humans and then they're always a little afraid of dogs after that. I understand. I'm always going to be a little afraid of great big bears. Not because they've bitten me, but because they're great and big and bears and they *can* bite me. So I get it.

<Very friendly!> Starbuck said, and he doesn't have much of a tail, but he tried to look as friendly as possible.

"They won't hurt you," Atticus told the man. "I promise."

"Well, keep them on a tight leash at least."

Atticus took up some slack but didn't pull our leashes tight. It only took a few sniffs to eliminate him.

<He's not the guy,> I said, and Starbuck agreed. We moved on to the next man. He was silent as we snuffled around his shoes and eliminated him.

<No squirrel,> Starbuck said. We padded over to the next person. It was one of the white guys. And one good whiff of his pant leg and I smelled that screaming lady's perfume. And then I smelled the killer's scent, the lady's scent, and even Big Dead Bill's scent on him. This was the guy! I growled. And Starbuck did too.

The first man who didn't like dogs said, "Oh, shit!" even though we weren't growling at him.

The man who tried to kill Atticus sneered at us and said, "What? You'd better control your mutts, lad," he said, and then I growled louder, because we were not mutts.

"Move on to the next, fellas," Atticus said, and then privately said, *We need to eliminate man number four. But after that, you can growl at three again as we exit.* "Hup!" he grunted, which is a thing that dog trainers always do, so Atticus says it to make other humans think we're just trained and he can't really talk to us.

We sniffed at the last man and he definitely wasn't the guy. He smelled like soap and toothpaste. We backed away from him and then growled at the white guy again.

"You tried to kill me earlier," Atticus whispered. "But you missed. You're gonna get got, though. I promise."

The man didn't say anything but his face went dark gray and blotchy in my sight, which meant he was blushing red. I could smell the anger on him, too. He was dressed in high-end walkabout gear from some catalog: crisp and clean khakis, buttery leather hiking boots with no dirt on them, a wide belt tooled with some sort of vine-like pattern, and a dark gray—probably deep red—kerchief around his neck. He looked middle-aged and a tiny bit jowly with blond hair and a neatly trimmed mustache grown to the edges of his mouth. He looked fit but wasn't swole like Constable Fosse. Under his bottom lip he had let the hair grow and shaped it into a V, but his chin was clean-shaven. His face looked accustomed to scowling. Atticus led us out as the constable loudly thanked us and said that would be all, opening the door for us.

Out in the hallway, the constable asked us to wait. The inspector joined us in the hallway shortly thereafter.

"So they're sure it's the third man? The white man?"

"One hundred percent. They don't growl like that for nothing. Who is he?"

Inspector Badgely blinked and hesitated, debating whether she should tell us anything, but I guess having cleared those cases in Oregon helped her decide in our favor. "His name is Royston Saxby."

"For real? His parents actually did that?" The inspector tried to stifle a smile and largely failed, but she only nodded. Atticus shook his head. "No wonder he's murderous, then."

"I wanted you to know that we won't be able to keep him, short of getting a confession out of him. We have no witnesses to the actual crime. But we'll see what his alibi is and maybe we can learn a thing or two besides, if you'd like to sit in on the interview. You can observe from that room." She hooked a thumb at the door from which she'd just emerged.

"Thanks."

"What did you say to him? It was too low to make out."

"Just that I knew it was him."

"Well, that made him mad. He's acting guilty, but that's not enough to convict. We don't have any idea why he'd want to do this."

"Did you find anything out about William Howe from Melbourne?"

The inspector shrugged. "He's a barista at some tiny espresso joint in Melbourne. No assets, no criminal record, no strong family ties. No obvious reason that he should be here or be killed for it. We're trying to find someone who might know why he was in Tasmania."

"This will be interesting, then," Atticus said.

We scooted into the room and there was a big window

that let us see into the other one. That was the one-way mirror made with science. Royston Saxby was fuming and the other three men had kind of drawn away from him, trying to look bored but really wanting to get out of there. They got their wish when the inspector opened the door and thanked them, telling them they were free to go. "Except you, Roy," she said to the killer, and he bared his teeth at her.

"It's *Royston*. Mr. Saxby to you."

Atticus chuckled and said to us privately since there was a constable in the room with us, *She called him Roy on purpose to see if he got mad, and he did.*

<Does she want him to be mad?>

*Not necessarily. She just wants to learn what motivates him. From that exchange we can tell he's used to being in charge and wants to assert his superiority. He's better than mere Roys, you see. He's* Royston. *He's unique! Special! And the police should feel ashamed for pestering someone as important as he is!*

<Is he important?>

*He thinks he is. Mostly it's important that we lock him up.*

"Thanks for coming down voluntarily. I'm Inspector Badgely and I have a few questions for you."

Saxby crossed his arms. "Fine. Get on with it."

He sounded pretty rude to me but Inspector Badgely didn't react. "Where were you this morning from sunrise to about eight A.M.?"

"At home, first, then I went out for breakfast and a morning constitutional with my cousin."

"What's your cousin's name?"

"Evelyn Bickford-Hicks."

The inspector asked for and received her phone number, then asked, "Where did you eat breakfast?"

"Samuel Pepy's Café on Yorktown Square. Evelyn requires a gluten-free diet and they have an excellent menu there for that sort of thing."

*They've had time to rehearse this. She's going to say the same thing when they talk to her,* Atticus said.

"Receipt?" the inspector asked.

"No, but I'm sure we'd show up on any security footage they may have."

"And after that, you had a morning constitutional?"

"Yes. We went to the Tamar River Conservation Area. Looked at the water birds feeding, you know, very scenic."

"You didn't go to the Cataract Gorge Reserve?"

Saxby blinked a few times. "No. I'm quite certain of where we went."

"Did you take your bow with you on your morning constitutional?"

"My bow? Whatever for?"

"Was it with you this morning?"

"No."

"Where is it now?"

"I presume it is in my trophy room, where I left it last season."

"What kind of vehicle did you drive this morning?"

"My Range Rover."

"How are you acquainted with William Howe?"

"Well, he's the—I mean, I don't know. I don't know anyone of that name."

The inspector's eyes bored into him.

*Ha! He almost admitted he knew the victim. She's asking questions fast and got him answering without thinking.*

"What's this all about?" Royston said.

"Just a few more questions. You said your bow would be in your trophy room. Does that mean you hunt big game?"

"It does. Though I also shoot competitively and I have trophies from those wins in there as well."

"Ever shoot something on the move?"

"Of course."

"In the back?"

"I beg your pardon?"

"What sort of arrows do you use for hunting? Could you describe them for me?"

"Not really. They're just normal arrows, nothing special about them."

*That's bullshit,* Atticus said. *This man who knows his brand names and cares about his appearance and his trophies would never buy anything he didn't think was special.*

"Do you keep them in your trophy room as well?"

"No, they'd be in storage."

"May we have a look at your arrows?"

"No, I don't think so. Not until I know what this is about."

"You're saying you don't know what this is about?"

"No, I—yes, that's what I'm saying!"

"This is about the murder of William Howe in the Cataract Gorge Reserve. He was shot in the back with a hunting arrow."

"How do you know it was murder?"

Inspector Badgely glared at him. "He was shot. In the back. With a hunting arrow."

"It could have been an accident."

The inspector tilted her head. "Someone accidentally went out to the reserve with hunting arrows when there is currently nothing in season and, instead of poaching something, mistakenly shot a man in the back?"

*Okay,* Atticus admitted, *I really like her.*

"Well, when you put it like that—look. I didn't know this was a murder investigation. If you're going to question me about that, I want my lawyer here."

"Who's your lawyer?"

"Cordelia Griffith."

Inspector Badgely nodded. "I know her. Okay. Do you have any plans to leave town?"

"Well, actually—"

"Cancel your plans."

"What? Here now, you can't just tell me what to do—"

"You are a person of interest in this case and I will need you at hand. I'll let Cordelia know. For now, you can go." The inspector didn't wait for him to leave. Instead, she just walked out of the room in front of him, leaving him to stand there and splutter. She came into our room right afterward and Atticus gave her a thumbs-up.

"Nicely done. He almost admitted to knowing the victim."

Inspector Badgely sighed. "I know; it was so close. Damn it. But right now, we don't have a motive and we can't place him at the scene."

"Maybe those tire tracks will come through as a match?"

"I'm sure they will, but even that is going to be pretty circumstantial."

"He'll be getting rid of all his hunting arrows if he hasn't already, and I'm sure his cousin will back up his story."

"Yes. We really need to prove he knew the victim or find the victim's phone—there's just not enough here to nail him."

<Hey, Atticus, what does this Royston guy do for a living?>

Atticus relayed the question to the inspector and she shrugged. "Some kind of investment banker."

"What about his cousin, Evelyn?"

"That I don't know yet. I'll bring her in next, but we'll have a lawyer to deal with, no doubt."

"That reminds me—why did he come down without one?"

"He knew it would look suspicious if he did. And he had an alibi prepared. Now he knows what we know and he's given nothing away."

"Hmm. Mind if I watch the cousin's questioning, too?"

The inspector shrugged. "I don't mind, but...don't you have better things to do?"

"If there's someone killing people in the woods where I'm working, I'd like to be sure they're caught. Hard to concentrate when you think someone might be stalking you out there."

"Fair enough," she said. "But it'll be a while. Especially if we have to get the lawyer involved. If you'd like, you can get out of here and grab a bite or something, and I'll make sure to give you a call when she comes in."

"Thanks, Inspector."

Her eyes dropped to me and Starbuck. "May I, uh..." she trailed off, and her eyes flicked back to Atticus, uncertain.

"Yes?" he said.

She pointed at us. "Would you mind if I just give them a nuzzle for a second? I am such a dog person but I'm not home enough to have one, you know? It wouldn't be fair to them, but damn, I wish I could pet dogs more often. It just makes me happy."

"Sure."

The inspector felt she had to elaborate, though, and do so very quickly, which is a thing humans do sometimes when they think other humans might not understand their need to snuggle a dog, which is silly because of course that doesn't need any explanation. "It's just that before, I was with Constable Fosse and I couldn't really relax in front of him, you know, gotta be professional and all that bollocks, and..."

She kept going but I lost track of what she was saying because Atticus started talking to us privately.

*Guys, be super friendly but super polite, okay? Do not lick her face unless she asks for a kiss, and do not under any circumstances hump any part of her, all right?*

<Geez, Atticus, I wasn't gonna—>

*Starbuck?* That's when I realized Atticus was mainly talking to him. Starbuck gets excited sometimes when he meets friendly humans and has humped a few legs on occasion, tenderly and softly.

<No humping!> the Boston said. <Will behave! Very good boy!>

*Thank you.* He used his voice after that. "Please, Inspector, nuzzle away. There is no shame here and I won't tell anyone."

"Thanks!" She promptly leaned over to me and made that happy, growly doggy voice that humans like to adopt whenever they ask us their favorite rhetorical question: "Who's a good boy?"

<Me!> I said, and I wagged my tail as she started scratching underneath my jaw on either side.

<Me too!> Starbuck said, and he kinda danced forward, his nails clicking on the tile, to let her know that he was there and was ready for scritches. One of her hands left me and reached down to my buddy.

"Oh, you're both very good boys, yes you are, yes you are!" And then her voice got really high-pitched as she said, "I could just eat you up!" and honestly, I've never understood why humans say that like it's a compliment, but apparently they think it's endearing when they threaten to eat you while they're petting you. Maybe we're supposed to feel grateful that they're petting us instead of eating us—and we are, for sure!—but I wish sometimes they had come up with a different way to express their affection. Like maybe they could say, "I'm gonna give you a cow!" or "I'll never let a cat in my house!" to let us know how much they love us.

She just made tiny happy screams after that, no words at all, and gave us a thorough petting and several hugs around the neck. She had tears in her eyes when she stood up, but she was smiling. She sniffed once and used a finger to dash tears from the corners of her eyes.

"Well," she said, her voice returned to normal. "I obviously needed that rather desperately. This job has its stresses, you know. Unconditional love is a blessing."

"Indeed it is," Atticus said.

"Thank you, Mr. Molloy. That was a lovely gift. I shan't take any more of your time."

"Not at all. It was my pleasure."

"You won't tell anyone?"

"Of course not."

"Good. We'll talk soon." She opened the door and stepped out into the hall but peeked her head back in before the door closed, keeping it open with one hand. She smiled at Atticus. "I really like your dogs. And you. Please don't turn out to be the murderer in the end, okay?"

"I promise," Atticus said, and the inspector waggled her fingers at him and closed the door.

<Atticus, what the heck?> I said.

*What?*

<Why didn't you say you liked her too? It was the perfect chance!>

*I think she knows, Oberon.*

<How?>

*Mostly body language.*

<Actual language is less likely to be misinterpreted, though!>

*Anybody hungry?*

<Yes food!> Starbuck shouted.

I know Atticus says that whenever he wants to change the subject. I mean, yeah, I always let him, because the subject means I'm going to get something delicious to eat, but that doesn't mean I don't know what he's up to.

He took us down to the marina just a block or two away from the police station to a place that was actually called Fish and Chips, where we got the featured food and wolfed it down. After that, he took us to the City Park, where we could pee on a tree and smell the pee of other dogs. Starbuck and I were just settling in for an afternoon nap in the grass when Atticus's phone rang. The inspector said that Evelyn Bickford-Hicks would be in soon with her lawyer to answer some questions if Atticus was still interested in hearing it.

"Yes, we'll be right there," he said. "Thank you."

We jogged back with full bellies to the police station and soon found ourselves in the same observation room as before. This time, there was a table and chairs in there.

Evelyn Bickford-Hicks was definitely the same lady we saw screaming that morning. She didn't have on the funny hat she had before so she looked younger now. But her eyes were all puffy and her skin was blotchy and she wiped at her nose with a tissue. She'd been crying a lot. Maybe we watched the same soap operas.

## CHAPTER 7:

# ABUZZ WITH CONTRADICTIONS

**Inspector** Badgely introduced herself to the crying lady and nodded to the woman sitting next to her, who turned out to be her lawyer, Cordelia Griffith. Cordelia had dark, wavy hair, some dangly blue earrings, and a blue scarf around her neck that looked pretty fabulous, so good for her. She had a confidence about her that might have been partly owing to the scarf and partly owing to her law degree. Law degrees can have that effect, I hear. Atticus said they're like +2 buffs to charisma or something. Scarfs are +1, so she was amply prepared for this interview.

"I just want to be clear that we're here voluntarily and Ms. Bickford-Hicks may refuse to answer any questions," she said.

"I appreciate that," the inspector said, and sat down. "Are you also representing Mr. Saxby?"

"I have in the past," Cordelia replied, "but he has not informed me yet of any need."

"I see. Ms. Bickford-Hicks, you seem upset. Did you know the deceased, William Robert Howe?"

She burst into fresh sobs and one of the soft screams sounded like "yes" to me, but I couldn't be sure. The inspector wasn't sure either.

"I'm sorry, I didn't quite catch that. You do know him?"

Evelyn nodded.

"And what is the nature of your acquaintance?"

"He's my business partner. Or he was."

Torrential sobs resumed, which I thought was a bit excessive for a business relationship. Evelyn put her head down on her crossed hands on the table, and her whole torso shook with her grief.

"I'm very sorry. When was the last time you saw him?"

Evelyn gulped and gasped and then said to the table, "This morning."

"Oh. When and where was this?"

"In the reserve."

"Tamar River?"

"No, Cataract Gorge. We were going to meet and I found him."

"When you say *we*, you mean..."

"I was going to meet William. He'd found this feral hive that had access to mixed flowers including leatherwood, and we were going to try to take a small bit of the honey and see how close it tasted to pure leatherwood. We were also going to see about transplanting it and making it our first commercial hive. I had the beekeeping gear with me but he didn't wait, I don't know why, and they stung him to death."

The inspector let her cry for a little while as she made notes. "Again, I'm sorry, Ms. Bickford-Hicks, but perhaps I can ask you to back up just a little bit. Did you find William by yourself?"

"Yes."

"And when you did, what did you do?"

"I screamed and ran. I just ran. I know I should have reported it, I know I should have, but I was so upset and not thinking clearly."

"Where did you run?"

"Back to the Range Rover."

"Your Range Rover?"

"No, my cousin's, Royston. He drove me there."

"Was he with you when you discovered William's body?"

"No, no. He never left the car. He was just waiting for me to return."

*Holy shit,* Atticus said. *He's guilty and she doesn't know it.*

<Heck yes he is! Guilty as that time when I—>

*When you what?*

<Never mind. I am here voluntarily and don't have to answer any questions.>

The inspector continued. "We spoke to your cousin earlier and he said you'd gone to the Tamar River Reserve this morning."

"I know, I know. But it's not his fault. He came up with that Tamar River story to protect me because I asked him what we should do. I was so scared because you hear about people spending years in jail for crimes they didn't commit. But I didn't do anything except lose my head. I mean, he was all stung by bees and it was supposed to be our ticket, I mean—" She dissolved into unintelligible sobbing again.

"Pardon me?"

Cordelia Griffith was just blinking and listening. Apparently, she was content to let Evelyn cry while she sat there earning $400 an hour in her +1 charisma scarf.

"We were going to be apiarists. Honey-gatherers. Start something that would last, you know? A business that's good for us and good for the environment. I'm very sorry I didn't report it."

"So William Howe was here in Tasmania to collect honey and possibly a feral hive with you?"

"Yes."

"And your cousin, Royston Saxby, drove you out to somewhere on the reserve this morning, parked the Range Rover, and you left the vehicle by yourself?"

"Yes. He stayed in the car."

"And he was in the car when you returned?"

"Yes."

"Did he know William Howe?"

"Of course he did. He knew we were in business together."

<Royston's pants are probably on fire,> I said, <because he's definitely a liar.>

"Do you know of any reason why your cousin might dislike William?"

Evelyn blinked rapidly and wiped at her nose, looking back and forth between the inspector and her lawyer.

"That's a strange question," she finally said. "Why do you ask?"

"Evelyn—sorry, may I call you Evelyn?"

"Yes."

"Evelyn, William Howe wasn't killed by bees."

"Yes he was! I saw him! It was an accident!"

"He was certainly stung, but no. He was murdered." The inspector flipped open her folder and whipped out a photograph from the crime scene, placing it on the table in front of Evelyn. "He was shot in the back with a hunting arrow. He fell on it, so you wouldn't have seen it. The shaft broke off and was trapped underneath his back."

"Someone shot him with a bow and arrow?"

"Yes. And your cousin is an expert archer, Evelyn. Were you gone from the Range Rover long enough for him to kill William Howe?"

"Don't answer that," Cordelia Griffith said, suddenly working hard for that hourly rate.

"No…no! He would never! He liked William!"

"Did he bear any grudge against you? Any resentment?"

"No! I mean…" She trailed off as something suddenly occurred to her. "Maybe? But no, wait! When I found him, there were two dogs there! Two dogs, off the leash, one huge, and one small! A cute Boston terrier! I don't know what breed the other one was, but it was huge."

<I'm an Irish wolfhound, Evelyn!>

<Ha ha, you just some huge dog,> Starbuck taunted me. <She know Bostons, though. We're cute!>

<I'm cute too! Tell him, Atticus.>

*You're both cute. Listen, I don't want to miss any of this.*

"Whoever owns those dogs probably did it!" Evelyn declared, a note of triumph in her voice.

"I know about those dogs already," Inspector Badgely said, "and we have spoken to the owner. He's the one who called in the murder and he cannot physically fire a bow. He has only one arm. So I ask again, were you absent from the Range Rover long enough for your cousin to have killed him and returned to the vehicle without your knowledge?"

"Do not answer," Cordelia said. "This interview is over."

"It is not," the inspector said. "She found the body but did not report it. She might be involved."

"She thought the bees killed him."

"Oh, yes, I heard what she said. But she could have wanted William dead for all kinds of reasons. If she didn't pull the bowstring herself, she could have had her cousin do it for her."

"What? No, I—I would never!"

"Then why would Royston want to kill him?"

"I don't know!"

The inspector pointed a finger. "But you have a suspicion."

"It's just—"

"Evelyn," Cordelia interrupted, "I advise you to say nothing."

"All right, I appreciate that. But Royston can deal with his own defense. This is mine."

Cordelia simply nodded, and Evelyn continued, her voice steely now and bereft of tears, maybe even a little fierce.

"I can't speak to anything Royston may have had against William. It would be irresponsible for me to speculate. But I myself have no motive whatsoever to kill him. I was—and still am—fully intending to start a honey business. William and I had no trouble."

"Okay. Leave motive out of it for the moment. Let's simply consider a basic fact: did Royston have enough time to leave the vehicle after you, shoot William before you reached him, and return to the vehicle before you did?"

She blinked and considered before replying. "Yes. I'm not saying it's likely, but it's technically possible. Because I was in no particular hurry to get to the rendezvous point. I was looking around at the flora to see what else the bees might have been feeding on. And William was texting me. In fact, I have his last text"—her voice quavered again as she reached for her phone—"which simply says, *Almost there*. And you can see my response: *On my way! See you soon*. But when I got there he was dead."

Inspector Badgely noted the times of the texts and said she would need to admit Evelyn's phone into evidence. "And afterward? Did you return straight to the vehicle?"

"No. After I found him, I was very distraught. A wreck, actually, even more than I am now, and I got a little lost. I was staggering more than walking, and I kept stopping to cry harder. When I got to the vehicle, I told Royston what I saw and asked what should we do and I didn't want to go to jail, and he came up with the Tamar River story, said we would phone in an anonymous tip to make sure William was found, and it would all come to nothing."

"Did you phone in a tip?"

"No."

"Did you breakfast together beforehand?"

"Yes. Samuel Pepy's in the square. I have celiac disease, so I love their gluten-free menu."

"All right. Please remain here and I will return in a moment."

Inspector Badgely exited the interview room and we left our room too, meeting her in the hall. She flashed a brief grin at us but then turned all serious as she called Sergeant Naseer and told her to arrest Royston Saxby for the murder of William Howe. "He lied to us all throughout his interview. Except about breakfast. Apparently, he has scruples there."

<Justice, Atticus! He's going down! Am I off snack penalty now?>

*We still don't have a motive. It's not over yet,* he said. Atticus was right.

CHAPTER 8:

# HIVE HAD ENOUGH ISOLATION

We were literally dog tired but could do nothing more that day and said farewell to the inspector, who was now super busy trying to clear her case. Atticus took us to dinner to truly finish us off—nothing like being tired *and* full—and then we returned to that Tasmanian devil den in the reserve as they were waking up for the evening. He cured the rest of them while we napped, and then we found a nice little hollow by the Esk River to curl up in together for the night.

About once a week, if we're near a city, Atticus will buy a night in a hotel so he can clean up and trim his face fur and stuff, but we all prefer staying outdoors as long as the weather's nice. He asks the elemental to watch over us while we sleep so that we don't get insect eggs laid in our ears or something like that.

When we woke up and stretched and peed on trees—Atticus does that too—I asked him if we were going to stick around in the area or move on. My Druid grinned at me.

"We can stick around for a little while. A day or two, perhaps. We've earned it."

<We have?>

"Yes. Do you remember me telling you about that bet I have going with Owen? Whoever heals more devils in Tasmania wins?"

<Yeah?>

"Well, he never came back after we left to fight in Ragnarok. He's been busy teaching his apprentices. I just checked with the elemental and we have now healed over half the sick devils in the country. That means even if he returns now, he can't possibly win."

<Oh, congratulations! So what do you get for that?>

"He's never going to tell anyone the story about me, the goat, and the Roman skirt again."

<Really? I never heard that one. What happened?>

"I'm never telling anyone about it either. Sorry."

<Awww! So that means we've been at this for a long time, huh?>

"A few months, if that is what you mean by a long time. Why do you ask?"

<I'm just wondering if that Ogma guy was supposed to be back yet. He was going to learn how to grow your arm back and then do it, right?>

Atticus snorted and waved his hand dismissively. "I don't think that's ever going to happen. He's disappeared. The Morrigan doesn't know where he went and neither does Brighid. He's not been to any of the Irish planes since we talked. And honestly, it's fine. When you look back and consider how other humans were punished for their hubris, I got off pretty easy. So I really don't mind. This is my life now and it's great. I like what we are doing and I like the elemental here. Perhaps we can work on something else in Australia after this, because I do like the flat whites in this country. Ready to go get breakfast?"

Starbuck performed a three-foot vertical leap. <Yes food!> he said.

We jogged to a place in town that served a very good flat white, according to Atticus, and I thought about what he said. Our lives truly are different now—we don't have a home or a reliable source of gravy, for example. Orlaith's puppies are all with Owen's apprentices and Granuaile moved out of the cabin, so Atticus has put it up for sale. We are nomads. And he's right: it's great. We smell new stuff every day, meet new critters, and occasionally fight crime. That's a dream life for most hounds.

I miss talking to Orlaith sometimes, but whenever we see each other, we just pick up where we left off. We will always be good friends, and since she had a litter, I think we did our part for the species. Hounds are not monogamous creatures and do not mate for life, so I am sure she will find a new hound to play with and be happy, and I will find someone new too. Maybe Atticus will take me to Melbourne, a magical place that he has suggested is full of poodles.

We sat outside in a patio area and Atticus ordered us all poached eggs and ham steaks. We squinted and smiled in the sun and then the phone rang. It was Inspector Badgely, and Atticus put her on speaker so we could hear.

"I know you've got your work to do," she said, "but since your dogs already have the scent of Royston Saxby and you're obviously good in the bush, I'm wondering if you'd like to take a wee trip?"

"A trip to find him? He's not in custody already?"

"No, turned out he was prepared for something like this. He scarpered off yesterday and we just got a report about his Range Rover parked outside the Savage River National Park. He's in the wilderness there and it's going to be tough to find him without a clue of his trail."

*Are you guys willing to hunt him down?* Atticus asked us.

<Well, yeah, I need to remove that snack penalty,> I said. <And serve justice.>

"We can try, Inspector, but that area is full of waterways. Any half-decent hunter will lose us in the streambeds."

<He won't lose us!> I said.

<No squirrel!> Starbuck added.

*It's better to underpromise and overdeliver,* Atticus told us on the down-low.

"I appreciate you giving it a try. It's about a two- or three-hour drive. I'm sending you with Sergeant Naseer and Constable Fosse."

"You're not going?"

"I'll be along later; I have much to do here before I can leave—paperwork allowing us to put this trip together and operate outside our normal jurisdiction—but I didn't want to let Saxby have any more time to extend his lead."

"Okay, we'll be at the station soon." He looked delighted at this development, and that got me thinking. Starbuck and I were having a great time being nomads, but Atticus obviously needed more than hanging out with us to feel complete.

When he hung up and asked for the bill, I said, <Atticus, are we going to get paid for this?>

He shrugged and spoke to us mentally since there were other people around on the patio. *Maybe they'll give me a medal.*

<No, I don't mean you. I mean me and Starbuck.>

*Oh, I see. Are we in a negotiation for exotic meats?*

<No,> I said at the same time Starbuck said, <Yes, food!> He looked at me with his head cocked to the side when he realized I wanted something else.

*What do you want, Oberon?*

<I want you to perform human mating rituals with Inspector Badgely.>

*Oh, gods below, Oberon, don't put it like that. Ever. Eughh.*

<You know what I mean. Ask her out.>

Starbuck made a tiny whimpering noise. <No food?>

*Why is this so important to you?*

<You like her and she likes you. We have heard both of you say it. So you should act on it. Because it will make you happy. You haven't been with anyone but us for months.>

*Yeah, well, being a bit antisocial can be good for you sometimes.*

<Being social can be great for you too.>

Atticus exhaled heavily through his nose and drummed his fingers on the table. *I haven't…been sure anyone would be interested in me without my arm, you know? Living like this is new to me, obviously, and I'm not comfortable with it yet. I guess it's been a rejection I've been trying to avoid. I'm conscious of the problem. I still don't want to face it. It's been easier to just work.*

<I don't think she cares about the arm, Atticus. She hasn't even asked you how you lost it.>

*No, she's too polite. But eventually, she'll ask.*

<So is that it? You don't want to be asked?>

*Yes. Because I'm not sure how best to answer.*

<I would answer as vaguely as possible, Atticus. But only because "It was taken as a trophy by a vengeful goddess" might not play as well as you think it might.>

*You advise me well.*

The bill came, Atticus paid, and then we trotted to the police station and piled into a car with Sergeant Naseer and Constable Fosse. The sergeant was kind enough to roll down the back window so that Starbuck and I could put our heads in the wind. I am not kidding: the air smelled of wombats and adventure.

We drove to some town called Burnie and then turned south down the A10 road. I only know this because Atticus asked. He still hadn't visited this part of Tasmania, and he figured he might heal some devils while he was in the wilderness, or at least note their locations for later.

The Range Rover was parked on the side of the road and empty, but it was full of scent to me and Starbuck. We were off the leash because Atticus asked Constable Fosse if we could walk free since we were going into a wilderness and weren't in range of Launceston's city ordinance, and he said yes. There were other Tasmanian constables there too, and they were going to join us.

"Find the scent," Atticus said, like this was something he always said to us. That was just performance for the coppers. Privately, he asked us, *Did he go around to the back of the vehicle?*

We sniffed around at the back and whoa dang, was Royston Saxby's scent strong there! <He most certainly did,> I said.

Atticus pointed at us and looked at the sergeant. "He spent a lot of time at the back of the vehicle. He probably has a full backpack and weapons besides. Might have all kinds of gear if he's a hunter—infrared, night-vision goggles. We should be careful."

"So they have the scent?" Sergeant Naseer asked.

"Yes."

"Excellent. We will gear up and I need to perform my midday prayer before we go in."

"By all means," Atticus said.

<We can't go after him yet?> I asked.

*Not yet. The sergeant has duties to perform. Let me get you a snack in the meantime.* He pulled out that bag of his.

<I'm off snack penalty?>

*Yes. You've been kind and considerate of me today and I appreciate it very much.*

I have to say: those were not the greatest snacks, and he'd been feeding them to us for a while. They were dry and tasted like artificial chicken and vegetable fillers. Unholy vegetable fillers! But they were fed to me with love. That made them delicious.

After twenty million seconds, Sergeant Naseer and all the other police were ready to go. They had packs and vests and weapons on. It was all a lot of bother on everyone's part, and I pointed it out to Atticus.

<Don't you think it's weird that we are totally certain Saxby killed Howe but not why?>

*It's a bit unusual. I suppose we'll have to ask him when we find him.*

<What if Evelyn is in on it? I mean, yeah, Saxby killed him, but maybe Evelyn put him up to it because she didn't want to work with Howe in the bee business anymore.>

*It didn't read that way to me, but I agree that we're missing something. Time to pretend we can't speak mind to mind.*

"Okay, Oberon and Starbuck," Atticus said aloud. "Let's go catch ourselves a murderer. Follow the scent. Find the man. Find the man."

We barked affirmatively and plunged into the Savage River wilderness.

CHAPTER 9:

# SETTING UP THE STING

The wilderness had significantly different plants to pee on than what we'd seen so far in Tasmania. Leaves were broad and spread out as if to offer luxurious beds to insects and frogs.

<Atticus, what kind of forest is this? I know there are different kinds.>

*This is a cool temperate rain forest.*

<Did David Attenborough ever narrate one of those *Planet Earth* episodes about these?>

*Probably not an entire episode, but I'm sure they were included in one of the forest episodes.*

<Are there devils in here we need to heal?>

*Without a doubt. But we need to find Royston Saxby first.*

<We seek! Annnnnd! Destroyyyy!> Starbuck said, his nose twitching near the ground and ears perked up. Bostons were originally bred to hunt down rats in garment factories, so he must feel this seek-and-destroy thing was his destiny. That worried me because I wasn't sure that he was built to take out an armed human.

I'm built that way, though. If I can get close enough to jump on him.

We ran into our first stream after only a few minutes, but Saxby didn't try to lose us there. We picked up his scent directly on the other side, and that worried Atticus.

*Hey, you guys. That's a little too easy, and this is a guy who likes to shoot people in the back. I want you to slow down. I'll bet you he's set up some kind of trap ahead. Look for wires or some dodgy footing that might be a pit, some leaves on the path that don't look like they'd naturally fall there, concealing a snare…*

<Dangerous human tricks. Understand,> Starbuck said.

"Take it slow," Atticus said aloud for the benefit of the constables.

"Why slow?" Constable Fosse asked. "We want to catch up."

"I suspect a trap. Triggering that trap and hurting my hounds would slow us down more than just being cautious."

"A trap? What kind of—"

Starbuck yelped as his right front paw sank beneath some leaves and he was suddenly chest down on the forest floor, his eyes wide in panic, and then he scrambled back.

<Trap! No ground!> he said, and I halted, going no further, but sat right next to him.

There was a hole where his paw had sunk, and Atticus came up to squat next to us.

"Hmm. Yes. A bit of a pit." He reached out with his hands and brushed some leaves away, revealing a thin lattice of branches. Underneath that was a shallow ditch with sharpened stakes at the bottom, just enough to injure paws or feet. Starbuck was small enough that his leg didn't go far enough down to get punctured. But if I had stepped in it first, it would have gotten me for sure. It was designed for me, I think.

"See here, constables?" Atticus said. "We need to be careful."

"How did he have time to do that?" Constable Fosse said.

"He probably came here right after leaving the station yesterday, so he had all night and most of the morning," Sergeant Naseer replied, then pointed at the pit. "That's shallow enough that he could do it in a few minutes with a spade. Cutting and sharpening the stakes probably took longer. Maybe a half hour, tops. I imagine other traps will be quicker setups, snares and the like."

Atticus carefully cleared away the edges so we could step around it. I saw him take off his sandals too, which meant he was probably talking to Tasmania.

<Are you contacting the elemental?> I asked him.

*Yes. Saxby is doubtless wearing boots, so the elemental cannot feel him directly, but he's disturbing plants and animals, being seen and smelled, that sort of thing. We might be able to get a read on his general location without having to follow his scent. I'd normally never try this, but he's probably the only human around here besides us.*

<Don't we want to follow his scent?>

*Not if that's going to lead us into traps. We might be able to come at him from a different direction and avoid those. Move faster. Ah, yes. Tasmania says he's to the southwest, but this trail is heading west. At some point ahead, he turns. We can skip that and move in a straight line in his direction. Sniff around here a bit and then veer off to the left, all right?*

<Okay.>

We trotted in the direction he indicated and Atticus said, "This way," to the constables, and soon they were all following us, except we had no whiff of Saxby in our noses anymore. There were plenty of other smells, and we enjoyed that—plants and lots of animal musk, that sort of thing. Atticus just told us to adjust our course every so often according to whatever directions he got from the elemental, and he said it would take a couple of hours at the very least to catch up to Saxby.

A couple is two, I know that much, and an hour is equivalent to sixty months, I think, which is either equal to ten weeks or five decades. So, two of those would be, uh...well, it was a long hike. We climbed some hills and crossed two more streams in between them, pausing at the second one to get a drink and to have a little bit of something to eat. The constables were wheezing a little bit and complimented Atticus on his stamina.

"Thanks," he said. "I'm out hiking all the time, though."

"Do you think we're getting close?" Sergeant Naseer said.

"No way of telling," Atticus said with a shrug. But privately he said to me and Starbuck, *He's probably only fifteen minutes away, near the top of the next hill.*

"Okay." She held up her phone, which looked a bit clunky compared to many I've seen. "I've been updating Inspector

Badgely on this sat phone. She's coming in to catch up, and I'm letting her know our coordinates. Do you mind if we wait here for her?"

"Not at all," Atticus replied. "We can take a quick nap. Or the hounds can, anyway."

<Really?>

*Yes, Oberon. I'd like him to start down the other side of the hill at least. Right now, he has the high ground and that's not ideal.*

<Does he know we're close?>

*If he heard us moving, perhaps. I doubt he's seen or smelled us. As long as no one yells or you don't bark, he'll probably remain unaware. Go ahead, take a rest.*

<Yes nap!> Starbuck said, and he immediately twirled around three times and plopped into the grass nearby the stream.

"Go ahead, Oberon," Atticus said out loud. "Go lie down."

I curled up next to Starbuck, and soon, lulled by the chuckling of the waters, I dreamt of bangers and mash in Melbourne and a mysterious poodle named Belladonna.

CHAPTER 10:

# HARK! THE HERALD WOLFHOUND SINGS

**Belladonna** bounded away all too soon; her poufy tail went poof! as I woke up to the sound of happy human voices. Inspector Badgely had arrived with another constable. Both had packs on, and they shrugged them off as they came to the stream and greeted the other constables. The inspector smiled widely at Atticus and asked how he was.

"Happy to be here. This wilderness is wonderful."

"Wonderful, is it? Well, yes. That is a word that we could use."

"I hope this remains a wilderness. There's so much valuable life in here. You haven't heard of anyone trying to remove its status and develop it, have you?"

"No, but I'm not usually attuned to such matters. What's so special about it?"

"Well, this is where most of your leatherwoods are. Did you notice on the hike in?"

"No, I was mostly trying to get to the coordinates as fast as possible. The leatherwoods are important why?"

"They're the basis of your world-famous honey industry. And they support your pollinators, which in turn support your crops. They're what William Howe got murdered for—indirectly, anyway. And they're only growing scarcer."

"Surely, we can plant more?"

"Absolutely. I'd recommend it. But it takes seventy years for them to produce nectar, and they don't regenerate in burns. Deforestation is therefore long-term damage."

"You know quite a bit about Tasmanian ecology."

Atticus shrugged. "Part of my job with the Gaia Stewardship," he said.

"Right, right. Well, I've done my job too. Turns out Mr. Saxby had a significant motive to kill William Howe after all."

"He did?"

"William Howe and Evelyn Bickford-Hicks weren't just in business together: they were engaged."

"Oh, wow. How'd you find out about that?"

"A wedding invitation at Saxby's house. Plus, once we got Evelyn's phone in evidence, it became clear in her other texts with William that they were a couple."

"Wild. So obviously he knew the victim. Was Evelyn in on it? Why would she keep that from us?"

"Precisely what I asked her! I called her back in. She claimed to be scared by television, because in so many of the mystery shows, it's always the girlfriend or significant other who did it. I told her that's often the way it is in real life, too; people are rarely murdered by perfect strangers. Then she admitted that she's often shy about admitting the relationship, since she was older than Mr. Howe. Said people tended to judge her about it and insinuate that Mr. Howe was a gold digger."

"A gold digger?"

Inspector Badgely nodded. "Ms. Bickford-Hicks inherited $3.4 million from her father's death a few months ago. Royston Saxby's uncle."

"Ah, and Saxby was no doubt one of those who insinuated William was after her money."

"Indeed he was, while nakedly pursuing it himself. He wanted her to invest the money with his firm. Ms. Bickford-Hicks admitted to me that she probably would have, with William out of the picture. So there's your motive. But William himself wasn't that sort; he had no idea her father was rich, and he proposed to her before she inherited anything. He wanted to open a honey business before the inheritance, and after the inheritance, his plans were unchanged."

"So they had a genuine shot at happiness together, however unconventional it may have seemed, and Saxby ruined it."

"That's about the size of it. She didn't want to believe her own cousin would do that to her, or else she might have thought of it earlier. So, Mr. Molloy. We have a solid case now but no criminal in custody. Are your hounds ready to continue?"

"Yes. Did you want to press on or rest for a while?"

"Oh, let's press on. I don't know if we can catch him before the sun sets, but that would be ideal."

"All right. Oberon! Starbuck! Let's go! Find the man."

<Is he still close by?> I asked, and Atticus replied mentally.

*He's moved a bit, but we should be able to catch up in a half hour or so. Cross the stream and head up the hill, please, pretending you have his scent in your nose.*

We forded the stream and started smelling stuff as we went uphill. Caterpillars smell like vegetable pudding, in case you were wondering. Not my favorite thing. Yuck!

I noticed when I looked back that Inspector Badgely was walking next to Atticus and both of them were smiling. Maybe it was a preliminary human mating ritual and maybe it was just talking, but proximity had to be good, I figured. Though I'm not very clear on that. Apparently, there are mating rituals now that involve texting and emojis. For some reason, eggplants are significant. Humans are strange.

Near the top of the hill we actually caught Royston Saxby's scent again.

<Hey! Bad guy!> Starbuck shouted.

*What?*

<We found his scent again, Atticus,> I explained.

*Okay, I want you to stop right there, turn around, and bark quietly at me, a single woof.*

We didn't understand why but did as he said, and Atticus used our barks to tell the police we'd found something.

"He must be close by," Atticus said, and after excusing himself from Inspector Badgely, he hurried to catch up to us, speaking to us mentally as he came.

*Same as before, be extra wary of traps now. He's only about ten minutes away—he must have been resting while we were, or setting a trap—and he has to be armed. I don't want either of you to get hurt. Once we find him, we can let the police capture him. But I might cast camouflage on you when you get near; he's a very good shot and I don't want him to be able to take aim. In fact...let's purposely flank him and not follow that scent again. I really don't trust him, and following him will force us to slow down instead of catch up. He may have heard us in the valley and prepared something nasty. So, go uphill but not in his tracks; I'll go with you and send you ahead to spot him when we get close.*

We continued straight up, but this time, Atticus was right behind us instead of like a thousand miles behind. The police lagged, discovering that Atticus had just been being polite before. We were moving fast the way a Druid and his hounds can.

Once we topped the hill and went a little way down the other side, out of sight of the police, Atticus told us to hold up while he communed with the elemental.

The undergrowth in the wilderness was thicker than in the east, lots of ferns and broad-leafed bushes, but it wasn't full-on choking jungle, either. I could see pretty well, and Starbuck perhaps less so due to his shorter stature. Atticus said the best that the elemental could tell, Royston Saxby was still on the same hillside as us but near the bottom. If he crossed over and got to high ground before we got there, that would be bad.

There were far too many trees and bushes in the way for me to see anything, but Starbuck cocked his head and his bat-like ears went straight up, then rotated a tiny bit as he tried to zero in on something downhill.

<I hear bad guy. Boot crunches. Leaf swishes.>

*Okay. Let's head down and try to spot him. Then we'll get the police involved.*

Atticus cast camouflage on us, and my fur and skin tingled like always. Starbuck and Atticus melted from my vision. It was the endgame.

*Straight down; I think he's off to the right*, Atticus said, and we plunged into the underbrush, Atticus following close behind.

We were making plenty of noise on our own; we were sacrificing stealth for speed. I heard Starbuck's little paws hitting the ground behind me and his cute little panting breaths, but he heard more than that.

<Bad man stops. No boot crunches. But other noises now. Swishing. Stretching.>

*He's arming himself. He's got his bow.*

A *twang* and *whap* reached my ears right before a searing line of pain cut across my chest. I yelped, because that's what you do when something startles you with pain.

*Oberon! What happened?* Atticus said, but the answer was clear as a *thunk* followed and a shaft quivered in a leatherwood tree trunk. Saxby had fired an arrow at the noise we were making and had nearly got me.

<Just scratched.>

*Okay. Stay very low to the ground and keep making as much noise as possible. It will distract him while we flank him.*

<Got it.>

I started howling. Or yodeling, maybe. Just making a bunch of racket, trying to sing like a human, unable to remember lyrics under stress, so I did my best imitation of Michael

Jackson's hoots and grunts. Atticus and Starbuck swung away to the right under cover of that noise while I continued to creep downhill and tried to ignore the stinging in my chest. Looking right, a gap in the underbrush allowed me to actually see Saxby standing flush against the trunk of a tree on his uphill side. He had another arrow nocked and was beginning to pull it back, aiming directly at me—or maybe a bit over my head. But my howls abruptly had some competition: Behind us, I heard the police shouting. My distress had summoned the proverbial cavalry.

Saxby snarled, peeked around the tree trunk, and swung his aim uphill, to my horror. Where were Atticus and Starbuck? I pivoted and started barking instead of howling to try to scare Saxby at the last second, but he let fly with his shot anyway, and a cry uphill told me he'd hit someone. It sounded a bit like Constable Fosse. I barked again, really mad, putting some growls in between each one, and Saxby drew another arrow from his quiver, his eyes searching for me. As he straightened his left arm, pointing the bow in my direction and nocking the arrow, a blur from uphill interrupted him. His left arm swung down with a sudden weight hung onto it, and he grunted in surprise and dropped both bow and arrow.

<No bad man!> Starbuck shouted, and I understood what had happened. My little Boston buddy had taken a flying leap and bitten him on the forearm or wrist. But Saxby dove toward his pack sitting nearby on the ground, and I heard Atticus in our heads:

*Starbuck, run! Get out of there!*

Saxby came up with a handgun, one of those modern kinds with lots of bullets, not a six-shooter. He began shooting at the blurred form making noise, cursing all the while.

<No booms! Very loud!> Starbuck complained, and I took a few steps forward and barked as loud as I could. Saxby swung around, expecting me to be right on top of him, but he couldn't see me, thanks to the camouflage. He hesitated and then his knee popped and erupted in blood. He went down but fired wildly uphill, pulling the trigger until it clicked on empty. He began to drag himself to his pack, presumably to get more ammunition, but Atticus dropped our camouflage at that point, appeared from behind a tree just downhill of Saxby's, and planted his knee in the villain's back as Sergeant Naseer and Inspector Badgely came downhill fast to make the arrest.

"Thank you, Mr. Molloy," the inspector said, keeping her gun trained on Saxby as the sergeant holstered her weapon and got out her handcuffs.

"My pleasure. Is Constable Fosse all right?"

"He'll live, but he took an arrow to the knee."

<Oh, no! Atticus, he's doomed to wander Tasmania and tell young adventurers he used to be just like them!>

*I am never playing video games with you again,* he said.

"So you popped him in the knee in return?" Atticus asked.

The inspector shook her head the tiniest bit. "The sergeant did that."

"Justice for Fosse and justice for William Howe," Sergeant Naseer said, and then formally arrested a moaning and bleeding Royston Saxby and put the handcuffs on him.

CHAPTER 11:

# ALL WILL BEE WELL

**Atticus** told me and Starbuck what incredibly good hounds we were and promised us an extraordinary meal once we got back to Launceston. He also spent some time healing up my scratch and making sure it wasn't infected.

*Are you feeling dizzy at all?* he asked. *Light-headed?*

<Only when I dream of Belladonna, the mysterious poodle of Melbourne.>

*When did you meet her?*

<I haven't. But someday, Atticus, we will frolic in the clover. I know she's there. My active imagination is certain of it. She pines. I pine. We pine together in our own pine forest. It's a deep bond, pining is.>

Atticus volunteered to help field-dress both Constable Fosse and Saxby's wounds because he claimed to have some medical training, and the police had brought along some first aid kits. It was really just an excuse to lay his hands on them and perform just enough magical healing to make sure they wouldn't bleed to death or get their wounds infected. Then they had to rig up two of these things that Atticus called a travois so that we could haul the wounded men out of the wilderness. One was going to be pulled by me; of course I wanted to help Constable Fosse get to a hospital! Inspector Badgely came over and gave me lots of pets and scratches and made those really adorable high-pitched noises of joy as she thanked me for my help.

Atticus and some of the other constables took turns hauling Saxby out. It wasn't a comfortable hike for anyone, and if everyone had been okay, we would have camped for the night, but since Constable Fosse needed medical attention, that was a priority, and we pushed on past sundown. We were all dang tired when we got back to the vehicles, and there were a couple of ambulances waiting there for Constable Fosse and Saxby. They were taken to North West Regional Hospital in Burnie and we followed behind in the inspector's car.

"I can't thank you enough for your help on this case, Mr. Molloy."

"You can call me Connor."

"Not yet. Until Mr. Saxby is sentenced, I need to remain completely formal. You're a witness and will need to testify and so on."

"Oh! Right. Yes, I understand completely."

"I'd be pleased to call you Connor after that."

She took her eyes off the road for a moment to smile at Atticus, and he smiled back.

"And would I be able to call you Rose?"

"Yes. I hope you will. You'd better."

"It's a deal, then, Inspector Badgely."

They didn't say anything for a while after that, but they were both grinning an awful lot.

<Atticus, was that a human mating ritual just now?>

*I do believe it was, Oberon. I'll be able to ask Rose out and she'll be able to say yes after the case is officially over. Your wish is granted.*

<But it's your wish too, right? Because you like her.>

*I do; you're right. While we were hiking out of there, I was thinking about Evelyn Bickford-Hicks and how she saw a chance to be happy and went after it in spite of what her family and friends might think of her or William, and I thought maybe I've been letting my responsibilities discourage me from accepting joy where I find it.*

<Yeah, Atticus! And ooh, hey, you know what she's like? That founding farmer who kept singing about how he was not throwing away his pot.>

*Do you mean Hamilton, the founding father who was not throwing away his shot?*

<Yeah, that's what I said!>

*Fair enough. It's good advice. If I have a shot at some happiness here, then I should take it. What are you going to call this case, anyway?*

<Oh, easy. This is *The Buzz Kill.*>

*That works. We'll have to see if we can find some great food in Burnie.*

<Yes food!> Starbuck said.

*Whether we find any there or not, I'll also take you to that place you like in Launceston when we get back. Because you're very good hounds,* Atticus said.

<You good human!> Starbuck replied, and that was true. Chasing butterflies and wombats and fighting crime were all great, but what made me happiest was that Atticus was feeling good about life again. I wanted that for him because he deserves it. He is my best friend.

# GRIST OF BEES

A SHADOW NOVELLA

Lila Bowen

**The** last goddamn thing Rhett Walker wanted was another adventure.

He'd made Sam a promise—that he would ignore his destiny and settle down—and he was hell-bent on keeping it.

From time to time over the last few years, he'd felt things pass nearby, dangerous and magical things that needed tending to. And he'd felt that familiar tug in his gut, that internal sense of the Shadow urging him to ride out into the sunset, guns a-blazing. And he'd ignored that and gone out back to milk the cow, facing no threat more dire than a pernicious billy goat who knew exactly when to sneak up on a feller while he was carrying a pail of frothy milk through a frost-crusted yard.

Did he feel bad about it? Maybe a little. He was the Shadow, and the Shadow was a legendary monster hunter sent to protect the innocent. But none of those tugs were as big as his three greatest foes had been: the Cannibal Owl, Bernard Trevisan the necromancer, or El Rey. And so, he'd let the monsters go on with their monstering and stayed close to home, close to Sam. It felt like penance: Sam was a vampire now because Rhett had shirked his duty and let a monster kill him, and now Rhett would stay home and let the monsters kill somebody else. Even if many an afternoon found him awake by Sam's side, eyeballs wide open and watering and seeing nothing but the pitch black of their sealed-up room in the pueblo complex, his hands in fists as he fought the Shadow for the right to run off and get himself killed by a stupid goddamn monster and, even worse, disappoint Samuel Hennessy. The Shadow always wanted to go, but Rhett Walker knew he had to stay.

This tug he was feeling right now, though? It was the worst one yet.

And it had taken the form of a peculiar little fuzzy insect, striped gold and black and round as a grape. It perched on Ol' Bess's speckled hide as Rhett milked her and seemed to stare at him with eyes as black as crystal, whisker-brows twitching at him.

"What the hell do you want?" Rhett asked, but not unkindly.

In response, the critter fluttered its veined wings and took to the sky, buzzing toward the barn door as if in invitation. Rhett figured that was just him putting people things on animal doings and went back to pulling teats, enjoying what seemed to be his only truly private moment. Every morning, right after Sam yawned wide to show his vampire fangs and settled down into the bed he'd made to sleep for the day, Rhett kissed him on the forehead and went outside to go about his daytime chores. Cows, after all, did not like being milked at midnight, and so

Rhett spent a quiet, thoughtful hour in the barn they'd built beyond the ridge of pueblos. He milked the cows, checked any young things that needed watching, gathered eggs, kilt snakes, and generally enjoyed the freedom of a complete lack of human or monster intrusion. As soon as the sun hit the ridge, Snappy the rooster would start his caterwauling, and Winifred's demon daughter would wake up, and pandemonium would ensue. But this quiet time, his cheek to the cow's warm flank, was as close as he got to feeling peace.

And now here was this bug—a bee? Is that what a bee was? And it buzzed right back over to him and bomped against his cheek, soft and inquisitive as a kitten's paw.

"Well, that's a bunch of goddamn nonsense," he replied.

The cow sighed against him, and he kept milking, but the bee kept buzzing at him. Not in a threatening way. More like a child who wanted something and would keep tugging on a feller's sleeve until he gave in. With his usual dogged stubbornness, Rhett filled the pail and left it in the communal kitchen with a cloth over the top, then collected the eggs in his pockets and shirt. The bee followed him all along in a patient sort of way, like it was willing to give him his hour of peace in good faith. Finally, when he'd done all his chores and heard the rooster getting all puffed up for his big crow, Rhett buckled on his gun belt, checked his knife's edge, and let out a huge yawn.

"Whatever you want, it had better be good," he told the bee. "It's getting on my bedtime."

As if understanding him perfectly, the bee buzzed right out the open door.

Rhett watched it hover, just outside, waiting. He put his thumbs in his pockets and rocked back on his heels.

"Look here, bee. I made a promise I wouldn't go out hunting monsters. A promise I kept for four years now and don't intend to break. And what's more, I been awake since dusk, and daylight is no longer my fond friend. I ain't a one to go following strange critters into trouble."

But the bee just waited, gilded by the sun's reaching rays.

"Well?"

With a little swoop that reminded him of a shrug, the bee took off.

Rhett tried to turn around but instead found his feet moving of their own will, as if he were being towed along behind a horse instead of a bitty little bug. The Shadow had not been this insistent in—hell. Four years. Not since El Rey. A feeling started up, a warm and growing thing, pressing tight against Rhett's heart, urging him to go, to leave, to do what needed to be done.

To kill what needed to be killed.

After throwing a guilty look back toward the locked door behind which Sam would sleep, insensate and still as a corpse until dusk, Rhett followed the bee out into the dawn.

OOO

**Of course, it** wasn't long before Rhett had decided the bee was a goddamn idiot.

"I got to get my horse," he told it, angling for the pen where his paint gelding, Puddin', waited for him, ears perked up where he stood at the gate beside Rhett's usual mount, Ragdoll, who was halfway into her pregnancy and frachetty for it and kept shoving Puddin' aside as if Rhett would even attempt to cinch a saddle around her enormous belly.

But the bee kept on buzzing toward the northwest, like it knew any damn thing.

"I ain't walking," he warned it. "I told you I'm tired, and I taken too many silver bullets to the buttmeat over the years. You don't got to wait for me to groom, but I'm by God gonna saddle my gelding." Quieter, to himself, he muttered, "And slip a brush and a pick in my saddle for later, as I ain't that kind of monster."

The bee buzzed up in his face like it was telling him off, and it reminded him so much of Winifred getting on to him about something or other that he almost laughed. But there was no time for frivolity; not only was the bee threatening to sting him, but as soon as Otter Paws or Dan or Winifred's mischievous daughter tumbled out of bed and moseyed out to the barn, Rhett would have to explain why he was following a bug's orders and was headed off into the north, where there wasn't a damn thing, to his knowledge. And that was gonna be awkward.

As the bee expressed its anger in *Zs*, Rhett caught Puddin', which wasn't hard, and walked the gelding back to the barn as quick as he could, ignoring his winged friend as he tossed on his blanket and saddle and tightened his girth and rammed his Henry repeating rifle home in its holster. He rarely bothered with a bridle these days with such a sweet little pony and just rode in his halter. The moment he was in the saddle, he said, "Well, go on, then," and the bee buzzed off like a shot.

If he'd been riding Ragdoll unencumbered by her next spotty foal, he would've just hopped on her back without a currycomb or a handful of grain, and the old bitch would've kept her ears pinned for the first hour at least, and her trot would've been a rough and jouncy thing. But little Puddin', a fat black-and-white paint pony Rhett still thought of as his brother's horse, just loped along pretty as you please. The bee was faster than it looked, and whatever business it had was definitely up north. If they kept up at this pace, they'd be into the foothills by noon, and Rhett knew after four years of scouting this area that there wasn't a goddamn thing of interest up that way. But he also knew from his time as the Shadow that monsters tended to pick lonesome places to do their foul deeds, places where passersby weren't too likely to witness and report on any evil.

Even though it had been many years since Rhett had played the Shadow, much less been a Durango Ranger, he kept to the habits of a fighting man, and they'd served him well. His knife was sharp, his saddlebags were always full of jerky, and his bullet pouch thumped against his hip. His guns were loaded, the last shot in each barrel a silver bullet, just in case. The little leather bag on its cord around his neck snuggled close to his heart under his rust-red shirt, carrying a lifetime full of memories in the form of teeth, buttons, quarters, and sand, mementos of all the folks Rhett had lost. Whatever this bee was leading him toward, he was ready.

Or he thought he was.

When the sun was high in the sky, a little village shimmered into being where no village had any right to be, almost like an oasis. Framed by mountains and edged in the green of a creek's path, the houses still smelled of fresh wood, and the fields and orchards planted around them were swollen with vegetables and fruit.

"Well, I'll be goddamned," Rhett muttered.

The bee kept on, and Rhett slowed his horse as they reached the first buildings. He'd seen a town like this once—Reveille, a trap of a place built to feed the unholy appetites of a siren. But that town had been empty, and this town was busy with folks going about their morning chores with an unusual amount of cheerfulness. Fresh laundry hung on lines, and fat chickens pecked at corn, and children filed by, carrying their slates and following a teacher with a kind look about her face. Even the street dogs looked well fed. The bee led Rhett past all these sights, past so many curious glances, and finally stopped in a verdant pasture filled with bright flowers, Queen Anne's lace and jolly white daisies and purple pincushions and crimson Turk's caps nodding like teardrops of blood. Bees buzzed everywhere, making a mighty hum, and Rhett's stripey-assed leader was soon lost in the tumult of fuzzy bodies buzzing around a semicircle of golden domes made of straw and placed upon old stumps. A figure in sprigged blue calico was curled on the ground amid the hives, the bees bumping around and over it but not quite touching it.

His senses on high, Rhett pulled his gun.

"What the hell are you?" he asked, voice low.

When the woman looked up, he knew that she was no monster, for all that her eyes glowed with rage and ferocity and heartbreak, her brown cheeks glossed over with tears as bright as snail tracks shining in moonlight.

"They took my child," she said.

It was then that Rhett knew he'd been right to follow the bee.

000

**Now, touching strange** women wasn't something that Rhett did on the regular. In fact, other than carrying Winifred's daughter Frederica around like a piglet, he hadn't touched a woman at all, not since Cora had left him and his mama had died. He wasn't even really comfortable with Winifred putting a hand on his shoulder while she cut his hair; it made him jumpy as a rabbit in a shadow. So, he dismounted and hooked his rope over Puddin's saddle horn. He shoved his gun back home in his holster and just kind of stood over the woman, feeling helpless and out of his depth, then squatted down so's to be on her level, then reached out, almost, then stood up and paced a bit. No space near her was comfortable, and not only because of the frantic bees. She carried her sadness wrapped around her like a shawl woven with rage and hopelessness. And Rhett didn't know how comforting a body even worked if that body wasn't Sam.

The woman stood too, and the bees drew protectively around her, hovering, buzzing, orbiting without really settling. She seemed to accept their presence with the same grim stoicism she showed Rhett. Her skin was the warm brown of a fine Morgan horse, and her oiled black hair was tidily contained by a colorful wrap of fabric. Everything about her seemed comfortably sensible, from her faded and much-mended blue calico dress to the sturdy man's boots on her feet. Her body was younger than Rhett's and looked like it had known more backbreaking work, and her eyes seemed a good deal more ancient. She wasn't a girl, and she wasn't a fool. Her mouth was a grim thing, and it wasn't smiling as she returned his stare with angry interest.

"Goddammit," Rhett finally said. "Who did it?"

She didn't mince words or simper or whine. "The oracle's servants. From up on the mountain."

"Well, what the Sam Hill is a oracle?"

She cocked her head at him like he was an idjit.

"Don't know what the oracle is? Damn, child. It's like a religion—but worse. The oracle lives up top the mountain, like a fortune-teller, and folks come from all around to make their offerings and learn their future. When we settled out here, it seemed like just another peculiarity. Every town has their witch, don't it? But this town seems to thrive on it. You ever seen bees in these parts, ever tasted such sweet honey? It don't seem possible. But here we are. And then three women came down from the mountain one night under a full moon, barefoot and carrying candles with flowers in their hair, and they took my little Valerie away, and when my husband tried to stop 'em, they kilt him."

Rhett shook his head, trying to make sense of the woman's story, which didn't make a damn lick of sense.

"They kilt him?"

She nodded, eyes going wet all over again. "He said he wouldn't let them take the child, and the head girl said it was the will of the goddess or some such bullshit, and when he put hands on her, he fell over dead. She said if I touched her, I'd die too—a wicked, green-eyed, red-headed thing. I tried to save him, my Elijah, but them girls went away, taking my baby. Turned out he'd been bee-stung and swole up like a tick. Couldn't breathe." She wrapped her arms around herself and put her chin on her shoulder. "Both my man and my child in one night. He's gone forever, but the child...well, the child lives. For now."

"What about the sheriff? Are there no good men here?"

She snorted. "We got no sheriff. No trouble, before this. No one here will face the wrath of the oracle, of her women, of their gods. These people love their soft life. They save the whitest calves, the blackest roosters, the most well-formed lambs with the bluest eyes. They put out thimbles of milk and round berries and flowers at little altars and whisper prayers and beg for mercy. They'd sacrifice my child gladly to keep their hands clean and their jam jars full. I didn't know it before, but I know it now." She cocked her head to look at him more carefully. "And why the hell do you care about a stranger's troubles?"

Rhett scratched his head under his hat and looked up toward the mountains, the way she'd pointed. Puddin' stole up behind him and rubbed his nose on Rhett's back, and he absentmindedly leaned into it so the horse could get a good scratch off him.

"Well, I reckon I got to go fetch your child," he said, frowning and trying not to fall over from Puddin's vigorous ministrations.

"And why would you do that?"

This time, he met her eyes, stepping away from the gelding so he wouldn't look silly while he did.

"Your story don't make much sense, and neither does mine, but I reckon I was brought here to help you. Whatever's up on that mountain calls to me, tells me I got to get over there and find your child while I can and kill whatever monster took her so it don't happen again."

"It wasn't monsters. It was women," she said, her voice dripping with fury. "Three white women who should know better."

"Even humans can be monsters."

The woman spit in the dust. "These are not normal women."

"Be that as it may, anyone who'd take a child from her mother and kill your man is the sort of monster that needs to die. So, I reckon it's mine to kill, and I'd best get on with it. You got anything else you can tell me about this place, or that mountain? They got lots of kids up there, or will I know your get?"

The woman stepped closer and really looked at Rhett for the first time, and he flinched under her scrutiny and hunched his shoulders and pulled his hat down low over the kerchief he wore over his gone eye. He wasn't a man who liked being looked at, not only because he'd spent most of his growing up being told he was ugly, but also because sharp eyes would start to pick out his more feminine features and come to conclusions about what was in his britches and start asking questions. Even after years of Sam telling him he was perfect and handsome and his scars were like a road map to his heart, the ol' softy, Rhett still figured most folks weren't ready to see past what he was on the surface.

"What's your name?" the woman asked.

"Kit Lawson."

It wasn't a lie, not really. He'd been using that name for years, just in case Nettie Lonesome, Nat Hennessy, or Rhett Walker was still wanted for murder in Durango. All the fellers in Rona and San Anton knew him as such, and he'd answer to Kit as well as he'd answered to anything else. Names, he'd long ago decided, didn't mean a goddamn thing and were only useful if a feller was being hollered at about dinner.

"Well, I'm Diana."

She stuck out her hand, and Rhett shook it, appreciating the calluses and roughness of her skin. She did laundry, he reckoned, noting the pinkness and wrinkles in her palms.

As for Diana, she crossed her arms again and leaned back, surveying him like he was a horse she might buy, if the price was right. And he narrowed his eyes like he was a stallion that couldn't be bought, pinning his ears at the insult of being judged. Puddin' innocently cropped grass nearby, flicking the bees away with his tail with more gentleness than one might expect.

"So, what is it you ask as a reward for a-hunting my baby, Mr. Kit Lawson? You want money?"

Rhett shook his head. "No."

"You want a night of my time? Because I tell you now, I ain't that kind of woman."

Rhett drew back, horrified. "And I ain't that kind of man."

She sighed heavily. "Well, if it's money, I can't help you there. We got food enough but we barely scrape by on my laundry money. If you like vegetables, I reckon you can fill your bags, but that don't seem like enough."

Sticking his hands in his pockets, Rhett again found his gaze aimed at the mountain over her shoulder. Most mountains in these parts were bare, bald, stark orange things, razor sharp and unforgiving. But these mountains had a softness to them, a sort of bounty. They were a cool, sweet green and a bit hazy, like maybe all them flowers and plants just couldn't stop growing even long enough for a feller to blink. A river that passed nearby snaked lazily up to the base of it, inviting as a well-trod road. A bee landed on Rhett's shoulder, and he stopped himself from flicking it off. That, he realized, oddly, would've been rude. After all, they'd spent their morning together, him and that bee.

"I reckon you won't owe me nothing. Although I wouldn't say no to some honey to take back home to my people. We don't get it much, you'll understand."

She chuckled, a rusty sound, like her throat had forgotten how. "Honey. That's all you want? I'll give you a whole damn hive. Just bring my baby back." She flapped a hand at him, the same irritable and exhausted but fond gesture he gave Winifred's pesky daughter or the more affectionate barn cats. "Go on, then. I reckon the day won't get any nicer."

She began to walk away, a purposeful stride, and Rhett waited a moment, as if expecting something further. When it didn't come, he swung up into the saddle and settled himself, turning his gelding to watch Diana's back.

"Mine's the house with extra wash out back," she called over her shoulder. "You get back around a meal time, I'll have something set aside."

And then she was out of range, and Rhett was alone with his horse and the bees.

"I guess we'd best get to it, then," he said, and when Puddin' didn't protest, he nudged him toward the river that would lead them to the mountain. Diana hadn't said anything about finding this oracle, which could be anywhere in the mountains up ahead. But Rhett knew the Shadow would take him right where he needed to go.

It always did.

000

**The air must've** been right thin, or perhaps his eyesight was going. The mountain had appeared decently close, like it would only be few hours of riding, if that, but night was somehow already falling, and he wasn't gonna make it. Sighing heavily, he steered Puddin' to an old stump in a pretty patch of green by the river he'd been following, and dismounted. He was accustomed to making camp on the sere orange ground, or maybe among the twisted little saplings by a creek. But here there were big, old trees with leafy boughs overhead and the constant tinkling rush of the water. This lush place felt so damp, so alive, like when he sat down, he'd smear something and get a stain on his britches. It had been years since he'd gone through the motions of making camp on the trail, and it always brought up memories both fond and sad.

As he untacked his horse and made up for the missed brushing that morning, he thought of all the fine mounts he'd sat in his day. Old Blue, the one-eyed mule, was dead, but they'd acquired a new mule from a drunk prospector in Rona and named it Solomon. Then there was Squirrel, who was now Digby's horse, and Big Bastard, the ancient unicorn he'd inherited from the Captain of the Durango Rangers Los

Moras Company, a beast of a critter who still rode like a colt newly broke. Ragdoll's first colt, Pie, was doing well in his second year under saddle, and they still had Samson pulling the wagon. He'd broke and ridden and sold and bought dozens of horses, first for Pap and now for himself, but none of them held a place in his heart like old Ragdoll.

"Excepting yourself, Puddin'," he assured the sweet little pony, letting him drink his fill from the river before he hobbled him for the night and began to set up camp.

As he collected kindling and branches for the fire, he thought of Earl, the cantankerous Irish donkey shifter who'd taught him two of life's greatest lessons, one about living and one about dying. Gathering wood had been Earl's job on the trail, and the feller had done a goddamn terrible job of it, but Rhett still missed him every time he watched fire catch on twigs.

As he pulled the packet of drunkard's matches out of his saddlebag and lit his fire, he thought about all those nights with Sam and Dan on this trail or that while hunting monsters, of fires that took half an hour to build up, gently blowing air and twisting sticks and praying the Durango elements would be kind. And now, thanks to their success with the cattle ranch and plenty of money, he could just snap his fingers, pretty much, to make a fire. Dan, of course, still tried his patience nearly as much as stubborn tinder once had, but they'd grown comfortable in their fussing.

Even though he didn't want to think about Sam just now, Rhett couldn't remember a moment in the past ten years when he hadn't done so. The night had become their solemn time together, whether for watching the stars or seeking comfort of a different sort, and Rhett physically ached, being so far away from his partner. Sam would be awake now, hurt and then angry to find Rhett gone with no explanation. He could imagine Sam standing outside, pale and slender in the moonlight, fine nostrils flaring as he sought a whiff of Rhett's scent. Rhett hadn't bothered to leave a note; how could he? He still couldn't write, after all these years, and he'd had no idea where he was going. Sam would be worried, and Rhett felt bad about that, but Rhett had no interest in just sitting around feeling feelings. He had work to do tomorrow, which meant he had sleep to get tonight. It was peculiar, doing as most folks did, sleeping in the dark and rising at dawn. He hadn't followed that pattern in four years. But now he swallowed down some jerky and laid out his blankets and put his head against the saddle, staring into the fire fully clothed and glad to be exhausted to the bone because that meant he was too tired to feel guilty.

Rhett had already started to drift off when Puddin' whinnied a hello, but he bolted upright, hand on his gun.

"Who's there?" he barked.

"Howdy, stranger," a familiar voice said.

"Howdy yourself, Buck."

Rhett rubbed his eye and adjusted his hat to hide his jumpiness from a feller he hadn't seen in forever. Of course, Buck hadn't aged a day. He was a god, or half a god, or some mixture of whatever a god was and whatever Buck was. The man was always dressed like a gambler who couldn't lose in all black with a bearish beard and a sharp hat. His teeth shone in the firelight and his eyes sparked and he took a hand-rolled cigarette from a slender case and stuck it between his lips as he grinned.

"This your land?" Rhett asked, as he'd been to Buck's town far to the east and couldn't imagine why the god-thing would leave his cozy grove.

Buck shook his head and looked down, eyes crinkling in amusement.

"You know it ain't. Let's just say…we're on the border I share with someone who doesn't take kindly to me."

"An enemy?"

The sound that escaped around Buck's cigarette was almost a warning hiss. "Nothing that important. Let's say a rival, maybe. Calls herself Melissa, these days, although she's got a list of names as long as yours or mine."

Rhett settled back down against his saddle and threw Buck a look that suggested he was sleepy and bored, and the feller could get on with things or get the hell out.

Buck just chuckled, and for him, the sound was well-oiled and cozy. "I forgot how short your temper is, Shadow. But I seem to remember how to sweeten you up."

A silver platter appeared at Rhett's side, the polished metal shining and the fire flickering off grapes and figs, fine cheeses and smoked meats and a symbolic can of peaches. A goblet of deep red wine waited on his other side. Rhett relaxed his frown and grabbed a bunch of grapes, shoving the fruit in his mouth with little grace.

"I ain't eating those peaches," he said reproachfully. "Nor drinking your wine. I know what that shit does."

"It has always been your choice, you know," Buck said. "What happens in my grove doesn't happen without consent. Without you wanting it somehow, in some deep-down crevasse of you."

Rhett tossed the goblet and the peaches into the fire, feeling an unexpected surge of relief. Yeah, he'd wanted what he'd drunkenly shared with Sam over that can of peaches a few years back, but Buck's statement meant Sam had wanted it too. It was a comfort, to know that even before they'd found their footing together, Sam had seen something to want.

But that didn't mean Rhett was gonna eat any peaches tonight.

"Just the same," he said.

Buck shrugged, smugly magnanimous. "As you wish."

Rhett noticed a new goblet had appeared by his side.

"What is it you want, Buck?"

Waving a hand, Buck settled back against the stump, fine black boots crossed near the fire. "Oh, eat up. What I got to say will keep a few minutes. How's things at the old homestead?"

"You mean how's that child you put in my friend Winifred? She's a heap of goddamn trouble, and you know it. Show up sometime and see for yourself."

"I don't reckon Winifred would like that very much."

"Nor I."

Rhett didn't have much taste for magic, but he did appreciate how Buck's grapevines were somehow never empty of grapes, and how his wheels of cheese could have wedges cut out all night and yet never disappear. After the dry old jerky, it was a treat to taste a juicy fig, seeds dripping down his chin. And he knew from experience that Buck was fussy as a cat, and he wouldn't talk until he was goddamn ready, and he wouldn't be goddamn ready until Rhett had et his fill. So he did, ignoring the wine and washing it all down with the cool river water he'd filled his waterskin with, and when he couldn't hold another grape or wedge of cheese, he wiped off his mouth with the back of his hand and turned to Buck and said, "Go on, then."

"I'll be frank, Shadow. I reckon you're here to kill Melissa, and I want to help you do it."

Rhett snorted. Help never came cheap.

"Why?"

Buck cracked his neck, sneering. "Let's say it's a public service."

"Doing you a favor, you mean. Taking out a rival. And what do I get out of it?" Because Rhett knew damn well that unless challenged, Buck would just take what he wanted.

Buck snorted and looked away and took a long drag off his cigarette. "What I am has no rivals. You'll be taking out a danger. And if you succeed, I'll make sure nothing else comes after you. No more monsters. Your little family can squat in that pueblo until the end of time."

Rhett belched and waved it away, trying to hide how his heart clutched at that hope. "Right charitable of you from my perspective, but I thought your kind couldn't die?"

Buck tossed away his cigarette and leaned close, lips to Rhett's ear, close enough for Rhett to smell hot bear breath that burned his nose hairs like an old copper sink full of pig's blood set afire. Dizziness rolled over him, and he struggled not to cower away from whatever the hell Buck was.

"Listen good now, Shadow. What I'm going to tell you ain't something you'll hear twice, nor anything I'll claim to know. There's a chink in every suit of armor, if you catch the warrior twisting at just the right time. Melissa has only one moment of vulnerability, and it's when she's not herself."

"What the Sam Hill does that mean?"

Buck leaned back, black eyes gleaming. "Suffice it to say that you'll know it when it happens, if you're half as clever as I reckon you've got to be, to still be alive after all the havoc you've wrought. If I could tell you more, I would, but it's worth more than my life, if you call what I do living. There's bigger things than me in the world, if you can believe it."

"Huh. Me, kill a god," Rhett mused. When Buck growled a bit in the back of his throat, he added, "Or something like it enough. I reckon that'll make a fine trophy for my wall. So, I just walk on up, wait for this Melissa to twist, and shoot her in the tender spot I'll magically discover?"

"You know it won't be that easy." Quick as a snake's strike, Buck was in Rhett's face, closer than Rhett wanted to be to anybody other than Sam. His dark eyes pierced Rhett's own, and his breath scalded like steam. "The supplicant's path is twisted, designed to test you. She'll learn what's on your mind, and if she knows what you're really about, you'll never get close enough to touch her. A supplicant's got to be pure. So, I'm going to give you a little gift to help you make it through the gauntlet."

Rhett reared back as much as his saddle would allow, his arms all prickled up. "What the hell's a gauntlet?"

But Buck did the unthinkable: He grabbed Rhett's jaw and kissed him.

It was no normal kiss, what the god did, and there was no consent.

Buck's unwelcome tongue parted Rhett's teeth and raked a hot, wet furrow up the roof of his mouth, stabbing and burning. Rhett put his hands against Buck's shoulders and tried to push him away, damn the god, but against Buck, even the Shadow was useless as a kitten. Thank all the heavens, the kiss was over with that one jab, and Buck withdrew, licking his lips and smiling.

"May not seem like a gift now, but it will be."

"Your tongue in my mouth is not a goddamn gift!" Rhett snarled, and he went to poke a finger into his mouth, as there was something wrong with the roof of his mouth now, some new pain on the ridged flesh there. But Buck caught his hands.

"Leave it. Don't touch it again. When the time comes, you'll know what to do. Now drink some water and wash away the taste of my...benevolence."

Rhett picked up his canteen, angrily muttering, "The taste of your bite my butt," but as soon as he'd started to swallow, he knew something was wrong. This wasn't the cold, clear water from the river. This was Buck's wine, red and deep and numbing, and it was already inside him.

"This is the second time you've violated me tonight," Rhett said in a low voice that most folks didn't survive hearing.

"And hopefully, it'll be the last. You feel better now, though, don't you? Lean back. Relax. Everything's going to be fine."

He did feel better, actually. Calm and sleepy and warm. He took Buck's excellent advice and leaned back. He relaxed. Everything was fine. Funny the way Buck was grinning at him, sharp as a crescent moon. Rhett considered that as he rummaged among the platter's offerings and picked up a chunk of honeycomb, glowing golden yellow. He turned it this way and that in his grubby fingers, admiring it, wishing Sam were around to enjoy Buck's bounty, that they might enjoy it together. And speaking of which, where was his bee? Was it asleep? Did bees even sleep?

"What's bees got to do with this mess, anyway?" he asked, slurring a little as he popped a chunk of comb in his mouth and chewed.

Buck winked a card shark's wink and shot his finger at Rhett like a gun. "Well, that's the real question now, Shadow, ain't it?"

A branch in the fire collapsed in a shower of sparks, and when Rhett looked back, Buck was gone. But he'd left his food behind as he generally did; not like a god needed the food he made himself, was it? And if it was needed, he could just make more. Rhett was always glad for the vittles, and the silver platter would fetch a good price back in Rona. He was a practical man, and he wouldn't turn away gifts. Well, except the shiny new can of peaches, although he couldn't quite remember why that was.

"You're a squirrelly shit, Buck," he said to the stars, as he knew the god was long gone, probably back to his grove. There was something else he'd been meaning to ask, some other bone to pick, but he took another swig of wine and reckoned it didn't matter. "I just wish I knew what your long game was."

Because if there was one thing he understood, even sleepy and tipsy, it was that folks like Buck did nothing for free, and that's why Winifred had a child with little antler nubs who could fall sixty feet off a tableland and walk away laughing.

"Only way to find out is to play the game," Buck said, somewhere in the night.

"Well, no shit, Buck," Rhett answered.

And then he settled down against his saddle, tipped his hat over his eye, and fell asleep.

000

**He woke at** dawn, which felt both intimately familiar and aggressively odd. For years, he'd gone to bed as the sun rose and blinked awake in the pitch black at dinner time, which made the indigo night outside seem downright friendly. But now he found a pinkish sky and a field of red flowers abuzz with bees, and his sweet little gelding snoring, his forelock over his eyes, just a few feet away. Rhett found breakfast almost too easily in the form of a strangely stupid rabbit and got back on the trail, which was easier than the trails he'd traveled in the old days. He'd once told his friend Digby Freeman that "the trail" wasn't so much an actual trail as the time you spent going somewhere useful, a thing you made as you trod it. But those trails were generally through the rangier parts of Durango and Azteca, and when a feller was on it, dust coated his tongue and settled in his hair, and he was glad to find and eat a scrawny rattlesnake, mostly cooked over a sputtering fire. When he burped, along with the rabbit, he tasted wine, which was right peculiar, as he hadn't tasted the stuff in years.

But this trail? Almost felt like cheating. The sweet little ribbon of blue water meandered like a child taking its first steps, headed for the big ol' mountain, and although Rhett didn't tarry, he didn't kick his horse too hard, neither. The lush red flowers were like a carpet, their petals spread lazily wide and their dark, secretive centers winking as they billowed in a light breeze. The air was golden with pollen and the bee stayed always in front of him, keeping him on the path when he'd start to meander away. The Shadow seemed...well, tranquil. Like he was headed the right way and nothing too pressing would spur him faster. Like he was right where he needed to be, bumbling along like a bee from flower to flower at exactly the right pace. Aside from the hunched shoulders of guilt at leaving Sam and the knowledge that he was in for a fight of some sort, it was a pleasant-enough morning. There was something he had to do, just a-niggling at him, but he couldn't remember what it was. Still, there were worse places to forget one's purpose.

At least until a few hours later, when his stomach jerked in a way both unwelcome and familiar, terrifying and most beguiling. Someone was walking toward him through the field.

Rhett knew who it was immediately. The Shadow told him, and his eyes told him, and his heart told him. The way she walked, head up, shoulders back, fingers dusting the tops of the bobbing flowers. The way she didn't look away like a coward, didn't simper like a coquette. The way she pushed her black hair behind her ear. The way the red of the flowers suited her golden skin. He'd never thought to see her again, and after all these years, here she was.

His heart jumped on up into his throat, and his gut threatened to fall out his back end, and his hands went cold and his cheeks went hot.

"Hello, Rhett," she said with a secretive smile.

"Well, howdy there, Cora."

She stopped, close enough to rub his pony's nose.

"This is not your usual horse."

"No, it ain't. But what are you doing out here? Awful far from Calafia, ain't it?"

Cora stepped to his horse's shoulder, and with anyone else, it would've been too near by far. But she was one of the few people he'd let close, for all that she'd cut him to the quick when she'd left.

"What I am can travel far." She covered her giggle with her hand; it was odd to think this small, seemingly gentle girl could turn into a dragon with wide, leathery wings. "And you, too, are far from home. What are you doing here?"

Rhett tongued the roof of his mouth as he searched for the answer.

"Why, I knew just a moment ago," he said, feeling off-balance. "It's on the tip of my tongue."

"Do you go to the mountain to speak with the oracle?" she pressed. "Is there some burning question about your future you wish to ask?" She put a hand on his leg and looked up into his eye. "Or perhaps it is something about your past? About what might have been?"

"The future." Rhett bit his lip. That sounded close. "Something about the future."

"About your lover? Your life? A child?"

"A child," he mused. "Well, that would beat all. I always known it was possible, for all that it never did seem like my path. But wait." He cocked his head, and a cloud seemed to pass over the sun, casting them in a cold shadow. "Why are you here, though? You got a question to ask yourself?"

She shook her head. She hadn't aged a day, hadn't even changed her hair. Or her clothes. Cora looked exactly the same as the day she'd left him. And then…

Every hair along Rhett's spine raised up. Clouds gathered overhead, promising rain. The dark red flowers bent over like mourners at a funeral. A chill settled in his gut. The Shadow suggested something was very wrong, but Cora's hand was wrapped around his ankle now, and there was no polite way to get some distance.

"I will always have questions," Cora said, her voice sad.

Rhett's hand stole up to the leather pouch he wore around his neck, and he snuck a finger inside and felt around all the amassed mementos.

There.

The lock of hair.

"Cora?" he said, voice breaking.

Both of her hands were wrapped around his boot now, pricking in like a tiger's claws. Or a dragon's.

"You did not choose me," she said, accusing.

"You left me first."

"Because you did not choose me."

He failed to kick her hands away from his boot. "That's a goddamn lie. And so are you."

Quick as a blink, he whipped out his gun, and the moment the steel kissed her forehead, she cried out as if it burned and let go of his leg and fell to the ground and sort of slithered backward into the mass of flowers. Pressed up on her hands, she turned the full force of her tears on him.

"You did this to me!" she shouted.

"No."

"I left because you didn't want me!"

He shook his head. "No."

"My sister died because of you!"

Rhett closed his eye and wiped away the stinging tears pooling there. "The real Cora wouldn't say such things," he said sadly.

"But I am—"

He shot her in the heart before she could finish that sentence with another goddamn lie.

Whatever she was, she didn't burst into sand like a proper monster, like the real Cora would have. She—it—withered like a dying vine, turning green and then brown as it twisted up in a curious coil, looking like nothing so much as the gnarled stem of a cut pumpkin.

Rhett dismounted and walked to it, mopping his tearstained face off with his bandanna. He thought about touching the twisted remains of the Cora-thing, but he was too smart to touch something that evil, so he pulled out his Henry and poked it, pushing it over. It didn't weigh a damn thing, and there wasn't anything the least bit Cora about it. Rhett reached into his leather pouch again and pulled out the twist of ink-black hair wrapped up with a bit of red thread and dusted with sand.

The real Cora, he knew, was dead.

And she'd been dead for years.

And yet, seeing her walk through the field like that, running a hand over the tall flowers that stretched up as if to kiss her palm, smiling that coy, confident smile…for a just a moment, he'd believed it.

"What is this bullshit?" he hollered at the mountain.

But in the way of mountains, it did not reply. So, he got back on his horse, steered Puddin' around the desiccated stem-thing, and kept on going, following the bee.

000

**The day got** hot despite the breezes that playfully tugged at Rhett from the creek, and by the time the sun was high, Rhett was more than ready for an excuse to find some shade and hunt down some vittles. Just up ahead, a grove of big, twisted trees waited. Oaks, maybe. The sort of thing that required more water than Rhett's usual stomping grounds, and in return provided shade to rival a springhouse. The cool shadow spread within their circle called to him, and Rhett let Puddin' drink from the river before he hobbled the gelding and pulled his gun, hoping for a quick squirrel or prairie hen taking advantage of the lush copse.

He could be quite silent, when he wanted to, but as he edged under the canopy, he heard noises within. The wrong type of noises. Human-type noises. He was just backing away when his friendly pony whinnied a hello, and something crashed through the underbrush toward him. The shape that appeared made his jaw clench, and he did not take his finger off the trigger of his gun.

Of all the people in Durango, why did it have to be this particular one?

"Well, of course it's you," Pap said.

The old man's skin was white as sour milk, except for his beet-red nose. He'd raised Rhett but never said a single kind thing, and his frown showed he wasn't happy to see his foundling again. But now his face went from disappointment to disgust to hope. His cloying smile was somehow worse than his honest frown.

"And good that it is you, because I seem to recall you're a girl of means these days."

Rhett bridged the distance between them, his gun to Pap's bulging belly.

"I'm no girl, and I got nothing for you except bullets."

Pap held up his hands and took on that crafty look that suggested he thought he was gonna try being clever. "Sure you are. And where's that young man of yours? Took right good care of us, and we wouldn't be sorry to see him again. That Sam Hennessy."

"Took care of you?" Rhett spit in the dirt. "Dropped you off at the saloon with a bottle of rotgut, I think you mean," he muttered.

Someone else crashed out of the shadows, shouting, "Who the hell are you talking to? Some other woman?" Seeing Rhett, she snorted. "Oh, it's you."

Rhett no longer felt hungry. Seeing them both here, Pap and his wife Mam, he felt sick. These two grifters had stolen him as a child and raised him as a slave, and he'd hoped to never see them again after Sam had dragged them off to Rona. But if someone was telling the future, surely they were on the trail to find out how to win at cards or otherwise cheat their way to fortune.

"Hello, Mam. You two varmints are far from home."

"No thanks to you!" she screeched. "We got stole because of you, and tortured because of you, and left without a cent to our names in some two-bit town while you lived high on the hog somewhere else!"

Rhett shoved his gun back home and cracked his knuckles. "I live in a haunted pueblo in the desert, and we don't abide drink. It ain't high on any hog I've ever seen."

"But you got money! Look at the silver on that saddle. We could live off the sale of it for a week!"

"Or you could get a job, or farm the land, or do anything other than drink yourselves to death and caterwaul about nonsense."

Pap spit at his feet. "Still an ungrateful little shit. After all we done for you."

Much to Rhett's surprise, someone else burst out of the trees, a bigger and angrier person still sitting pretty high on the list of folks he never wanted to see again. It was Herbert, a man he'd tangled with near San Anton while tussling with the necromancer Trevisan. Last he'd seen Herbert, the man had been missing a finger and gathering up lawmen to come after Rhett and his posse and hang them for kidnapping a child...who had actually been said necromancer in disguise.

"You!" the big man thundered, his jowls quivering. "I'll have the sheriff on you! We've been looking for you for quite some time, and now the fox has finally come home to roost!"

Rhett tiredly rubbed his forehead. "Don't know much about animals, do you?"

"How dare you speak to me, you impudent cur? I'll box your ears!"

Not that Herbert made a move to do so; he was panting from exertion and sweating, and he wore no weapons at his hip.

"What are you shouting about, Herbert?" a woman called, and Herbert's wife Josephina emerged from the grove, stopping dead in her tracks and going white as a goddamn sheet.

"It is him! The killer! The child-stealer! Arrest him immediately!" she howled.

"I'm the closest thing to a lawman in fifty miles, and I don't think so," Rhett said. He put his hands on his hips and looked at the semicircle of bastard people that had formed around him.

Pap, Mam, Herbert, Josephina.

For all the monsters he'd faced, these monsters wore the face of human men and still thought themselves superior.

"I ain't got time for this," he muttered, turning back to his betraying horse.

"And why's that?" Pap said, falling in step with him as if they were sharing a secret. "You got somewhere to be? Somewhere in a city, maybe?"

Pap reached out to touch the silver conchos on Rhett's saddle, and Rhett slapped his hand.

"No, fool. I got a job to do."

Pap's grin was a dark thing, and not just because several of his teeth were black pegs. "Thought you gave up on jobs. That Sam said you were giving it all up for him. Going to ground. Settling down. Nettie, are you trotting out behind that nice boy's back? Be a shame if somebody told him."

Rage flared in Rhett's chest, burning like acid up his throat, and he made fists so he wouldn't pull his gun.

"My business is none of yours. And you can't tell Sam nothing because you don't even know where you are, much less where Sam is. After all these years, I reckon you still can't tell your ass from an alligator when it comes to gettin' places."

Pap reared back like he might slap Rhett, and although Rhett had hunched and shuddered away from the man's beatings for years, curling in like a goddamn armadillo, now he stepped forward, chest to chest, right into Pap, forcing the man to step back.

"You don't scare me anymore," he said, and in that moment, he knew it to be true.

"And what of me, then?" Herbert barreled over, close enough to make Puddin' dance back in alarm. "I have the law on my side. Posters of your face are pasted all over San Anton, and the reward money goes up every year. Are you asking the oracle if you'll ever get caught and hang for your crimes? Because I assure you: vengeance will find you."

Rhett looked him up and down, his eye cold. "Unless you're gonna sling me over your round little shoulders and carry me to San Anton on foot, I don't see that as much of a threat."

Pap looked at Herbert. "Sounds like we're of a similar aim, sir. I reckon I'd like to collect on that reward."

Now Rhett stepped back, both guns drawn. "You'll both take a bullet in the gut if either one of you tries a goddamn thing. Now, why are y'all out here?"

"Why are you?" Mam squawked. "Only thing nearby's the oracle."

"Yeah, Nettie. What big question brought you so far out here?" Pap said, all sly.

"The oracle," Rhett said to himself. "So, that's it for all of you. You're going to the oracle. Pap probably wants to know where to dig up another man's corpse to steal his gold teeth, and I reckon Herbert wants to know where he can steal another child." Rhett shook his head. "Baby-stealers, the lot of you."

For it was true. Pap and Mam had stolen Rhett, and Herbert and Josephine had found a little child in the middle of nowhere and decided to take her in, very much against her will—Cora's sister.

"Some children are bound for better," Josephina said, sounding all gentle like a teacher holding a ruler behind her back. "It's not stealing if you improve a child's life, give them a proper destiny."

Rhett looked from Rhett to Mam. "You ain't God. You don't know what's better. You just want everybody to be like you."

He turned Puddin' so the horse was between him and the four folks he hated most in the world. Before Pap could intercept him or interfere, he mounted up and kicked his horse to a canter. The little gelding was surprised, but he obliged, and for all that they hollered in his wake, threatening and cajoling and begging and threatening again, he didn't turn back around. Let them go to the damn oracle, if they could find it. He would get there first and...do whatever he meant to do there, whatever the Shadow required. It was slippery in his mind, floppy and single-minded as a fish on the dock, but he knew he had to go there. To ask a question? He shook his head. Too many emotions, roiling around in there like angry bees. He needed to get some space. And he needed to get to that mountain. A bee buzzed around his head, and he swatted at it.

"Cut that out. I got shit to do," he mumbled at it.

He kicked his horse again, and they cantered until the bee was gone and the shouts were replaced by the peaceful quiet of the prairie and the gentle swishing of red flowers and the soft laughter of the stream.

Whatever Rhett was doing there, it was better and more pure than whatever those other assholes were doing. And eventually, he'd remember what it was.

OOO

**The afternoon lulled** him into a daze, half-asleep among the nodding flowers, kissed by a warm breeze. Puddin' kept on like he knew his job, and Rhett was grateful for the quiet. He loved the pueblo, loved his simple life, loved Sam, but it felt damn fine to be out in the afternoon and alone to enjoy the world on his own terms, nobody tugging at his shirt or scolding him about the chickens or silently begging him to be there, come dusk. He was, he realized, enjoying himself.

At least until his stomach tugged up and a wide black shadow passed over him. He looked into the sky, squinting behind his hand, and saw a monster he'd long been avoiding, the very sort of creature that had dogged his steps on his first time on the trail.

A harpy.

No. Three of the goddamn things.

Oh, sure, a harpy looked like a vulture to your average man, but Rhett was no average man. To him, each hulking, razor-feathered beast of a bird had a woman's bright blue eyes and the wrinkled, swinging dugs of an old hag. Even worse, each foul bitch-thing had a mouth.

"Varmint!" called one, swooping down to clutch at Rhett's hat with her talons and send his poor horse skittering. Ol' Ragdoll would've been steady, knowing what she was up against and prepared for a fight, but Puddin' had never beheld a harpy before. The next beast swung low, grazing the pony's rump with sharp claws, and Puddin' took off like a shot.

"Heh heh. Meat on the hoof!" a harpy yelled, but it was everything Rhett could do to stay in the saddle as his horse scrambled across ground thick with flower stems and twisting roots. Plunging and tripping, Puddin' finally threw him, and Rhett tumbled over his horse's head and onto his back in the carpet of flowers. His back ached to hell, and he reckoned a regular ol' human would be in a world of pain and possibly unable to get up again, but one of the few benefits of being a monster himself was the speed with which he healed. He gave himself three breaths on the ground, feeling the hot zip of monster bones knitting up—but he spent those three breaths pulling his gun. Puddin's muzzle appeared, blocking the sun as he whuffled his apologies.

"Not now, silly critter," Rhett mumbled. "Don't you know when a fight's coming?"

But he didn't. He'd never been in one. Not like this.

Rhett's life had gotten a lot more peaceful, and for all that Ragdoll and BB had seen him through necromancers and werewolves and shapeshifters and chupacabras, goddamn their lizard eyes, it'd been a long time since he'd been in a tussle. The sweet little pony was gonna get himself killed, caring that much.

Instead of slapping him away to safety, Rhett rubbed Puddin's nose, and that was a mistake, as another harpy, laughing like fire in fall brush, swept in to leave long scores in the painted hide and send the innocent creature galloping his heart out to be anywhere else.

"Goddammit," Rhett muttered. "I'm out of practice."

He stood, ignoring the pain, gun in hand, and scanned the sky for the harpies. But that was foolish too, and he barely had time to throw himself to the side before one of the bitch-birds plucked out his remaining eye. She barely missed, her claws catching in his hat. Furious with himself and the monsters in equal measure, he recalled his extra sense and listened to the Shadow's dependable tug in his gut. If there was one thing the Shadow knew, it was how to find monsters.

There. Two birds wheeling while one dove for him; that was their strategy. Not the smartest things, harpies. Instead of looking up at the betraying sun, Rhett flopped on his back and followed his gut, tracking the three monsters hunting him through the sky. As the next one plunged for his heart, he squinted and blew her out of the sky.

The harpy screamed and tumbled to the ground, and Rhett rolled over and lunged at her, putting the gun against where her heart should be and pausing for a breath before pulling the trigger. Once, a long time ago, he might've asked a few questions, made some demands, called the bird a few choice names—or tried to figure out their game. But he knew enough about villains now to kill first and ask questions later of whatever critters were more interested in striking up a deal than taking chunks out of his hide.

And then he pulled the trigger, and the harpy exploded in a cloud of black sand, leaving nothing behind.

Overhead, the other two birds screamed their rage, and his gut told him the moment the next one swooped down, diving like a falcon for a mouse. As he wasn't a mouse, Rhett just shot that hell-buzzard out of the sky, too, then finished the job the moment she hit the ground. Sand filled his nose, grit ground between his teeth, and he could feel the hateful slip of grains and pebbles in his boots. He realized he was smiling, an old, vicious, fierce smile, the smile that said that only one monster was walking away from this tussle.

Goddamn, he'd missed killing shit.

Twisting a rooster's neck for supper or slaughtering a pig for bacon felt like a sad, pathetic pantomime of what death meant when it was a fight between equals.

Well, not equals. Harpies weren't people, goddammit. They could barely sling together more than a sentence, and they did nothing but eat babies and crap their nastiness over everything in sight. Vultures were useful, effective things, but harpies were a mad perversion of a decent scavenger, which was something Rhett knew more than a bit about.

His gut tugged in the wrong direction, and he looked up to find the last harpy flying away from him, wide wings flapping.

"Oh, no, you don't," he muttered.

Stripping off his clothes and boots and hat, he tracked the bird, noting that it wasn't going toward the mountain but out into the prairie. And that wouldn't goddamn do. Once he was free of his human encumbrances, Rhett took a running start, leaped into the air, and felt the warm, familiar, golden string that seemed to run down his middle and turn him inside out. Soon, he had his own wings, his own bald head, his own sharp talons, his own cruelly hooked beak, and as the Lammergeier, he flapped after the harpy, screaming his fury at being denied his prey.

He'd once thought his alternate shape was a regular sort of vulture and considered that fitting. But then the necromancer had taught him the words for what he was, for this giant vulture from Africa: lammergeier, ossifrage, lambhawk. He was bigger and stranger than anything else in the skies of Durango, and even if his daily life had grown quiet and tranquil, he still took regular trips to the clouds, soaring over their settlement and casting wide circles until he was sure everything under his purview was safe. He'd even followed Ragdoll a few times, in this form, to see which wild mustang stallion she'd select to sire her next painted foal. He had great control now, and even in this form, with this brain, he knew what he was about, which was chasing down that harpy, knocking her out of the sky, and demanding at the point of gun or claw that she reveal why the hell she'd attacked him when he was minding his own goddamn business.

The harpy put on speed, but she was no match for him—and he wasn't weighed down by swinging dugs. Everything about him heated and quickened as the predator neared his prey, and his talons stretched and fisted, stretched and fisted as he dreamt on the feeling of flesh parting beneath his sharp beak. Wingbeat by wingbeat he neared her, just a little higher up, before he pinned his wings and dove, screeching his defiance in a voice that felt as much a part of his soul as his human one.

Talons struck and held, and the harpy cried out, and they tumbled together, spinning and spinning until they landed in an ungainly heap. The harpy tried to struggle away, her bright blue eyes blinking fear, so Rhett aimed for that ring of sky and stabbed it out in a spurt of oily black blood. She only fought harder after that, and Rhett longed to turn human again, but without his gun or knife, she'd have the advantage. He was hard to kill—but it was not impossible. Grappling and grinding his beak, he stabbed out her other eye, then snapped at her neck, but not hard enough to sever it. The harpy flopped there, almost sad in her pathetic misery, but Rhett wasn't one to forget a grudge in either of his bodies.

"Trash bird," the harpy spat. "Stupid bitch."

With a feral growl, Rhett took back his human form and wrapped his fingers around the pins of the harpy's razor-sharp flight feathers, ripping them out in great gouts of inky blood. Neck snapped, eyes pecked out, unable to take to the sky, the harpy jiggered like a broken marionette, and Rhett stood and grabbed her by the neck and yanked her back to where her fellows had left nothing but sad piles of ash-colored sand behind. He could feel her growing stronger with each step, her body just as resilient as his, her neck bones knitting, and he took up a jog. Her feathers cut up his hands, his feet hit rocks and burrs, but he kept on, knowing full well now after a lifetime of pain that nearly everything could fix itself, in time.

There—his clothes and revolver. He didn't let go of the harpy's neck as he sank to his knees, naked as the morning, and put the gun to her chest.

"Why'd you attack me?" he asked.

But the harpy just laughed, a vile, wet sound.

"Bitch," she spat. "Know what you are."

"Well, no shit. I ain't hiding from you. Now tell me why you're after me. Were you there with the Cannibal Owl? Was it your sister who tracked me across the desert? What?"

Still the harpy just laughed. So, Rhett pressed the gun harder, right between her flapping, hot dugs.

"I could snap your wings," he suggested.

Her answer was yet more laughter.

It was a strange, long moment. Rhett, naked in the tall grass, holding down a half-broken bird and finding himself gone soft.

Well, no. Not soft. After all, he'd done his damage. But soft*er*, somehow. He wasn't willing to snap off bits of this creature to get answers, wasn't going to sink to torture.

Hell, he was asking a monster to explain motives, which seemed downright stupid.

"Well, shit," he muttered, and as the harpy kept laughing, he shot her, turning his head away so he wouldn't get more sand in his mouth.

The prairie was quiet for about thirty seconds, and then the sounds came back. The drone of bugs and bees in the flowers and the booms and chirrups of frogs in the crick and the inquisitive twitters of the birds who weren't quite sure it was safe to sing again. Rhett stood, dusting the sand off himself, watching as the razor-feather wounds on his arms began to close.

"Well, hell."

He went to the stream and stepped in, all cautious, his skin dimpling as it hit the freezing cold water. Sam had taught him to swim, and it still didn't seem safe or like a pleasant sort of thing to do, but the creek wasn't deep enough for that to be a problem. Splashing water up his body, hissing against the cold, he had no choice but to see his old scars, the pink twists of silver bullets and the thin lines of knife blades writing their jagged secrets across his brown skin. He caught a glimpse of himself in the water and quickly looked away. He'd never liked his face or his body, and time hadn't done anything to sweeten that feeling. At least Sam didn't seem to mind.

Puddin' met him as he exited the creek and found his clothes, dressing quickly as if someone else's eyes had suddenly reminded him he was out in his all-together in enemy territory. He buckled on his gun belt and reloaded, making a mental note to pay a bit more attention to what might be headed toward him, looking for trouble. To think: harpies, out there, just being assholes. It perturbed him, not knowing if they'd wanted a quick meal of something stupid and alone or if they'd been after something more sinister. His Shadow powers meant other critters didn't know he was a monster too, so they might've just seen easy prey. But the way they'd called him names—called him *girl* names—suggested they knew more about him than he was comfortable with.

His horse, however, had nothing magical about him, and the cuts on Puddin's rump didn't look good. Sam did most of the critter-doctoring back home, but the softhearted cowpoke made sure Rhett always kept a basic healing salve in his saddlebags, so he pulled it out and dabbed it on the pony's hide while he danced and twitched, his instincts telling him to stay near Rhett for safety while also to get the hell away from whatever pungent business was being glopped all over him.

"Quiet, you," Rhett murmured. "You took your licks, and now you got to take your remedy, even if it stings. That's why you can't be softhearted in this world."

Puddin' blinked as if to say, "Look who's talking."

OOO

**The mountain was** sort of like somebody staring at you from across the room while you were drunk. You thought you saw it all right, and then you got closer, and it was different and maybe a little less what you'd hoped it would be. Most of the mountains in these parts were stark, orange things cut through with black shadows and the barest fuzz of green, but this little group of mountains was almost purple, always hazy, with little cloud hats that never seemed to float away. They looked like maybe they'd been snatched up in some other part of the world and slapped down in the desert and reckoned it was everybody else that was peculiar. So, as Rhett got closer and closer and they didn't get any clearer, he understood well and good that magic was afoot. Nothing in these parts, other than a healing bruise, had any right to be that lavender and green and blobby.

With the harpies gone, the bee bustled back into view and kept on, and the river they'd been following didn't change much, at least. The water stayed cold and sweet, and neither he nor his horse complained. The land changed gradually and reminded him all too much of Buck's grove: the red flowers petered out and gave way to neat orchards, gardens busting with leafy greens, and pastures of sleek white goats and glossy black cows, mooing their welcomes. A few farmhouses sprang up, not quite a city, their boards still yellow with sap. The trees grew gradually bigger, their canopies spreading out in great dappled shade, and here and there a vibrant lea busting with lacy flowers sheltered a few golden bee skeps, although no bees personally approached Rhett with any sort of business—not like *his* bee. A great rushing sound built as he got closer to the towering stone itself, and he found a waterfall gushing down the side of the mountain and surrounded by lush, twisted fruit trees, candy-colored flowers, and strange little clay statues of ladies stuck toe-down in the black dirt. Some were round as balls and some were skinny and holding snakes, and the lot of them were eyeless…and yet Rhett felt watched.

He'd expected a cave, or a passel of fighting men, or something dark and threatening, but all he found was a twisty little dirt trail up the side of the mountain. Although he'd seen people tending their farms, he hadn't yet been approached, and even if there'd been signs, it's not like he could've read the dang things. Shielding his eye, he looked up the mountain and saw a building high up top, all boxy lines like a child's building blocks with triangles on top. The afternoon sun gave it a sort of halo thing like he'd seen around various saints in paintings in Ines's old chapel, and he reckoned that meant whatever was up there thought it was right holy.

"We'll see about that," he muttered, dismounting with a creak in his back.

Feeling altogether disturbed, Rhett hobbled his horse so he could graze and drink as he needed, filled his canteen from the waterfall, and methodically checked his weapons. Both guns in his holster were loaded, the last bullet in each hand-cast in silver. His Bowie knife, the same one he'd carried all these years, was sharp as a harpy's feather. After a moment's consideration, he pulled the Henry repeating rifle off his saddle and slung its strap over his shoulder. He had a bullet pouch hanging off his belt, and even a little stick knife he'd taken to keeping in a sheath on his boot. He hadn't needed to be so deadly in many years, but he'd watched too many good people die to assume that fate would stop throwing shit into his path when he least expected it. The bee buzzed at the base of the trail, expectant.

"Meh!"

Rhett looked down, startled, to find a tiny goat staring up at him, tongue poking out and blue eyes shining up. It was white as snow and looked, in his mind, a bit stupid.

"What the hell?" he muttered.

"Meh!"

"Well, I don't see how that's my business," he told the goat, because he'd always been the sort of feller who gave animals the benefit of the doubt, and it had worked out pretty well.

"Meh!"

He looked around the clearing but didn't see any mama goats anywhere, nor any annoyed goatherds about to shake a stick at him. He went down to one knee, and the peculiar little thing butted him in the hip.

"You'd best go back to your folks," he told the goat, which was twitching its tail like a mad thing and trying to nurse off his hand. "You're too little to be out here all by your lone. Something big'll come along and eat you."

"Meh!"

The goat offered no thoughts on that as they struggled up a path growing increasingly more challenging. It was narrow and so close to the ledge that Rhett decided even for a hard-to-kill thing that could turn into a bird, he didn't much feel like looking down. At least when he'd thrown himself off the ledge that first time, when he'd discovered he could change into the bird, he'd reckoned that if he failed, he'd die a quick death, the question answered for all time. Now he knew that if he fell, he'd just get the hell beat out of him, break a bunch of bones, and end up in a bloody heap at the bottom of the mountain, slowly waiting for his body to heal itself as the sun baked his flesh.

"It's not easy, being a monster, you know," he said to the goat. "You ain't one; I can tell. But the thing is that after having a hard life, you get real accustomed to things being easy. To letting stuff go when before, you might've chased it. I reckon I forget how to hunt, once I got everything I needed."

In response, the goat unloaded an ass full of pellets, and Rhett figured that was about how he felt about it, too. He didn't like the thought of how he'd gone soft, but he hadn't noticed it at the time, seeing as how it'd happened slowly, over time.

"Too much time to think," he told the goat. "Gets dreamy on horseback, but this is just nonsense."

"Meh."

"Don't I know it, buddy."

The top of the mountain was near enough that Rhett could now see the triangular roof of the peculiar building up top poking out against the blood-orange sky. He began to pass lit braziers, wide metal bowls filled with fire and the peculiar scent of burning herbs. Statuary appeared, men and women and silly little fellers with goat legs, posed in limber sorts of ways and wearing bedsheets and feeding one another grapes and honeycomb and sipping from goblets and waving branches around. They looked like layabouts, which Rhett didn't approve of, but at least he was fairly sure they weren't the sorts of statues Ines the gorgon made, as they all looked too smooth and pretty to have ever been real people. He could feel eyes on him now, but nothing new tugged at the Shadow's sense, meaning nobody meant any real harm. He hadn't felt it in years, but surely he would recall the skin-crawling, neck-prickling, bowel-liquefying feel of a weapon pointed at him from the darkness?

"Hello?" he called.

"Meh?" the goat echoed.

The bee just buzzed.

"You two stay out of it."

The path ended at the base of a set of dove-gray stairs, their smooth stone too clean for anything that dared plop down in the Azteca dirt. Yet more braziers lined either side of the stairs, which led to a strange and somewhat cavernous darkness beyond. Rhett took the first few steps, gun drawn and senses on alert, but he turned back around when he heard the frustrated clicks and butts of the tiny goat, who couldn't manage the stairs and was upset about it.

"Oh, goddammit," he barked.

But he hurried down, scooped up the goat in his left arm just like he'd carried an infant Frederica, and kept on with the gun in his right hand. The steps were slippery under the smooth soles of his boots, and the mountain up here seemed awful quiet, other than the whispering wind and the faraway splash of the waterfall down below. For all that he liked high places and loved his time with Sam atop their favorite tableland, this place felt…other. Wrong. Like it shouldn't be there at all.

And that made Rhett jumpy.

As he neared the top step, he heard the slap of bare feet on stone, quiet and soft, and he aimed his gun for where whoever-it-was would appear. The footsteps didn't sound furtive, and nobody fought barefoot if they could help it, but still Rhett felt like he was in the belly of the goddamn beast, and he'd sworn long ago that he'd never get taken prisoner again.

"Who's there?" he barked.

The only answer was laughter, girlish giggling. The footsteps had stopped.

"Welcome, petitioner, to Melissa's temple," a breathy voice said.

In response, Rhett cocked his gun.

"What the hell's that mean?"

A woman appeared at the top, looking down from on high, the temple's columns framing her face. She was young, beautiful, half-naked and draped in bedsheets, smiling at him like he was a naughty child. Her hair was the color of sweet potato pie, her eyes altogether too green and lit from within. Two more women flanked her, each beautiful in a completely different and equally unnerving way. Gold bracelets bit into their bare upper arms, and their wet teeth glinted in the moonlight like wolves approaching a fire. One woman held out a silver platter of fruit and cheese and honeycomb; the other offered a goblet identical to the ones held by the playful statues Rhett had sneered at on the way up the mountain. The Shadow told

Rhett these women weren't monsters, but every other bit of him said they were. Things this beautiful could not be trusted. The woman in front, the one who looked like another man's whorehouse dreams come to life, opened her soft, white arms.

"It means the oracle welcomes you."

000

**For a long** moment, Rhett just stood there, gun in one hand and goat in the other, feeling conflicted. If they'd been monsters, if the Shadow had given him any reason at all, he would've shot each of these women. *Bang bang bang*, right in the heart. Monster or no, if the Shadow suggested he shoot, he generally did, and he'd nipped many a problem in the bud that way, so to speak. He was pretty goddamn sure these women were up to no good, and they didn't have a single goddamned reason to be cavorting atop a mountain, but it's not like their white bedsheet dresses were splattered with fresh blood. There were words carved in the smooth stone overhead, but it's not like Rhett could read it. And it's not like it would've said THESE BITCHES ARE BAD NEWS, in any case. It looked older then the hills, this place, and somehow wrong. He set the kid goat down on the top step, where it waited with a patience it hadn't shown before. The bee, he noticed, was gone.

"Well, where's this oracle, then?" Rhett finally said, as that was the one thing he could rightly focus on. He was supposed to see the oracle, and that was really all he knew. He ran his tongue over the roof of his mouth, feeling the strange bump there and worrying at it. "Let's get on with things."

"The oracle will appear when she has been purified," the red-headed woman said, and she held out her arms like she wanted to give him a hug, which made him skittish as a mare in foal.

"Uh, okay. So, I reckon we wait. You-all got some chairs or something? Or I can sit on the steps?"

The women giggled behind their hands, their eyes as bright as their teeth. "Oh, no. You must enter the temple. Bathe in the holy spring and drink of the honeyed mead and taste of Melissa's bounty."

Rhett fidgeted a bit. "I reckon I could do that, but y'all are blocking the way up, far as I can tell. And I hope you don't mind goats, as this little critter don't seem to take no as an answer."

The red-headed woman looked at the goat and licked her lips. "All pure things are welcome here."

A brief flare of annoyance raged up from Rhett's chest. "Then I reckon I'll leave."

But she grabbed his arm in hands as strong as irons, pulled him up the remaining stairs, and half-dragged, half-danced him over to a peculiar stone fountain. The building was open on the sides, held up by columns, but the roof overhead shielded Rhett from the stars. A deep black hole led into the mountain in back, the gush of water within suggesting it was connected to the waterfall far below. Lanterns and braziers glowed everywhere, giving the women's skin the appearance of something living, shifting, like hot brands dancing behind a silk screen.

"Unnerving," Rhett said to himself, but the woman just laughed. And that was unnerving, too.

She stopped in front of the fountain. "Wash your face with the sacred waters," she intoned.

Figuring it couldn't hurt anything, Rhett rolled up his sleeves a little and dipped his hands into the cool water, dashing it over his face and rubbing it over his neck like he did before dinner so Ines and Winifred wouldn't scold him too much for looking like he'd been making mud pies. The water was as soothing as his mother's touch had been, the few times he'd felt it, and it rippled over his lips like a kiss. When he stood again, the water dripped down his hair and collarbones to trickle down the inside of his shirt, over the twin pink scars that marked him.

"Okay. What now?"

She grabbed his arm again and pulled him over to a peculiar little half-couch, tufted and fine as anything in a banker's house, and he wasn't sure if he ended up on his rump because he'd sat or she'd pushed him. The black-haired girl placed the platter of food on one side, and the girl with hair the color of sickly corn silk placed the heavy goblet in his hands. The odor wafting out drew him in until his nose was about in the liquid. He couldn't see the color by the flickering firelight, but it smelled like heaviness, like honey that knew things, and he sipped it delicately before just tossing it back in long swallows. The girl had to pry it out of his hands, and then another girl was holding a bunch of grapes just above his lips.

"Eat," she said in another language that he still somehow understood.

"I had grapes before," he informed her, and then he showed her that he damn well knew how to eat them. He realized he'd skipped lunch for some pesky reason he couldn't remember, and dinner, too, maybe, and he started gobbling things off the platter like a starving dog. Cheese and fruit and some wretched, greenish globe that tasted like saltwater and sadness. He spit that out and reached for bits of meat, thin-sliced ham and thick sausage that left grease painting his lips. The women laughed gaily at him, handing him choice tidbits when he paused too long, pressing the heavy goblet against his mouth, kicking the little white goat kid away as it butted and kicked him and shouted, "Meh!" in an insistent sort of way.

Suddenly, for no reason Rhett could name, the three women stood at attention as if they'd forgotten Rhett existed. He smuggled a few more grapes off the platter and stood, but he had trouble seeing past all their bedsheets and tangled hair.

"Mother, are you purified?" the three women asked, all at the same time, perfectly, and their voices melded together like the hum of a hive of bees.

"I grow ready," a new voice said. It was a normal voice, a woman's voice, but a woman feeling her years. She sounded exhausted, bled out, seared by the sun, her voice as dry and twisted as something or other Rhett couldn't quite remember, something he'd found lying among the flowers.

He peeked between two of the women blocking his view and saw a figure hidden by robes of a deep purple Rhett had never before seen. Slowly, as if in pain, the figure limped to the fountain. Hands curled into claws carefully grasped the purple hood, drawing it back to reveal possibly the oldest woman Rhett had ever seen. White hair like old cotton struggled over her bald head, and age spots covered most of her skin, and her lips curled down over a toothless skull. Her fingers shook as she washed her face in the fountain's cool water, and she sighed like everything hurt—except the sweet water dribbling down her wrinkles. Then she hobbled over to a peculiar golden stool Rhett hadn't noticed before and dropped her purple robe to puddle on the smooth, gray stone. Underneath it, she wore a younger woman's nightshirt, white and billowy around her spare frame. When she sat, her back curled over as round as a spoon, and she groaned and creaked like old timber.

"Hellfire, how old is that gal?" he said.

"Too old," the red-headed woman said, her voice like acid. "This will be her last prophecy before the next queen rises."

"Watch, child," the old woman said, crooking a finger at the shadows, and Rhett noticed round eyes glowing in the dark corner, a hunched shape in faded calico hiding behind a brazier like a cat in an alley.

It was as if the Shadow had punched Rhett in the goddamn stomach. This, whatever it was—this child had something to do with why he was here. But he didn't know what. And he didn't know why he was watching this peculiar scene play out, why he didn't just shoot everybody but the little girl and be done with it.

"Wait for it," a voice said—someone familiar but unseen. A man's voice, bold as a bear.

Rhett's hand moved to his gun, but the little goat butted him in the shin, hard, and he looked down.

"Bring the sacrifice," the old woman said.

"Bring the what now?"

She curled a claw at Rhett now, shot him an impatient look, as if he'd forgotten something important. "The sacrifice. The goat kid. Bring it to me."

Rhett looked down at the little goat, and the little goat looked up at him, and its blue eyes, fringed in snowy lashes, seemed too big, and it blinked at him with complete innocence and trust. He took a step back.

"Lady, whatever you want with this goat, I reckon it ain't good. Nor something a child should see."

"Fool."

The red-headed woman snatched the goat kid up by the back legs and strode to the old woman, to a stone table beside her golden stool. She didn't so much place the goat on the table as press it down on its side, and the little thing bleated in terror and scrabbled with its tiny, pointy feet. A flash of movement caught Rhett's eye, and he saw the little girl behind the brazier creeping out, a hand over her mouth in fear.

His hand was yet again on his gun, but something stayed it there, as if the revolver weighed as much as the mountain itself. He tried his Bowie knife and likewise found it cemented into its sheath. His teeth ground as he tried all three of his weapons again and again and found them unmovable; even the Henry clung to his back like a vine. The wound on the roof of his mouth pained him something awful, and he jabbed it with his tongue as the black-haired woman brought a dipper of water from the fountain and splashed it all over the little goat like a goddamn fool.

"None of this makes sense," he shouted.

The red-headed woman pointed at him. "More mead. He's not in the proper state."

"I'm either in Durango or Azteca, and—"

The cup pressed against his lips, hard, clanking against his teeth, and the thick liquid splashed down his throat like sweet honey fire he had no choice but to swallow. He tried to pull away, but the woman had the back of his head, her fingernails digging in like harpy claws, and she held him tight as a goddamn vise until the goblet was drained.

"The conditions are favorable!" the red-headed woman shouted, and Rhett smelled smoke and roasting meat. His stomach turned and tears sprang to his eye. That tiny goat on the table, the fires everywhere, the look in the women's eyes that suggested murder wasn't even interesting anymore, that this was just business. He didn't want to look, but he had to, and he saw the red-haired woman holding up a bunch of stringy, steaming innards as the little girl behind the brazier sobbed her heart out.

"You will get used to it," the old woman said in a kindly but exhausted sort of way. "It only hurts the first time. We must do as the goddess demands, as we have always done. When we do not please the goddess, the gardens wither and the river dries up and the plagues come, and the supplicants never finish their journey. Do you see?"

Perhaps the little girl nodded, and perhaps she didn't, but Rhett was trying his weapons again and finding them stubbornly locked down, and he ran a thumb over the roof of his mouth, worrying at the wound there. He tried and failed to lift a foot to run and found himself pinned in place, and a cold sweat broke out across his brow and down his back as he realized he was, somehow, impossibly, stupidly helpless. These insane, heartless monsters had killed the goatling—what would they do to the child? What other sacrifices were required for their sick sort of magic? The Shadow flopped in his belly like a fish fighting a line, and a dribble of blood leaked out the corner of his mouth from biting his tongue.

"Now, watch," the old woman said. "The Thriae will help you, but it's always you who must do the part." She dipped one thumb into the goat's blood and another into a little pot of honey and smeared them over her face in a peculiar sort of pattern, almost like a cross.

"Melissa, goddess, your oracle calls!" she said, softer than Rhett would've expected.

A peculiar hum started up somewhere, an echoing thrum in Rhett's blood answering like nightingales calling at midnight, and it was as if the mountain shook under his feet, for all that nothing changed. The air grew heavy and twinkly, and the fires all stilled to nothing, and the three unnatural women in their bedsheets were on their knees, their fine faces plastered against the stone, and the little girl hid herself deep behind her brazier, her animal panting in counterpoint to the thrum. The old woman jerked, her curved spine straightening, her hair curling out into fat, golden spirals, her skin washing over the color of honey. Her mouth opened, and a voice like a million bees rang from every inch of sky, saying, "Your goddess answers."

000

**It was a** long moment, the sort of moment when Rhett figured a more urbane man, a more worldly man, would know what came next. But all he could do was stand there, frozen, the world likewise frozen around him, as the now young and beautiful woman in her short white dress sashayed toward him, bountiful hips swinging. She was a lush thing, golden all over and somehow bigger than herself, and the Shadow's desperate tug told Rhett she was now more, much more, than just a woman.

"Bow to your goddess, supplicant," she said, the corners of her mouth curling up.

Rhett found that was indeed something he could do, for all that his feet were stuck, and he bent at the waist, feeling awkward and small.

"Now rise and greet me."

He stood, and the world spun around him. The woman stood a few paces away, easy and powerful in her body and unashamed to have most of it on display. Rhett had never met anybody more important than a sheriff, but to him, she appeared a queen. He worried at the roof of his mouth, knowing there was something he was supposed to do, something he was supposed to remember. He opened his mouth, but all he could think to say was, "Well, howdy."

The woman raised one eyebrow, and he added, "Ma'am."

She snorted gently and walked around him.

"You do not know the ritual," she observed.

"I reckon not."

"But you made the journey. You passed the tests, if roughly. You bathed in the spring without fear and drank the holy mead and brought unto me my sacrifice."

Rhett winced, remembering the kid goat. At least the woman's face was no longer marked in its blood.

"So, ask."

He cocked his head. "Ask?"

The woman put her hands on her hips and pinned him with a fierce glare. "Ask your question. You are a supplicant and I am the oracle. So ask, and I will speak."

Rhett's mouth fell open. He was supposed to ask a question? Had he known that bit? He had come here for some reason, and the Shadow was on full alert, trying to remind him what it was.

"A question about what?"

"The future, usually. That's what people care about. They already know the past. The journey is meant to teach you the proper question."

Well, and the journey was awful hard to remember, just then. Rhett had gone to great trouble to learn his own past, and he needed no reminders of that now, of what he had lost. The future, then. He was supposed to ask a question about the future.

It came to him, and he nodded his head.

"Will me and Sam be happy for a long time?"

The woman shook her head like it was a stupid question, and annoyance plucked at Rhett's heart.

"Yes," she said, like it was that simple.

"And that's it?"

She turned in a whirl of white fabric and headed back for her little gold stool.

"You asked a yes-or-no question, and all I can do is answer it truthfully. Perhaps next time, you will go to the trouble of thinking up a better question. Foolish mortal."

The annoyance bloomed into rage. Foolish? Who did she think she was?

The wound on the roof of his mouth thrummed with pain, so hard that Rhett's whole body quivered, and he reached a fingernail up there and scratched like hell. To his horror, he dug out a little stone and held it in his palm, all covered with blood.

"What the Sam Hill?" he said, tasting copper, but then it hit him like a goddamn bolt of lightning.

Rhett remembered why he was there.

He remembered everything.

He had to take back the little girl.

And he had to kill the oracle while the goddess, Melissa, was still in her skin.

The moment he remembered, her magic had no further power.

Without a peep, Rhett pulled out his gun and shot the woman in the back, aiming for something like her heart.

Of course she didn't burst into sand—that would've been all too easy. But the bullet did find home, and red flowered against the white fabric. The bullet was the loudest thing in the world, louder even than the hum the world had taken up, and in its wake, all fell silent. Melissa turned, slow and deadly as a predator sure of its prey, and lunged for him, hands up like claws and lush mouth in a feral howl. But Rhett was ready for that, had been waiting for that, and he shot her again and again, aiming for head and heart. She reached him before he'd gotten to his silver bullet and wrenched the gun free, tossing it off the side of the mountain and slapping him across the face hard enough to send him flying. Rhett landed on the stone floor and rolled until he fetched up against something hard and cold. Legs.

The women. The Thriae, whatever the hell that meant.

The red-headed one was giving him a look that said she'd been waiting her whole life to tear him limb from limb, and the brunette and blonde grabbed his arms and yanked him to standing to help her do just that.

"What are you to a goddess?" the red-head said.

"Death," Rhett answered, kicking her hard in the belly while silently congratulating himself on not kicking her in the crotch.

She doubled over, and Rhett took that moment of weakness to kick her in the face. The women holding him gasped and slightly loosened their grip, and he yanked his arms away from them and whipped out his remaining gun, shooting each of them in the belly. They weren't fighters, these women, weren't monsters or goddesses either, and Rhett felt a little bad, but…well, it wasn't like the goddess thing was just gonna let him walk away now. If he wanted to take back the stolen child and live up to his goddamn agreement with Buck, he had to end whatever the hell they'd been doing up on this mountain.

He stepped back, popped off a shot at the writhing red-headed woman, and hunted around for Melissa. He didn't see her, and that felt pretty nice right up until someone wrapped hard fingers around his neck from behind and let their nails bite in.

"Who put you up to this?" Melissa hissed in his ear.

"Maybe I just wanted to kill you. Ever think about that?"

The fingers tightened. "No."

Rhett couldn't do much with his gun with the woman behind him, so he whipped out his Bowie knife and stabbed her in the thigh. But instead of dropping him, she squeezed tighter, and he began to see stars and panic.

"I am bounty," she hissed. "I am the old ways. I am the hive and the queen and the promise of grubs snugged in wax. I am summer and winter and birth and plague. I am death and honey. This place blooms for me. My children come for me, to suckle at my breast and hear their future in forgotten rituals. I am life."

"Not to that little goat, you weren't," Rhett whispered. "Not to that little girl over there."

His vision was going over red, but he pulled his knife out of Melissa's thigh, switched it to his other hand, and stuck it in her other thigh. She just laughed.

"Life requires death. It's the simplest of understandings. Everything that is born ripens and withers and dies to feed something else. Every creature is born a sacrifice whether it knows it or not. One small creature is only a tiny fraction of the whole. And some creatures..." She squeezed hard enough that he heard something crunch in his throat. "Some creatures don't know their place."

"No!" a tiny voice shouted, and Rhett fell to his knees, reaching for his broken throat.

Melissa had released him.

And it was because she was on fire.

The short white gown billowed with flames, catching and dancing upward, dry fabric the ultimate tinder. And there, just a little away, teeth bared like a goddamn badger, was the child, Valerie, holding a lit torch.

Melissa screamed, and Rhett's attention refocused on the goddess, who didn't look quite so smug and powerful as she realized she was about to get burned alive. Behind him, the red-headed woman screamed and ran past him toward the fountain, carrying the goblet, and dashing water onto her mistress.

"It ain't enough," he whispered to himself in a cracked voice. But he wasn't going to take the chance that it might be, either. Melissa had taken his Bowie knife with her, and it was poking out of her thigh as she danced around, her hair now on fire and billowing white smoke into the night. But Rhett still had one gun and a couple bullets, and he took careful aim at the red-headed woman, hit her right in the head, and watched her fall over, the goblet tumbling out of those beautiful white hands and dashing cool, sweet water all over the ground.

"You," Melissa growled, and Rhett turned to face her, gun up and ready.

"Yeah?" he answered.

"You don't know what you've done."

"Oh, I reckon I do. I ended whatever bullshit operation thinks it's okay to steal a child from her mama in the night."

"Death will come for you, too, one day."

Rhett shook his head. "But not today, you bitch."

On fire from head to toe, Melissa suddenly seemed to recall who and what she was. The humming came back, and she walked toward him, swinging her hips, billowing smoke, smiling through the flames.

"The child was to be the next oracle. Raised lovingly with every need met. She would serve until she was a hundred, longer than most folk live. She would never know illness or hunger, never feel pain or suffer loss. And you've stolen all that from her. This mountain will crumble. The river will dry up. The fields below will wither, the crops dying in the sun. The people will—"

"The people will go on as they always have, and maybe they'll have the goddamn sense to move somewhere that ain't supposed to be a desert," he interrupted. "This is a wild place, and nobody who comes here expects grapes and sweetness. It's a hard life, but it's honest. All this?" He gestured to the severe stone building, the fountain, the statues. "This is just bullshit. It don't belong here. And neither do you."

Melissa fell to her knees, suddenly, and then to the ground. She opened her mouth, and the sound that came out was like the world breaking, like a thousand furious wasps, and Rhett put his hands over his ears to try to keep his eardrums from bursting. The little girl did likewise, and he wanted to protect her, but it was all he could do to protect himself as his bones threatened to explode under his skin. The sound rose to a crescendo and broke, and the world went silent.

Rhett dared open his eye, and through the flames, he could see Melissa's lavish curves melting away to show old knobbed bones and hanging flesh and straggling gray hair. The fire went out suddenly, leaving a gently smoking naked body sprawled on the stone.

"She didn't belong here. I don't suppose I do, either." The old woman's voice sounded resigned. And, Rhett noted, relieved.

"Is the goddess gone?" he asked, his voice funny and cracked in his own ears and the silence of the night suddenly unbearably loud, punctuated only by the hesitant songs of night birds and the quiet sobs of a frightened child.

"She's gone." The old woman laughed, a rusty sound. "I always hate it when she leaves, you know. Like getting everything you wanted and then losing it. To feel that young, even for a few moments. I'd say it was a blessing, but it's more like a cruel curse." She looked up and saw Valerie crying beside the blackened torch, the girl's face covered with her arms. "Look, child. It's over. Forget everything I told you. You're free."

Valerie looked up a moment but quickly returned to sobbing.

"Children," the old woman said with a shrug of her bony shoulders. "They don't even know how good it is, not knowing anything."

Rhett didn't ram his gun home yet, but he did walk over a few steps and look down at the old woman, trying not to focus too much on her body while also trying to figure out how she wasn't on fire.

"You okay?" he asked, holding out his free hand to help her up, if that was what she needed.

She laughed, and something sweet and bubbly in the sound reminded Rhett that she'd once been young, too. "Oh, lord no. I'm dying, boy. You stabbed me good." When she moved her hands, he saw what he'd missed: his Bowie knife, still in one thigh, the other thigh bleeding a puddle that winked black as ink in the firelight.

"I'm sorry," he said on reflex, then quickly corrected himself. "Not for killing her and ending this shit—I was right honest about that. I'm sorry you had to get hurt, too. Is there anything I can do? Fetch a sawbones, maybe? I got a horse at the bottom of the stairs, but I'll have to carry you down..."

He trailed off, trying to figure the woman's chances of getting even to Puddin' alive with that much blood loss. A monster could live through it, but she was no monster, and she was old, and he could already hear her breathing going funny.

"Just help me onto my back."

He did, and it was awkward, and her body was like the map to a place he'd long ago sworn never to visit. But she looked so pathetic, so fragile, that he went and fetched the rich purple robe and spread it over her, and she sighed and stroked a hand over the fabric. "Pretty thing, for a cage," she said. "I won't miss it."

"Can I—"

"Stop saying stupid things and listen. I got things to say. First of all, you done good here. That needed to happen. I was going to die anyway, but with that little one's soul on my ledger." She waved a curled claw at the child, who had stopped crying to listen. "Secondly, the goddess didn't lie. This place is gonna wither up right quick. You'd best fill your skins and take what food you can find, because underneath this fine pelt of a temple is a bony skeleton that ain't long for this world." She looked down at the purple robe and croaked a laugh. "Lot of that going around."

"But what about—"

"Shh, child. You already broke the toy. No point in regretting it. Just do one more thing for me."

Rhett leaned in, dreading whatever came next. He couldn't take on another goddamn quest—this one had already made him break his promise.

"Help the bees," the woman said. "They were always kind to me."

"The bees?" Rhett asked.

But her eyes went faraway and then glassy, and the light left them, and she was just an empty corpse under a pretty robe. Rhett closed her eyes and pulled the robe up to cover her face and stood. He checked to make sure Melissa's women were dead—and dispatched the last one clinging to life, in a merciful sort of way. He reckoned that, like the old woman, these women were stolen or drugged or somehow compelled, and even if they had to go, they didn't need to suffer. As he looked over the havoc he'd wrought, at the dead and twisted bodies and the puddles of moon-black blood flowing over the cracking stone, he felt something he hadn't felt in quite some time:

Satisfaction.

Satisfaction at a job well done, at justice meted, at violence doled out to monsters who deserved it. Satisfaction at knowing he'd done good, that he'd triumphed over evil. Goddamn, but sometimes he missed being the Shadow. Missed the excuse to give in to his temper and punch a feller in the teeth. Missed the simplicity of killing what needed to die. Missed the feel of galloping toward victory, of standing over a pile of sand with a gun in his hand, of watching the light leave a foe's eyes gone wide with surprise. It had been good, to have a destiny.

All these years, it had nagged at him, a chore left unfinished. And he'd ground his teeth and told it to fuck off; he had promises to keep.

But now, as the Shadow returned home to roost, its hunger slaked...all he could think about was getting home to Sam.

A whimper recalled him to the present.

His job? Wasn't over.

The Shadow was like a tornado, a force of destruction and chaos. But Rhett Walker had to deal with the aftermath. His eye skittered sideways; the little girl was still scared. He'd have to sidle up like she was a jumpy colt.

Humming an old saloon song, he stopped to fill his waterskin at the fountain, which was already going dry, and passed by the stone table where the little white goat lay, eyes open to the night sky, beyond saving. He closed its eyes, too. Finally, when she crept out from behind the urn, he approached her.

"Valerie?"

The little girl looked up, surprised. "They said I didn't have a name anymore."

Rhett squatted down and tried to look harmless, which was pretty difficult for a murderous monster cowpoke with only one good eye and a body that was mostly scar tissue. He'd been told his smile could be disturbing, so he didn't smile. He just returned her serious stare.

"You have a name. I was told it's Valerie, but I'm glad to call you whatever you like. My name is Kit Lawson, and your mama sent me to fetch you home."

"What about Daddy?"

Rhett scratched the back of his head and looked away. "I reckon that's a different conversation. Point is, I'll take you home now, if you'd like to go."

"Mama said I shouldn't trust strange men."

Rhett stood and looked around the odd little building. The stone had been smooth and whitish gray when he'd arrived, and now it was pockmarked and rough, aged and streaked with black. The waterfall was silent, and the fountain was still, and a pall of death had settled over everything.

"Well, you can stay here if you like and see if somebody better comes along, but I'm the one who's available just now and has a nice pony named Puddin' you could ride. Also, your mama said there'd be some stew back home, and I find I like stew. Do you?"

"Yes."

He held out his hand. Not out to her, in an expectant way that had any sort of weight to it, but more hanging from his side like it needed something to do.

It took a few long minutes, and he had to scratch at his eye and yawn, but eventually, a tiny and soot-stained hand slipped into his.

OOO

**As they inched** their way down the path in near pitch-black darkness, they passed toppled statues with broken faces, braziers full of ash, and the sort of small, skittery rocks that could send a body plummeting into oblivion. Rhett had never been good with people, but he'd learned that if he treated a child like a jumpy colt, they could get along fine. He went slow, helping the girl scramble around tight corners and keeping a tight grip on the back of her dress as she skidded on pebbles. Valerie, at least, wasn't a troublesome child; she was a serious thing, and she applied herself to the work at hand instead of whining or caterwauling or causing the sort of problems Winifred's godlet would've caused. They didn't talk much, and Rhett knew enough about recovering from terror to let that lie and not go asking the sorts of stupid questions adults sometimes inflicted on folks who's come out the other side of hard times.

Like "Are you okay?"

Hell, no, the child wasn't okay. She'd just watched an old woman slaughter a goat and turn into a goddess, which the child herself had set on fire as adults tried to murder each other all over the place. She might never be all right. But giving her space right now, treating her like everything was normal? That would be a start. Rhett personally knew that the world could be a terrifying place, and for all his stony demeanor, he didn't expect anyone to suddenly be fine with things when things were nowhere close to fine.

In between the child and his own footing and the distinct lack of light, Rhett didn't spend any time looking down at the world below, and when they finally stood on flat ground, the area had changed. The waterfall had dried up to a sick, black trickle, the pool below it scummed with green. Puddin' stood by it, tail twitching in annoyance and lips pursed.

"Sorry, fussy," Rhett told him. "Hope you drunk big before this, as it could be awhile."

The child, at least, wasn't scared of his horse, and she snatched up a handful of crispy dry grass and held her palm properly flat as the pony delicately cropped up the offering.

"You been on horseback before?" Rhett asked the child, and she looked at him like he was dumb as a possum.

"Of course I rode before," she told him, and that's when he knew she was going to be okay.

He unhobbled his horse and tightened the saddle before swinging up, and Valerie had already scrambled up a boulder, knowing how to find her proper place on Puddin's rump. As he kicked the gelding to an annoyed walk, he couldn't help thinking it would be quite a boon if only Winifred's child had half this good sense.

The river was no longer a lush blue ribbon. It was as if the ground had sucked up all the water, leaving only a pebbled arroyo behind. The scent of carrion and decay made the night air heavy. The bright green grass had gone a sickly white in the moonlight, and the trees had dropped their leaves and stood stark as skeletons against the indigo sky. Puddin's hooves clip-clopped on hard, unforgiving ground.

They followed the bee and the bones of the river, passing places that were familiar to Rhett yet seemed as far away as forgotten dreams. A stained sandy patch of land that made the place between his shoulders itch. A copse of twisted old trees that looked like a witch's dance. A field that had once seemed endlessly alive with flowers, now lying flat and dead as if the very land had given up.

It struck him that he had done this, that his actions had caused the world to wither. But as he looked back at the mountain, staring hard at a crumbling ruin at the summit, he felt in his heart he could've done nothing else. The bee had drawn him, and the Shadow had pushed him, and Buck had...well, *forced* didn't seem quite the word, because Buck was altogether too smooth for that. Tricked him? Enabled him? He remembered that night now, recalled the pebble planted in the roof of his mouth and the stone-cold fact that if he hadn't been made to forget everything, none of this could've come to pass. This child would now be a vessel for a goddess, unwillingly kept all her days. And for a creature like Rhett who shunned cages, that was a fate worse than the death of a place that maybe didn't deserve to exist, anyway.

The child fell asleep against his back, tiny arms wrapped around his scant waist, a hot cheek against his ribs. He normally squirmed at any physical contact with folks that weren't Sam or on four legs, but this felt more like...well, like having a puppy fall asleep on a feller. Not that bad. He steered Puddin' around the trickier bits to keep him on solid footing so the kid wouldn't be disturbed. Rhett couldn't have slept if somebody had paid him, and as he was accustomed to moving about the night, he felt mostly at home. It was decently lit, at least, a fat white moon reflected off high, puffy clouds, and the way seemed faster than it had been heading in. It didn't get any prettier as he went along, though—everything was all dried up like a peach pit, wrinkled and rattling. He could only hope there was still a water trough in the little town, or that their wells were still pulling water. If not...well, it was gonna be a long night either way.

It wasn't even close to dawn as the town came into view—if it could even be called a town anymore. Now it looked like a collection of falling sticks, like old, wind-scoured clapboard buildings held together with spit and dead dreams. The orchard trees were bare claws; the neat vegetable patches were rotted black mush and hard, twisted stems. The laundry flapping in the dry breeze behind one of the houses was the closest thing to alive Rhett could see, other than a confused dog scratching in the dirt. Rhett felt right bad for the homesteaders. He knew what it was to see a favorite calf go weak and die for no

discernible reason, and these folks had gone to bed in a land of plenty and would wake up with nothing but whatever they kept in their larders. Hell, maybe even that small boon would be gone, the jams and jellies turned to old, black mush and the onion and garlic braids withered where they dangled from rafters gone gray and dusty. Rhett had once dreamed of magic that would lift him from his terrible home life, but he'd since learned that magic would take away far more than it gave, if a feller let it run amok.

He steered his horse up behind the house with the laundry, as Diana had ordered him to do, and tied Puddin' up to the small barn, where another horse whinnied a confused greeting that woke the child.

She startled awake and pressed away from his back, asking, "Where are we?"

Before Rhett could answer, a door banged open and Diana rushed out of the house in her nightclothes and cap, her shawl flapping and her bare feet sending up clouds of dust in a yard that had been thick with grass not long before.

"Valerie! Baby! My baby!" she cried, over and over again, lifting the child off Puddin's rump and dragging her into a tight embrace that made Rhett's heart ache for the arms of his own mama, who was well and surely dead.

He just stood there feeling awkward and beat to hell and thirsty, digging a toe in the sand and watching the bee hover in midair as if it still had business.

"You did it," the woman said, stating the obvious because there was really nothing better to say. "And…sweet lord. What else did you do?" She looked around, the changed world evident even in the darkest part of morning. "The fields. The trees? And even my garden."

"The oracle is gone. It was the only way. That wasn't something I'd planned on, but I reckon you'd rather have your child than..." Rhett waved his hands around. "Everything else."

Diana nodded, her mouth set. "True enough. So, I owe you my thanks. And a hive of bees. Looks like they'll be better off going with you, anyways." She knelt down, looked her daughter in the eye. "You go on inside and take up anything you got to have in my old carpet bag. We got to leave, child."

"But why, Mama? I just got home."

Diana stood, hands on her hips, wind whipping her skirt around her legs as she stared at the mountain, a jagged black thing in the distance.

"Because this ain't home anymore. Run along."

As soon as Valerie was gone, Diana went about her business with the fury of a storm. She pulled a little goat cart out of the barn and called Rhett over to help her wrestle one of several bee skeps into the cart. When he hesitated, she *tsk*ed at him. "Bees are asleep. And even if they weren't, they won't sting you, fool."

She was right—they managed to load the cart without incident, and the skep fit in just right, and soon she was hooking up an old nanny goat to the traces.

"Might as well take old Nan with you," she said. "No grass means no milk, and we'd eat her before we got to a living town. She'll pull fine. Just pony her off your horse."

Rhett checked out the rig, and it looked right fine to him. Returning home with a hive full of honeybees and a goat would please his little community, but he'd have to come up with an easy lie about how they came about. No one back home could know about this jaunt, about his dinner with Buck and his tussle with another god. Even now, as far from home as he was, he half-expected Sam to come galloping out of the night and flutter his hands all over Rhett in that sweet, fussy way he did when he forgot Rhett wasn't mortal and easily broken.

"Where will you-all go?" Rhett asked.

Diana was pulling sheets down from the wash lines now, stuffing them in an old reed basket, and Rhett couldn't stand to watch anyone do work while he loafed, so he joined her.

"Go south again," she said, exhaustion in every corner of her voice. "All I need is a dusty town and my washtub. It used to matter which one, but it doesn't so much, anymore."

After Rhett balled up the last crisp white sheet and chucked it in the basket, he realized that maybe there was something he could do. She carried the wash in, and he went to his saddlebag and pulled out Buck's silver platter.

"This is solid silver," he told Diana when she returned, holding it out.

She jerked her head back like an offended horse. "Where'd you steal it from, then? Because you ain't the sort for finery, I can well see."

Rhett cocked his head and told a little white lie. "I got it from the temple," he said. "And there's nobody left there to ask about it, so sell it and use it to find a better place."

The woman hesitated, and Rhett just shoved it in her arms and turned back for his horse. Leavetakings weren't a thing he cherished, and there was too much sadness and spite wrapped up in this one for his taste. He told himself he wasn't a person who liked people, a feller who was better off with horses and other reasonable, four-legged critters. And yet, seeing a woman with nearly everything ripped from her in just a few short days through no fault of her own, he knew what he had to do.

"And if you don't mind living in a pueblo, we got a settlement near enough here. Not a proper town, mind, but solid folk who do their work. Plenty of laundry, if that's what you choose. We got our peculiarities, but nothing will be able to harm you there." He gave the mountain a significant look. "Nobody like that could touch your life, ever again."

Her eyes went over hard.

"I ain't looking for a man, Kit."

He chuckled; he had to. "And I already told you I ain't looking for a woman. But I'd hate to think of that sweet child dying on the trail after what I been through to save her. This is a harsh place, and it's only gonna get harsher."

Diana thought for a minute, gave it her full attention with eyes going far off and her brow drawn down. And then she shook her head.

"That's right kindly of you, but I reckon we'll make our own way. I won't be a burden—" Rhett opened his mouth to protest that, and she slashed a hand, silencing him. "Charity don't suit. You done your good deed. You gave me back the last thing I cared about in the world. I'll take that gift and find something new to care about on my own terms; you see if I don't."

"Ma'am, I do believe you could send a bear crying for his mama," Rhett said, meaning it. Funny how, long ago, when he'd been a girl himself, he'd thought women useless, fragile, stupid things. The older he got and the more women he met, the more he realized there was nothing tougher that a critter that could go through what any woman did and still get out of bed in the morning. And this one was gonna just strike out across the razed prairie, no idea where she was aimed but bull-headed enough to find it.

"You got a gun?" he asked.

She nodded, her face hard. "I got a shotgun. Know how to use it, too."

"Well, then."

"Well, then."

Rhett tipped his hat, mounted up, and aimed his horse for home. Behind him, the nanny goat bleated in surprise and planted her hooves, but Diana swatted her and got her moving. Rhett thought Valerie might run out to wave goodbye, but then he also thought Diana might've told the child to stay inside, where it was safe. Or perhaps the little critter was asleep, or still in shock. He also realized he had not been offered the promised stew. Still, he had a beehive and a goat and a nicely made cart, and that was thanks enough.

A quiet buzz at his ear made his head whip around, his hand going to his gun. But it was just a single bee, his bee, and it was giving him his space, and it took off toward the place Rhett called home.

So, he followed.

**Rhett followed that** bee through morning and afternoon and rolled into the pueblo's valley at dinner time, the goat bleating her complaints loud enough to bring Dan and Digby and Winifred and her get hopping outside to see what the fuss was about. Their little flock of goats took off, hollering their fool heads off, and Solomon the mule brayed his greeting, and it was right friendly if a bit loud.

"Shadow, what the hell is this?" Dan said, skipping his friendly self and his preachy self to go straight to his exhausted-parent self.

"Well, it's a goat, a cart, and a beehive, Dan. I thought any fool could see that."

"So, you disappeared this morning with no warning and came back with...bees?"

Rhett counted the days in his head, figuring he'd been gone at least three days, but if Dan thought he'd only been gone for one day, he wasn't gonna argue the point.

"Sometimes, a feller gets a hankering for some honey," he said with as much innocence as he could scrape up, and Winifred smirked like she knew there was more to the story but wouldn't expose him, considering how much she liked sweets.

"Bees don't do well in a place like this," Dan warned him.

That one bee still buzzed around Rhett's head, and its buzz almost sounded like laughter.

"Oh, these bees are special, Dan. I reckon they'll do fine wherever they land."

Dan threw up his hands, a familiar gesture. "And a goat?"

"Well if you don't like her, you can eat her, but I'll warn you: I renamed her."

"What's her name?"

It took everything Rhett had to keep a straight face.

"Danielle."

Dan left, muttering to himself under his breath, and Rhett felt a wash of comfort. It was good to be back in the comfortable, hidden valley, surrounded by people he was used to that were used to him. Digby took possession of the goat, already talking to her in that calming way of his and promising her fresh water. Rhett wheeled the little cart over to a flat sort of boulder and chucked his chin at Otter Paws, who hurried over to help him move the skep. It settled down on the stone, and although it had been quiet all this time, a soft and steady hum took up. Otter Paws took a few steps back, ever a cautious man, for all that he'd shacked up with Winifred.

"Bees bite?" he asked.

"Not these bees," Rhett said. "I think."

Dinner was more than welcome, and as much as they all would've enjoyed hearing Rhett's fantastic story of danger and salvation, he didn't breathe a word of it. The day had been uneventful for everyone else. He ate his fill and drank the fresh, cold water from the well and was just grateful as hell that the mountain's devastation seemed to keep within its radius. After about an hour, the land had greened up again, and by the time it was lunch, everything was just as alive as it should've been. And here, at home, everything went on as usual. A whole tragedy had happened just a bit north, in a place they'd never heard of, and now that place, Rhett was sure, would be off the map and torn apart by dust storms as if it had never existed.

When Sam woke up in the dark of their bedroom, Rhett was there with a lantern and a little mug full of honeycomb.

"Where'd you get the honey, Rhett?" Sam asked, his vampire nose picking up on it immediately.

"Oh, I was out and about. We got a hive now. I figured you needed all the sweetness you could get, seeing as how you're stuck with a cantankerous old coot like me."

Sam sat up, ignoring the honey, and pressed his lips to Rhett's.

"You're sweet enough in secret," he said. "You just hide it from the rest of the world. Now, hand over that honey and tell me the gossip."

Rhett gave Sam the honey and watched him lick the comb, just a little. Vampires lived on blood, but Sam had always loved honey, and he'd learned that he could have a little lick, as long as it wasn't too much. But Rhett was getting sleepy, the full exhaustion of what he'd done sinking into his bones. One day or three, he'd ridden for hours, climbed a mountain, and killed four people and maybe a god. He had a right to a jaw-cracking yawn. But this was their ritual, and he had a part to play, relaying for Sam what he'd heard at the dinner table.

"We got a new goat," he said. "And the bees."

"That's it? Nobody got in a fight or stepped on a rattlesnake? Winifred's child didn't leap out of a tree and land on her head? Just a goat and some bees?"

Rhett yawned again and settled down into the pillows.

"That's it. We lead a simple life, Sam."

Sam chuckled and gently ruffled Rhett's short hair. "Well, then, I'm gonna go to Rona and have me an adventure."

Rhett smiled. "You mean you're gonna ride over there and drink from some bad guy you caught kicking a donkey in an alley."

"That's all the excitement I need, Rhett."

"Me, too, Sam. Me, too."

And with that, Rhett fell asleep, a smear of honey on his cheek, feeling like he'd made his choice and earned his rest.

# INTERLUDE: TANAGER

A WREN NOVELLA

Chuck Wendig

# 1. THAT WAS THEN...

Miriam called her on the hospital phone; the girl, young at the time, not even a teenager yet, leaned over the bedrail, the IV tangling around her elbow before she answered. "Hey, psycho," Wren—aka Lauren Martin—said. She maneuvered her arm free from the IV serpent.

"Still charming as ever," Miriam said.

Wren apologized: "Sorry." Not an easy task for her. She'd lived so much of life willfully, purposefully not apologizing. Saying sorry was a sign of weakness—like exposing your belly for someone to sucker-punch you. How often she'd opened her arms to her mother only to be abused, abandoned, hit, spat on, or ignored...but here, she meant it, because Miriam had done a thing no one had done for Wren before: Miriam saved her. She stood up for her against stupid odds. Went against not one serial killer but a whole *family* of them, a family that had designs on Wren, designs that involved her death. Killing her to right the world in some twisted, delusional fantasy.

It *was* just a fantasy, wasn't it?

Either way, the matriarch of the Caldecott family, Eleanor, took Wren and dragged her down in the river. The muddy churn. The slither of slime-slick weeds. Wren didn't remember much about it. But she remembered the wetness. And the dark. Like being held in a monster's mouth for minutes before the beast finally swallowed you down into its bowels. But Miriam had jumped in after her, and Miriam's—boyfriend?—Louis jumped in after Miriam, and together, they somehow made it out. Alive.

"No, it's cool. I like that about you. You remind me of me."

Wren liked that. She *liked* Miriam. That felt strange too. Like the other woman was her big sister or—well, no, not her mother. Her mother didn't want her. And Miriam did. Mothers were terrible and Miriam was not. That made Miriam different and better. "They said I was a bad girl. That's why they wanted to kill me."

"They did," Miriam answered. "They thought you were going to turn out to be a real bad apple and so they figured on killing the tree before it could…drop the fruit. Ugh. Metaphors. You know what, fuck metaphors. They thought one day you were going to grow up and be a bad person and hurt other people."

"Will I?"

There came a pause before Miriam said, "You won't if you don't want to. Fate isn't written. This life leaves room for choice, but only if you want it real bad."

"I want to be good."

"Then be good."

"Will you help me?"

Miriam sighed. Wren could hear the crispy crackle of a cigarette. Then: the exhale, whoosh. Miriam sniffed. "I'll be back for you in a few years. Check on your smart ass, make sure you're not a total shitbird."

"Thanks. For that *and* for saving my life."

"Ain't no thing."

A shadow passed by the window to Wren's hospital room. She saw the hint of a police officer's hat. "There are cops outside my room."

"I know. That's why I'm calling you."

"I told them you were one of the good guys."

"Not a bad girl?"

"Not a bad girl."

Another drag off the cigarette. "Thanks, Wren. I'll catch up with you one day. Keep your grapes peeled."

"Bye, Miriam."

*Click.*

# 2. ...THIS IS NOW

**Kansas,** July 4th.

Wren bolted through the corn, in the dark.

She did not travel down a single row but rather, she crashed through the rows, one after the next, the sharp fronds of the stalks slicing at her, tasting blood.

The girl, freshly sixteen by only a few days, had made a terrible error.

She wasn't alone out there. The sound rose up behind her, like an echo of her own passage through the field: more crashing, trampling, stalk-snapping. And something else, too: a man, grunting as he followed behind. Whacking at the young corn with a piece of steel pipe, the end of it fitted with a corroded elbow joint. A man, she knew, who wore a rubber pig mask with bulging, grotesque cartoon eyes, a mask that was filthy and old and was rotting at the bottom in an uneven fringe.

Wren had been following Pigface now for days. Following him since she had seen him at the little farm stand outside of Lawrence. She saw him—no mask, then—holding up a head of cauliflower like he was regarding *it* regarding *him*, as if it had eyes to see him, a gaze to meet. He just stood like that for the longest time until the girl behind the stand, a freckle-faced girl with a nose like a button, asked him if she could help. Then he put that cauliflower down hard, as if startled. As if caught doing something shameful. He hurried off. A big man, but somehow scurrying.

She was pretty sure after that he masturbated in his pickup truck.

It was plain as day to Wren and nobody else:

The man was a murderer. Or would be one.

A liquid line of silver shone around him—*he's one of the Mercury Men,* she thought, using the term she came up for them. He stood out from the rest of the world like he was extra-3D, like he hovered above everything else, an image in a book popping out on a short spring. Wren told herself, *I'm not gonna do anything, I'm gonna leave him alone*, because she wasn't doing this anymore. Wasn't killing anybody. She'd had enough of that. The young woman felt tired at being used like some tool, as if she were a knife held in the hand of an attacker she couldn't see. So: no more killing. Even though the world was full of Mercury Men, their murderous intent shining like light on a brand-new nickel…

Then she found Pigface.

She'd been hanging around the farm stand, sleeping in the motel just down the highway, using money she'd stolen from that trucker, the one hauling liquid air across the country, whatever the hell liquid air was. She had enough for five nights, and was on her second night when she popped down to the stand to buy some late-season berries, maybe a beef jerky stick, a couple carrots to eat. That's when she saw Pigface—who at the time had no mask. Instead, it was just his face: meaty, jowly, pale at the front but red on the neck, as if he stood outside sometimes in the sun, his neck bent, his nose pointed toward the earth, so that the back of him grew rust-dark while the front of him stayed grub-pale. That first day he went and polished the knob in his truck—jerking off as his eyes sometimes strayed up over the steering wheel to gaze at that freckle-faced girl behind the stand—and then he drove off, tires throwing up stones as he peeled out of the lot and onto the highway.

He came back the next day.

And the next after that.

And earlier today.

Each day, the same: He'd fondle some produce, and then hurry off as the girl noticed him. Then he'd fondle himself in the truck. This time, her father was there, a ruddy-faced fella in a Kubota tractor hat. He told Pigface to buy something or don't, but to stop hanging around.

Today, when that happened, Pigface didn't go back to the truck to masturbate. All he did was leave. Then, as Wren was paying for her purchase (more berries today, and a cold milk in a glass bottle), he passed by the stand again another three times. Each time staring out. Little eyes nested in the puffy, uneven pillows of his face.

Wren asked the girl if she knew him.

"Nah," Freckles said. "He came by first time a few days ago. Never saw him before. We get a lot of weirdos around here. You checking out the fireworks tonight?"

"What?" Wren asked.

"It's the Fourth of July," the girl said, and she said it like, *duh, dumbass.*

"Oh. Yeah. No." Wren pulled her arms inward, suddenly awkward. "I dunno. Why are you even open?"

Here, the father stepped over and butted in: "Because money's money and farmers gotta eat. You gonna buy anything else?"

"No. See you."

"Later," Freckles said.

The girl didn't seem worried about the stranger.

Wren, though, *was* worried. So, she set off in the direction he went, away from the motel, away from the farm stand. All the while, she told herself to turn back around, stop walking, forget this guy. *You don't need to do this. The world turns with or without you. People are bad. You can't fix that, because you're bad too.*

*A killer killing killers. You're no better,* she reminded herself.

And yet, she kept walking.

She walked for a few miles, found a little pull-off winding its way through the corn, across the street from an open-air park where some people had gone to grill out and the like. And there, heading down it, gauzy behind a curtain of limestone dust, was a pickup truck. *The* pickup truck, same she came to follow. Wren bit her lip, told herself *again* to turn around.

She didn't have anything. No weapon but for a rusty penknife in her pocket. *This isn't who you are anymore.* Of course that opened herself up to the follow-up question: *Well, who the fuck are you, then? Do you even know?* She felt like a leaf in a fast stream. Nothing but a vessel for bugs, swept by the current.

Wren took a step down the pull-off. Kids laughing burbled up behind her—kids at the park, flying a kite, or trying to. Music kicked up. Country music bullshit. Twangy.

Another step.

And then another.

And then suddenly she was walking, a quarter-mile, then a half, then a full mile—eating berries along the way until there were no more berries to eat, and all the while, the afternoon sky started to go dark like the berry stains on her fingertips. Evening settled in, coloring everything the hue of smashed cherries. That's when she found the truck.

And the man, just outside of it.

He was parked dead in the center of this little gravel road. The man moved his bulk around the back bumper—his back was to her, and even in the growing dark she could see the sweat stains across his white T-shirt. He had the back gate of the truck down, and the man was rooting around; she heard a bang and a clamor, until she saw he had something in his hand: the length of pipe with the elbow joint fitted at the end.

Then, something else. Something loose and rubbery. Dangling at his side in his free hand. She didn't know then it was his mask, but it didn't take long to see how he set that pipe down on the end of the tailgate before pulling the mask clumsily over his head.

He turned. In profile she saw the smashed-flat pig snoot, the comical bug eyes shining in the last light of day and the first light of the moon.

Wren must've gasped. Because he turned. He saw her.

The two of them regarded one another for what felt like an eternity.

With a fast hand he pawed at the tailgate, finding the pipe. He gave it a spin—a surprisingly graceful move for such a brutish pile of man, and he charged toward her like a barrel rolling down a hill. She thought to stand and fight him; she knew from her days at the Caldecott School how to defend herself by going for all the sensitive parts, from the eyes to the throat all the way down to the tender coin purse between every man's legs. But one hit from that pipe and she'd be laid out. So, she ran.

Into the rows, then against them, like a minotaur escaping the maze not by winding through its contours but rather by headbutting every wall until it bashed open a straight path through. In here, in the corn, it was dark: waves of black stalks punctuated by ribbons of night above. Wren cried out, not meaning to; her ankle tweaked as she landed hard on an uneven rise of ground between the rows. She caught herself and grabbed momentum—but it was enough. A roar rose behind her. Like that of a great beast in dogged pursuit. Something came crashing through the corn—

*Whish whish WHISH*

*WHUD*

It felt like a hard fist meteored into her back.

Wren staggered and fell, a thatch of corn stalks bending as she tumbled against them, doing just enough to ease her fall so she didn't faceplant into the hard, rain-starved earth. She planted her hands hard, gasping for air—whatever hit her blasted the wind out of her lungs, and now she keened for breath like wind whistling through a broken windowpane. Behind her arose the sound of corn smashing flat under heavy boots.

Pigface was there.

She pushed off the ground, her lungs finally relaxing enough for her to draw a breath, and it was then something glinted nearby—as she stood, she saw the man's weapon there in the dirt. The pipe. That's what hit her. He had *thrown* it.

Her back reminded her as she straightened up, a blip of pain radiating out from the middle of her torso. It nearly staggered her. *Don't fall. Get up. Stay up.*

There, ten feet away from her, he stood.

The bulk of the man, looming there, sweat pressing through the thin fabric of his white T-shirt like grease through a paper towel. The rubber pig mask sat askew on his head, the bulbous eyes like a pair of cartoon breasts drawn by an overeager thirteen-year-old boy. Pigface bleated.

"*You* were at the farm stand," he growled.

"*You* were going to hurt that girl."

He shrugged. "Still gonna. I'll get her after I get you. I'll smash your head like a pumpkin. Then I'll fuck it. I'll fuck it real good."

"You look like a pumpkin-fucker."

It was the wrong thing to say. Or, maybe, the right thing. Enraged, he rushed toward her—but this wasn't her first fight, and she prayed like hell it wouldn't be her last. She sidestepped one of his clubbing fists, then delivered a flurry of hits. She slammed the flat of her hand up under his mask, against his throat. Then a high knee in his side. Then her other knee between his legs, smashing into his balls.

And all the while, he just stood there.

Taking it like a department store mannequin.

She took a step back. He hadn't moved.

"People can't hurt me," he said. He sounded almost sad about that.

Then he hit her in the side of the head with a tree trunk. Or that's what it felt like, at least, when he brought his hand against the side of her head—it was like a grizzly bear's paw. His meaty palm smashed into her and she went down.

Her ears rang. Dizziness was like a drain drawing her down, down, down.

Pigface kicked aside a stray stalk and bent down to retrieve his pipe. Once again, he twirled it upon rescuing it. Then slapped it against his hand a few times.

He stood over her. He raised the pipe high in the air.

Then his head twitched. He grunted. The gesture of someone who had just walked through an unseen spider's web. Again he raised the pipe—

And again he twitched, this time in the other direction. "Get out!" he barked. To who? Her? And then, like that—

There came a shrill whistle streaking across the sky from right to left. And then the sky lit up above his head: a flash of hot pink light streaked across the black from a center point as the fireworks show began. The air popped; lights crackled. It left colors bleeding across her vision. Pigface pirouetted suddenly, swiping at the air with the pipe, and again with his other open hand. As the one exploding firework went dark, another fired up like a rocket, erupting in blue light that cascaded outward before falling like a rain of electric fire. And in that light, Wren saw—

Movement. All around Pigface. Little black shapes silhouetted against the electric dark. Not still. But moving. And moving fast.

He grunted again—"Unngh!"—and pulled at the bottom of his mask.

*What the hell is happening?*

Another whistle, pop, and crackle: this time, a multicolor spray of lights above.

And this time, it was bright enough for her to see what was around him.

Insects.

*Bees.*

More coming in from all directions, fast forming a horrible dark cloud around him—the buzzing of their wings now competed with the sound of the fireworks above. Pigface was whirling about now, bleating inhuman, animal sounds as the insects covered him. They formed a carpet on his chest, and that carpet undulated as it squeezed its way under his mask. As green light lit the sky and the corn, Wren could see his bug-eyed swine mask swelling, *distending*—pushed and stretched by what must've been the insects swarming underneath. The man's bleats turned to screams, and those screams were suddenly lost beneath a tide of gagging and choking.

*They're in his mouth*, she realized.

Quickly she clambered to stand—

Just as he teetered like an axe-chipped tree. Pigface toppled. And the bees kept on him. Hundreds of them. Thousands. A black, buzzing hurricane. His body began to swell everywhere, bloating like so much summer sausage. Soon, his gabbled cries and gargling sounds died back. His body stopped thrashing. Wren, shaken, turned and ran. She ran hard and fast, charging through the corn, until she once again found the gravel road and his pickup truck, and it was then that she threw up on the side of it, her vomit spattering the dust-crusted tire.

What had just transpired, she did not know and could not say, and it made her feel sick not just in her body but somewhere deeper, all the way down to her soul.

# 3. MEMORY, ALL ALONE IN THE MOONLIGHT

*"The line from the Bible," Miriam growled. "Thine eye shall not pity, but life shall go for life. Eye for eye. Tooth for tooth. Hand for hand and foot for foot. My mother used to say that. She'd say that to remind me that the world worked that way—it demanded grim balance, and I've always been an agent of that. I take one life so that another may go. I balance those scales. Now, you took a life. A very big, very beautiful life. I don't meet many nice people, but he was one of them. Killing you won't even begin to balance the scales."*

*Wren dropped the gun. "I know."*

*Miriam's finger coiled around the trigger. "I should have let you drown in the river. Eleanor Caldecott was right about you. She told me; she said you were a bad little girl. That I was part of your wreckage. That you would rob me of something, some important piece. And here we are. Prophecy fulfilled."*

# 4. OR MAYBE NOT ALONE, AFTER ALL

**Wren** tossed and turned in the shitty motel bed. Her last night in the motel, and she wanted to enjoy it—as much as you could enjoy sleeping in a bed that stabbed you in the back with unruly, errant springs, as much as you could enjoy the musty stink and the near-certainty that you're sleeping on some underestimated percentage of blood and semen. But sleep came to her in sudden falls, and wakefulness came quickly after, delivered in sharp jabs. Soon as she'd fall asleep, dreams would rise up out of the dark and take her down, and then she'd spasm, a leg kicking out, an arm flailing sideways, and then she'd be awake once more. Bathed in sweat. Shivering cold despite the heat.

The last dream that fled back to the darkness of Wren's mind was one of Miriam. The last time she saw Miriam was in that cabin. Miriam and Louis had come for Wren and saved her. They saved her not just by swooping her up before the cops found her, but they also saved her from the life she had been living. Wren had been out in the world, finding those who were gilded with the gleaming mercury lining of murderous intent—she had the ability to see those who would one day kill. When she found them, she killed them. The ghost in her head—Miriam called it a Trespasser, and to Wren it looked just like Miriam—egged her on. Or maybe worse. It felt in a way that the Trespasser had filled her up, had taken her hand, had held her in its grip the way a murderer holds a knife, way a sniper cuddles a rifle.

Miriam, outside the cabin, in the snow, had asked Wren how she knew that was she was doing was just. That it was both right and righteous. Wren saw things simply, and she said that she saw people who were going to kill, so she killed them first. Wasn't that what Miriam did? Even though she knew it wasn't. Miriam saw how people were going to die—she saw the full-throated vision in the dark of her mind, got to live with the person as they died sometime in the future. When Miriam killed, it was to preempt what was to come, yes, but she *knew* what was to come.

Wren did not.

If she found someone gleaming in the knife-bright light of silver, what did that mean? That they would kill? Yes. But what did *that* mean, exactly? Maybe they'd kill because they were monsters. Maybe they'd kill to protect a loved one. Maybe they'd kill accidentally—like if they were driving drunk, or if a pedestrian stepped out in front of their car. Maybe their fault, maybe not. And without knowing that, *really* knowing that, what could Wren say? How could she defend ending someone's life without all the details? Wren decided, *I'll do better, I'll be better.*

Then came that night.

In the snow. Upstate Pennsylvania. Miriam had a way of cultivating enemies—and one of them had somehow returned from the dead. Wren didn't know how then, didn't know now, and all she knew was that Miriam went outside to find and kill this woman, Harriet, before Harriet could kill her. And while she was gone, Wren was left with Louis and a woman Louis was intending to marry. Samantha. He was ragged. On the edge. Angry. And the silver lines ran around his margins like mercury spilled from an old thermometer. Wren's own Trespasser appeared in the guise of Miriam, and Not-Miriam whispered to her, told her that Louis was going to kill this woman, Samantha. That he was a murderer. That he would stop at nothing. Wren didn't believe it, but Not-Miriam's words slithered into her earholes and into her mind like worms ineluctably chewing into the heart of an apple. The thoughts drove her mad, like hearing wasps in the wall, like hearing rats chewing somewhere but you can't find them, like an itch so deep you can't scratch it and it slowly, surely drives you mad. And Louis *was* upset—afraid for Miriam, angry with Samantha, who had lied to him. (The woman had apparently become his fiancée only to get close to Miriam. That, another of Miriam's many non-supernatural

She remembered the gun in her hand.

The way it bucked in her grip.

She barely heard the sound.

He'd knelt down and was looking at Samantha, and Wren remembered Not-Miriam telling her, *This is when he does it*, and then she pointed the gun and shot him in the head and even as it happened she was yelling, screaming for *real* Miriam to come back, to stop her from doing this, screaming at the bullet to reverse out of his skull and slink back into the gun, but it was done. Over. His head was slumped. The blood was oozing. The cabin smelled like chemical eggs. And then, to cap it all off, the real corker was that Samantha lifted her chin, drawing a loud, keening gasp—

Then *she* died too.

It had all been for naught.

The demon that haunted her—Not-Miriam—laughed and said, *Oops*, and then told her to run. And any other day, she would've. Wren had gotten pretty good at running. But this time, she stayed. She hid in the corner. Gun in her hand. The blood-stink and gunpowder reek hanging in the air like a fog.

Eventually, Miriam returned.

She found Louis, dead. Samantha's corpse draped across his lap.

Wren wanted to die. She stepped out. Let Miriam see what she had done. *Kill me*, she thought. A coward's suicide: let someone else do the work for you. Like all those shooters who shot innocent people for the sole purpose of committing Death by Police.

Wren was committing Death by Vengeful Miriam.

And boy, if Miriam did not look the spitting image of vengeance that night. She was covered in blood. A lot of it smeared around her mouth—red, dripping, gummy.

But Miriam didn't kill her.

(Which still threw Wren for a loop.)

No, Miriam said, "I can't do it. I can't kill any more people. I don't have my owl. I don't have my Louis. You need to *go*. Take the car. Drive far the fuck away. Live a life of reparation and repentance. And if you ever cross paths with me, you dire little beast, I will cut out your heart and eat it."

(*Cut your heart out and eat it.* Even now, Wren wondered: was that what Miriam had done that night? Killed Harriet by eating her heart?)

Wren did as she was told. She fucked off.

And ever since, she's thought about that line:

*Live a life of reparation and repentance.*

An impossible goal. She hadn't lived up to it one fucking iota. The best she could manage is that she hadn't killed anybody.

Tonight, she thought about breaking that. Tracking Pigface. Then running from him as he put on his mask. She wondered how exactly she would, or could, kill him. Not just in the way that it would take her summoning something that she'd kept squashed for the last several months—that murderous urge—but in the way that he was huge, and had a pipe, and did not seem to be affected by whatever pain she visited upon him.

*People can't hurt me…*

Then the bees came. Descending out of the dark. Lit by the spray of colorful chemical fire in the sky above. Stinging him. Filling his mask. Hanging from his underarms like writhing, buzz-wing tumors. Pigface fell and she ran and now here she was once more, in bed, catching sleep the way one caught fireflies, trying dearly to outrun her dreams and memories. She was alone.

Until she wasn't.

Someone was here with her.

It was Miriam. Or the Trespasser in the guise of Miriam—the ghost that pretended to be her. Not-Miriam. A lean feminine shape stood at the edge of her bed, between it and the set of dressers that had a lean to it because one of the bottom legs was missing. But Wren hadn't seen Not-Miriam in a while—and whenever that wraith visited her, it always came with a whiskey stink and a cloud of sharp, unfiltered cigarette smoke. (Ironic, given that the *real* Miriam had since given up cigarettes—proof that if she could quit, anybody could.) Now she did not smell that acrid tang. Didn't see the bright red cigarette cherry glowing there in the darkness, either.

Her second thought was: Pigface.

He wasn't dead.

And now here he sat. Pipe in hand. Mask on face. Ready to club her head into red pudding.

But the shadow that stood there did not match his uneven, monstrous girth.

Could it be the real Miriam?

"Who are you?" she asked. Wren's voice was a rough, raggedy croak. The sound of it, the rawness, disturbed even her.

A deep breath slid through the dark. "My name is Lissa." Her voice was soft and rich—light and airy, yes, but with a resonance behind it, a comforting hum. *Golden*, Wren thought. That was the word for it. *Golden*. Like warm honey. "Lissa Larson."

Wren sat up straight. Her hands balled into fists. "The fuck did you get in here?"

"You're not staying in the most…secure location. I paid the man at the front desk—not even all that much, to be honest. He gave me a key."

"Get out."

"I will. In a moment. First, I'd like to talk."

"You don't get out, I'll put a bullet in your heart."

"Mm. If you had a weapon, why didn't you use it tonight? On Merton Myers."

"Who?"

"The man in the pig mask."

*Pigface.*

"You were there?" Wren asked.

"I was."

"You saw what happened to him."

"I did."

And then, a new sound arose in the darkness of the motel room. A faint buzz. Not high-pitched like a fly. But a deeper, more resonant buzz. A rough, saw-cut hum. It flew around her head, orbiting her from one ear to the next—close, but not so close she could feel the air from its wings. Only the sound reached her, Dopplering back and forth. *Vvvvm. Vvvvvm. Vvvz.* Wren's breath caught in her chest, trapped there like a frog in a cup, unable to hop away and escape.

"That's a…" she started to say, but the words rotted on her tongue.

"A bee," the woman said plainly and clearly. No, not just that. *Proudly.* A little spike of bona fide pride in that declaration. "A friend of mine."

"You. You killed him. Pigface."

"Merton Myers. I did. Well—" she said, reversing course. "I suppose the strictest reading would say that the swarm killed him. Certainly, whoever finds his body there in the corn—a farmer, most likely—will think that's all that it was."

Miriam, Wren knew, could control birds.

Did this woman have a similar power? But with…insects?

In the dark of the room, Wren shuddered. Even as she heard the lone bee buzzing, unseen, around her margins.

"You're wayward," Lissa said. "A lost little bird. But you're special, too. You have promise and power. If you want to make use of that promise and power and do something good, come find me. I've left an address on the nightstand. It's a farm. It's not far. You could walk or catch a ride. I'll be there if you decide to come."

"And if I do?"

"Then I can show you what I did, how I did it, and why."

"To Pigface. Myers."

"Mm-hmm."

"I'm not coming to your fuckin' farm. I can smell a trap. I've had enough of people telling me what they want me to do."

"That's perfectly understandable. You can remain on your own, and I wouldn't begrudge you that decision." A pause before she said, "But I'd ask you to consider: being alone, out here, without plan or purpose. How is that working out for you?"

"*Just fine,*" Wren lied.

"Then it was good to meet you, and the best of luck."

There came a few footsteps, and the shadow eased away from her. The door to her room opened, framing the woman with the light of the hallway—her silhouette showing someone tall, thin, like a wispy willow tree sapling. She eased through the space, into the interstices of liminal space, and was gone again. Gone like she'd never existed. Like she had only been a dream, an intruder like the spectral interloper of Not-Miriam.

Wren buried her head under the pillow and stayed, ratcheted awake and charged like a live wire, until dawn.

# 5. SUCCOR

**There,** on the dresser, sat a note. Nice paper, creased down the middle. Plain white, or cream, she guessed. The script inside it was elegant as fuck:

*The Farm.*

*North 1550 Rd*

*I hope to see you there.*

It was sealed shut with a wax stamp of a honeybee, like in a woodcut style.

And atop it, keeping the notecard closed, was a small jar of what looked like honey. It had no label, just a bit of pink ribbon looped around where the lid met the glass. Wren unscrewed it and took a smell: it was heady and sweet-smelling. It perfumed the air around her with a floral cloud, nearly dizzying in its intensity.

She capped it, pocketed it, and then left the room, leaving the note behind.

She wasn't going to that farm.

She wasn't going to meet that lady.

Because fuck that shit.

# 6. A WAYWARD'S CHOICE

**Wren** didn't have a car. She did, once. When she left Miriam the last time—her parting gift being Louis's dead body—she took Samantha's car, as directed. But she ditched it soon after. The cops would be looking for her, wouldn't they? Eventually, they'd find the bodies. They'd know. They'd come for her. They were already looking for her—though, then again, her dressing like Miriam meant they were also looking for Miriam. And if they caught Miriam, they'd stop looking for *her.*

That troubled her too. Another burden. Another cost. Another cross-beam borne across the breadth of her narrow, skinny-ass little shoulders.

*God, I have fucked everything up.* What irony, too: her nickname for Miriam was what? Psycho. *Psy-cho*, said almost singsongily. And she turned out to be ten times the psycho that Miriam ever was. Couldn't put that monster back under the bed, right?

She stood out front of the motel on a road adjacent to the Kansas Turnpike. The asphalt lot underneath her feet and the road ahead were blasted and scoured by time and sun and dirt. The plan was, what? There existed no plan. She was trash. Blowing wherever the wind took her. Thumb out, wiggle-wiggle, grab a ride with whatever hopefully-not-handsy motherfucker would pick her up. If they did get handsy, she'd make her warning. If they kept on keeping on, she'd stick them quick with the small lockback penknife she carried, then get the fresh hot hell out of there. If she could.

It was a shit plan.

Why even bother?

Why not just lie down here on the asphalt, wait for a car to run over her? Or, forgoing such passivity, maybe the best bet would be, instead of popping up her thumb to hitchhike, she could just catch a ride on the front grill of a tractor-trailer by stepping out in front of it at the very last second. She'd turn to paste, they could take her wherever. Maybe they'd hose her viscera off at the next truck stop. Maybe she'd be a meal for flies, same as every bloat-belly truck-struck deer or tire-smashed fox along the highway.

Or maybe the best bet was to turn herself in.

Go to the cops. The Feds. Hold up her hands, wrists together, like they do in the movies, say, *Cuff me, I'm a killer, a real sicko psy-cho.* Confess to everything. Go away for good. Maybe live out her life in a steel and concrete box, eventually get shanked by some block-skulled meth-bitch outside the prison showers, or hey, maybe they'd eventually just pump her full of some chemical cocktails, and she would die there in a chair, watched by whatever gross shit-hogs liked to come and voyeuristically watch people die. That was as good a plan as the one she had.

*You're wayward. A lost little bird. But you're special, too. You have promise and power. If you want to make use of that promise and power and do something good, come find me. I've left an address on the nightstand. It's a farm. It's not far. You could walk or catch a ride. I'll be there if you decide to come...*

Then, with Lissa's words, Miriam's came back to haunt her, too—

*Live a life of reparation and repentance...*

Fuck.

Fuck!

"Fuck," she said.

Wren started walking.

# 7. THE FARM

**The** farm sat, a strange tree-lined oasis nestled in the wide, flat Kansas expanse. White farmhouse, old but well maintained. A little farther back sat a metal pole barn, and a rust-red tractor sat outside it, framed by a spray of wild grasses and tangled weeds. Big round haybales lined the outside of the pole barn. A couple doves sat together on a powerline above, like a pair of feathered potatoes snuggling.

Wren drew a deep breath and stepped onto the property. Gravel complained under her feet. She saw Lissa by the house, kneeling down by a set of flowerbeds at the margin of the front porch. Her hands and arms were dirty up to the elbows, and her hair was pulled back as sweat slicked her forehead. A few bees buzzed around her. Plastic flower planter pots—some individual, others in trays—sat around her, some still filled, some now emptied. As Wren approached, a few more bees found her, *vvviiip*ping about, circumnavigating her once, then twice, before disappearing.

*Scouts*, she thought. A strange thought, but it proved itself quickly true: Lissa's head popped up like a dog that had caught a scent. She turned to face Wren.

"I was hoping you'd come," Lissa said.

"I'm here," Wren said, her mouth a dire line.

Lissa stood, brushing crumbs of soil off her forearms.

In the bed behind her, a series of flowers thrust up, freshly planted. Purples and pinks and reds. Wild, strange varieties. Exotic-looking. She must've caught Wren looking at them, because she said, "They're local flowers. We prefer to plant from native varieties. Lupine, gayfeather, musk thistle, and such."

"Good time to plant," Wren said, not knowing if that was true or not.

"It's a bad time, actually," Lissa said, which made Wren feel stupid, but Lissa didn't seem dismissive about it. She just smiled and added, "I was busy earlier in the season, and we had a lot of rain. So, I'm late to planting."

"Oh."

They stood across from each other, the silence an awkward, ever-expanding void.

"I wanna know what you want from me," Wren said, abruptly. "I want to know why I'm here."

Lissa offered a pained smile. "Why any of us are here is one of the biggest, most troubling questions of them all."

"That's great on a motivational poster with a kitty cat, but I want to know why *you* invited *me* here, specifically. What's your bag?"

"Why don't we take a walk?"

"Are you going to kill me?"

Lissa laughed. "Is that a problem for you, usually?"

Wren hesitated.

"Maybe," she said, finally.

"No, if I wanted to do that, I would've done it while you slept in your motel bed. Come on. Walk with me. Then we can have some tea and I'll tell you my proposition."

# 8. THE TREE

**They** walked straight back from the house, into a field—a field that may have once been for planting crops like corn or soy, as many were. Now it had been repurposed. If Wren thought the flowers at the front of the house were pretty, she had no idea how to describe the massive spread of them here. Wildflowers of every color stretched out before her. Some already dry, going to seed. Others just starting to bloom. Many yet in full-bore colors, downright flirty with one another—like a peacock with his tailfeathers in a fireworks array. She realized ironically, that's what this was, wasn't it? Flowers flirting with each other. Or, rather, flirting with the insects and birds that would pollinate them. *Everything looks the way it does because it's trying to get laid*, she thought. Nature, red in tooth and claw, sure. But also, nature, red in petal, and tailfeather, and lipstick. Ugh, gross. Wren didn't care for it. Not for any of it. Grimly, she decided that the world would be better off if everyone and everything just stopped fucking and let it all slow to a crawl, let the wheels come off this thing, let it all end.

*That was fuckin' dark*, she told herself.

*The world is fuckin' dark*, she answered herself.

Whatever.

They waded into the field, and all around them, bees buzzed. Some were honeybees, but also little hovering bees and a few wasps whose waists were as thin as pins, whose wings were as blue as a rifle barrel. A handful of puffball bumblebees ping-ponged about too, tapping into flowers drunkenly before clinging to one and rolling in the pollen the way a dog rolls in a dead thing.

"It's all right," Lissa said. "They're not interested in you."

"Are you sure?"

A cheeky smile. "Quite. Come on."

Deeper they went, toward the center of the field, where a single tree stood tall. The tree, Wren could see, had died—it was a giant skeleton's hand, thrust up out of the earth, reaching implacably toward the heavens, its black-bark bones twisted into a mad, desperate shape. It seemed to vibrate in the very air, a black shimmer like flies—

No, not flies.

Bees.

She could hear it now, and *feel* it up through her feet, and in the hinge of her jaw. A maddening, saw-cut buzzing. It made her eyes water. She wanted to turn around and go back. But

Lissa kept walking and she trailed after, wincing as the sound grew louder and louder, as it thrummed in her *teeth*.

Then, amid the black haze of insects—

A dart of bold, brash red.

A bird. It came straight down, spiraling—its wings extended outward as a brake before it disappeared under cover of the meadow flowers. Moments ticked past. Lissa stopped walking. She held up her hand, index finger aloft. Tick, tick, tick.

Then: the red bird popped back out, snatching something out of the air. A bee, black and wriggling, pinned in its beak. It flew out away from the tree, over the flowers.

Movement. Off to Wren's right.

*Boom.*

A sudden, concussive blast cut the air. The bird ceased flying straight and did a pinwheel flip, wing over wing. A spray of feathers and blood, and then it dropped like a thrown stone into the field. The movement off to the side continued—someone stood up, having been hidden there in the flowers. They had a small gun in their hands. Wren knew enough now about firearms to know it was not a rifle—it was a little shotgun, single barrel, a hammer at the back. Draw it back, pull the trigger, and that's what makes it go boom. The gun was a small caliber, too—no, wait, gauge. They count shotguns in gauges, right? On that, Wren was no expert. And she didn't much care to become one.

Her heart pounded.

That bird—

It was beautiful. A splash of red amid the buzzing black.

Gone now. Dead.

The man with the gun was barely a man at all. A young man—maybe Wren's age. His hair a messy, sweaty shock of red. His cheeks speckled with fat, smeary freckles. He gave the two of them a nod and then shrank back into the field. As he moved, the light around him gleamed: an unnatural light. Silver and fluid.

*He's a Mercury Man*, Wren realized. Meant he was a killer, or would be one someday. A murderer now, or later.

"That's James," Lissa said.

"He—you—that bird. That beautiful bird!" Wren felt her heart beating not in her chest but right at her temples, each like a timpani drum banging *thoom thoom thoom*. "Why the *fuck* would you do that?"

"That *bird*," Lissa said, "is what I wanted to show you. It is a summer tanager—a bee-eater. Already bee populations are struggling, and this songbird—precious and showy as it may seem—can decimate a hive with just a few of its avian cohorts."

"So what? They're just…they're just fucking *bees*. That bird was…red and pretty and, and, it was *special*."

Lissa's mood darkened. "Is that why we keep it around? Because it's special? The bees are common? Just bugs, so we can watch them die? The tanager does nothing for us. But the bees are an ecological niche unto themselves. Strong, social creatures—a veritable community doing so much for the ecosystem all around them, for flowers, for trees, for us, too. The one 'special' bird does not deserve to feast on the bees."

Wren held up both hands. She wanted to press them to her head to shut out the buzzing, but it was all in her—not just in her ears but singing in the marrow within her bones. Instead, she held them up in a fuck-you gesture of surrender. "Fuck this. I'm leaving. I don't know what the hell this even is—but I don't want any part of it."

A snap of Lissa's fingers, and everything changed.

The bees left their dead tree, whirling about in a black serpent that called to mind a susurration of blackbirds in the sky—a dark, porous serpent of buzzing creatures. They whipped around behind Wren, forming a humming, dashing perimeter that enclosed her in with Lissa. "Not yet," Lissa said. "Stay for a moment."

"I don't want to stay."

"I ask only for the time it takes for us to drink some tea."

"Fuck you."

"I have honey. Good honey. *The best* honey."

Wren turned. She flexed her fists. Tensed her calves. The honeybees—carving a fence in the air—stayed eerily in this pattern. The woman, Lissa, had to be controlling them. *I can sprint,* Wren thought. She could make it. Take off running, break through the insects, charge hard through the field—the woman's powers had to have a limit of distance, didn't they? But Miriam's didn't. Miriam could ride a bird halfway across the Pacific Ocean. Shit. Shit!

But then the fence broke apart. The bees peeled away, like old images of the Red Sea parting under the staff of Moses. And just like that, they dissipated, zipping back to the tree from whence they came. Though the humming was loud still, it was considerably quieter now that they weren't circling her and Lissa so closely. Wren caught her breath.

"If you want to go, I understand," Lissa said.

"Good," Wren said, though her feet did not yet move.

"I'm not here to hurt you. It was just to show you that I'm serious. I need your help. That man in the cornfield, the one you call Pigface? Myers was a bad man. And he was special, too, like the tanager. He wanted to hurt people, kill them. Girls and young women like yourself. Like the girl at that farm stand. Like the tanager with the bees, he could pluck one, or ten, and in the grand scheme of things, it wouldn't matter much, would it? He couldn't kill enough to change the human ecosystem. But those individuals, their pain, the loss of them—it would do so much damage. No matter how special he was. No matter how his abilities seemed to earn his place as an apex predator. He was bad. Like the birds are bad. And so, I had to stop him like I have to stop the tanagers. Do you understand? I want to offer you a chance. A chance to be better. To do good."

"I. . .should go."

"And you can. But then you won't see what we can do together. And you'll miss out on the tea. The honey of killer bees is quite something else."

"Killer bees?"

Lissa smirked. "You didn't think these were normal bees, did you?

# 9. KILL OR BEE KILLED, GET IT, BEE KILLED, SHUT UP, NEVER MIND

Tink, *tink, tink.*

Lissa tapped her spoon against the teacup. The honey was thick and strangely granular—the glob of it oozed off the spoon without any urgency, like a torpid, overfed penguin sliding off its ice floe. All the while, she kept her eyes fixed on Wren. Holding her like a pair of tweezers.

Wren's tea was black, without any sweetness at all.

Because that honey was killer bee honey.

A thing she did not know existed. A thing she did not know *could* exist.

Surely, it was poison.

"It's not toxic," Lissa said, seeming to read Wren's expression. The two of them sat at a small nook table in a farmhouse kitchen: white wooden cabinets, a pellet stove in the corner, an old fifties-style oven next to it, turquoise-lacquered. "The honey. It's safe. It's delicious, honestly. There *is* toxic honey out there. The so-called Mad Honey of Turkey or of the Nepalese honeybees—the honey contains compounds that are hallucinogenic. And then there's imported honey from China, which is often not honey at all, and because it isn't tested may contain lead, mercury, or other poisons. But that's not from killer bees." The honey finally left its spoon and plopped into the tea. *Ker-bloop.* "It's not even fair to call these creatures 'killer bees'—many call them 'Africanized honeybees,' which I'd argue carries some... racial implications. Honestly, they're not even supposed to be this far north, but climate change has modified their borders, and that leads people to be scared. But they shouldn't be. The bees are aggressive *defenders*, and only that. They do not seek out prey to kill. They do mount a considerable defense of their hive and queen, which is to be lauded, I say, not demonized."

"Do you control them?"

"I prefer not to think of it that way. I...urge them, when needed."

"Does that make you their queen?"

That seemed to strike a nerve. Lissa visibly flinched, as if prodded. "Let's talk about you. And why you're here." The woman leaned over to the side, pulling out a soft leather briefcase. From it she withdrew a file folder, and from that folder she pulled out a series of photos and news clippings. Each seemed to contain information about a killing—or a series of killings. *Seven Dead at Camp Do-More; The Convenience Store Killer Strikes Again; Ten More Bodies Found in Shallow Grave by Elementary School; Masked Madman Seen Fleeing Scene of Massacre in Released Video.* There were crime scene photos, too: bloody, garish, lit by camera flashes, limbs off, faces gone, some dressed in outfits (like a child's doll, or in latex, or in the outfits of a 1980s camp counselor). Lissa spread them out, and as she did, she continued to talk: "They have names given to them by investigators, or sometimes by the press. The Convenience Store Killer. The Zodiac. The Taxman. The Lollipop Man. The Starfucker. Pigface." On that one, she looked up, met Wren's eyes once more. Then she dropped a pair of bombs: "The Mockingbird. The Angel of Death."

On those last two, it was Wren's turn to flinch.

The Mockingbird—that was the killer who once wanted to end her life on a table, bound by barbed wire, beheaded with an axe by a lunatic wearing a beaked plague doctor mask. Though it wasn't just one killer: it was the whole damn Caldecott clan, a family sharing the role, even if only one of them, Carl Keener, wore the mask most of the time.

And the second one...

The Angel of Death.

That, the name they gave to both Wren and Miriam—Wren, killing people looking like her. Miriam, doing her thing, too. Both a Reddit sensation. Both earning that name together, believing—in maybe the same way as the Mockingbird—that it was just one of them doing the deeds, not two. Though therein lurked a considerable difference: Miriam did not consent to the killings Wren committed. Which was the whole fucking problem in the first place, wasn't it?

*Live a life of reparation and repentance…*

Lissa knew. She must have. Though her expression seemed not to change, she didn't bring that up just to bring it up. Wren figured, fuck it, it's like a Band-Aid: just tear that fucker off and get to, and through, the pain of it.

"I'm the Angel of Death," Wren said.

"I know."

"Of course you do."

"It's why you're here now. To make things right."

Wren shifted uncomfortably in her chair. She crossed her arms hard across her chest, then uncrossed them again because suddenly she felt like, *What if I need a hand free to go for my knife?* Would she even be fast enough? Could this woman from here, in her kitchen, snap her fingers and bring a swarm of stinging monsters to kill her?

"Listen, just spit it out. Speak your truth, tell me what you want—stop, like, dancing around it, and lay it out. Or I'm the fuck out of here."

"These killers are both unhinged and enhanced. And those two characteristics? They're inexplicably linked. You know that as well as anybody. The powers we have are made out of pain and trauma. Something breaks inside us, and… *this thing* comes out."

Wren sneered. "What's *your* trauma?"

But Lissa ignored that question.

"Those who are traumatized into power are not often to be trusted with it. They have been broken, and no one is putting them back together again. Sometimes, an extreme aberration results: these killers. Serial killers. Slasher murderers. People so fundamentally abused and tortured that they break in all directions—and now they have psychic abilities that they can bring to bear against an unsuspecting world."

"So what?"

"So. I want you to help me hunt them."

"No."

"No?"

"No! What the fuck? N. O." Wren stood up so suddenly, the chair she was in nearly fell backward before she caught it. "I…I don't want to do that anymore. That's not who I am. I… can't. I won't."

"Don't you want to be better?"

Wren forced a fake, bitter laugh. "I do. That's why I'm not going to *kill a bunch of dudes*. I'm going to live a life of, oh, I dunno, *not killing people anymore*."

Lissa sighed. "So, a more selfish life."

"The fuck you say?"

"I just mean, you know these people exist. Not just because I'm showing you. You saw Merton Myers. You've been out there. You know what the Mockingbird did, and could do. If nobody had stopped the Mockingbird, how many more girls would that killer have killed? Hm?"

*Me*, a small voice said in the back of Wren's head.

Lissa continued: "To know that this is happening, that these broken people are out there, and you'll do nothing about it? You'll stand aside and let them die?"

To this, Wren said nothing.

"The Convenience Store Killer," Lissa said. "Do you know how he did it?"

"Obviously, I don't," Wren said, replete with weaponized eyeroll.

"His mask—so many of them wear masks, I assume because they don't like to look at themselves in the mirror—was as simple as they come: a brown paper bag with eyeholes clumsily cut out. Different bag every time, as one supposed they do not hold up to duress. He would walk into a store, and then anyone inside would be paralyzed. Instantly. That was his gift—or his curse. When he willed it so, those nearby him—within, I don't know, fifty, a hundred feet—could no longer move. They could barely make a sound, just a squeak. On the security camera footage, that's what you hear first: all of them squeaking and squealing in a chorus of it, like strange little night-frogs. Their eyes popping in panic. Shallow breaths in tight chests. With his victims unable to move, the CSK could do…whatever he wanted. And he did. He walked around the store, leisurely as anything, like a man out for an amble in a rose garden, smelling the flowers, drinking it in. He touched the women, forcing his hands down their pants, under their dresses. He slit the throats of the men. He killed most of them but left some alive—with missing ears, fingers, flaps of skin. Any who walked in on him doing it would freeze too. And they'd become another victim."

Wren swallowed a hard knot. "Is he still out there?"

The next word, perfectly formed, knowingly enunciated.

"*No.*"

"You stopped him."

"I did."

"How?"

"It was…hard. Hard to find him. I tracked the stories, followed the trail of his crimes. He did this six times, across the Midwest, here. I have some money, and I used it to pay a private detective to do some work for me on it, though he didn't know to what end. The cops couldn't catch any leads, in part because they did not understand what was happening or what to look for. I did. I found him, finally, in Illinois, in Elgin. That's where he was from. He worked there. A mild-mannered office worker, middle manager. Worked with kids as an art therapy teacher, of all things—and he did sculptures. It took me a while to find him. A year or more. He did his thing two more times in that span of months. I can see when people have powers. But *you*, you can see when they're killers. Together, we can see so much. We can find these people. And you're an efficient exterminator of such villainous vermin, aren't you? A weapon held in a steady hand."

"I have to go."

Lissa looked crestfallen. No—she looked fucking *desperate*.

"Don't. Please. We can do this. Together."

"I can't."

Wren turned and walked out the door.

And she told herself she'd never come back.

It was, of course, a lie.

# 10. FORGIVE US OUR TRESPASSES

**Wren** stood out at the end of the driveway. Wondering where she would wander next, like a piece of trash blown onto the road and down it, tumbling, tumbling, just looking for a landfill to call home. Her feet rooted hard in the rough stone, and she couldn't decide where to go. Left. Right. Straight ahead. Back to the motel. Back east, onward west, to the mountains or to the beach, to heaven or to hell.

Behind her, the gentle crunch of gravel perked up her ear.

Lissa, she expected. But when she turned—her nose wrinkling at the stinging scent of a burning cigarette—she saw her.

"You," Wren said.

Miriam.

Or, as it were, Not-Miriam. *The Trespasser.* This Miriam was an illusion: an uncertain percentage of *ghost* and *hallucination.* Wren expected she was somewhat, somehow real, by some measure: the other Miriam, the *real* Miriam, had her own Trespasser, too, which meant this was a product of their abilities.

Abilities, Lissa had reminded her, that were born of trauma.

Somehow, when she and Miriam broke, this *thing*—spirit, demon, angel, wraith, avatar, whatfuckingever—crept into the cracks. Maybe it's how they gained their abilities. Or maybe it was just a parasite.

*Parasite.*

That made a lot of sense, didn't it?

"That's what I'm going to call you from now on," Wren said.

"What's that?" Not-Miriam said, thumbing the end of her cigarette, flicking ash.

"Parasite. Not Trespasser. You're feeding off me. Aren't you?"

A wry smirk from Not-Miriam, who currently wore a pair of cherry-red cheap plastic sunglasses. She tilted them down over her nose. "Whatever makes your grapefruit squirt, little girl. So, you gonna take the, ahhh—the job?"

"Job?"

"Hunting freakshows."

"I already told her no."

"And yet," Not-Miriam said, clicking her tongue against the roof of her mouth, *tsk.* "Here you are. Your feet irrevocably fixed to the fucking earth."

"Fuck you, psy-cho."

"Trespasser, Parasite, *Psy-cho.* You're just not very nice to me." Not-Miriam mimed an exaggerated pout around the stem of her cigarette. "I don't know why I stay."

"So, don't stay. Go."

"Maybe I will."

"Maybe you should."

*Sniff.* "You'd miss me. You fucking *need* me, little girl. Your mother didn't want you, and now she's all dead and shit. Miriam didn't want you either—not that you made a good case for yourself, what with, ohh, *shooting her boyfriend in the fucking head.*"

"You told me to do that. You *made* me—"

"I don't make anybody do anything."

But that somehow felt like a lie, didn't it?

"You probably *want* me to go back in there," Wren said. "You get off on me killing those people."

Not-Miriam shifted uncomfortably. "I dunno."

"You *do* want me to take her up on her offer, don't you?"

The Parasite said nothing. Just suck, suck, puff. Illusory cancer cloud.

What did that mean?

Did she *not* want Wren to take it? Wren couldn't figure it out. What was the Parasite's play here, exactly? "I'm gonna take it," Wren said, suddenly, pivoting heel to toe and moving to march back down the driveway. "I'll help her."

*Whoosh.* Not-Miriam moved fast—faster than was human, floating like a ghost in a spectral wind. Suddenly, she was right before Wren, hands up, palms out, saying, "No, no, no. Think about this. You're right. Hit the road. Let's…let's go, fuck it, let's be free again, okay? We don't need that bitch in there."

"Why?"

"Why what?"

"Why don't you want this?"

Not-Miriam offered a wicked, fishhook grin. "Not about what I want. Just trying to do what's best for you, is all."

"You don't give a damn about me."

"That hurts me. That hurts me in my soul." Not-Miriam cocked her head like a dog not understanding something. "Wait, do I have a soul? Jury's out."

That decided it for Wren. It was just a bluff moments before, but now—*now*, it felt like she had to take it. If this wretched wraith didn't want her to go back in there, well…

Then she had to go back in there.

Wren stalked straight toward Not-Miriam, forcing the specter to juggle her steps sideways so she got out of the way. "Wren. Lauren. Wait. Wait!"

"Fuck you," Wren said, and walked back down the driveway, to the farmhouse, to the door. Didn't bother knocking. She just walked inside.

Lissa was waiting there. "I saw you out there having a conversation with…" Her hand arose like a butterfly, fingers tickling the air like its wings. "No one. Did you find an answer you were looking for, or one you were not?"

"I'm going to help you," Wren said. "That's all you need to know."

"Gorgeous," Lissa said, beaming. "I'm so happy."

She reached in and hugged Wren.

It felt…

…

*Nice.*

"When do we start?" Wren asked.

"In the morning, dear. Always start in the morning, after a good sleep, and a bracing cup of French press coffee."

# 11. BUT FIRST, COFFEE

**Lissa** wasn't kidding. As the morning light pried its way under the curtains, Wren stood blearily in the same farmhouse kitchen, watching coffee grounds steep in the glass tube of the French press. The smell was fabulous, and the patience required to get to the actual *drinking* of the coffee was killing her like a slow cancer. She wanted to grab that thing, smash it to the ground, and pour the scalding coffee into her face. And she wasn't even a huge coffee drinker—honestly, she couldn't afford it. But now? With that smell? Her teeth pressed together so hard, they felt like crumbling chalk.

Someone stepped into the kitchen next to her—the young man from the day before. He wore simple jeans, a blue T-shirt that advertised the Douglas County Fair. He moved ringlets of red hair out of his eyes and gave her a small smile. "Hey," he said. "I'm James. Jimmy."

"Jimmy," she said, dour and suspicious. Still, she saw the *shine* along him: that silver glow, the mercury sliding along his margins. *You're a killer, Jimmy.*

Or he was gonna be.

"You okay?"

"I want coffee. And you killed that bird."

His smile died. "I had to. The tanagers eat the bees."

"Not all of them."

"They can do a number on the hive. And if one comes, others show up. Like a buffet."

"Maybe that's how it's supposed to be. A natural order of things."

"If that's the case, why are you here?"

Her frown deepened. Lissa cautiously watched the exchange. As she (finally!) began to press the plunger on the French press, she said, "James here has been with us for a...year and a half now? Eighteen months?"

"That's right," Jimmy said.

Wren asked, "Who exactly is 'us'?"

"Others come and go," Lissa said, guardedly. "All have roles to play."

"And does Jimmy-James here have...an ability?"

He hesitated.

"He can shoot," Lissa said.

"I saw."

"No, I mean—"

"I never miss," Jimmy said, interrupting. Wren cocked an eyebrow and he explained: "What I point at, I hit. I don't even have to aim. I just...shoot with my heart and hit what I shoot."

That's when it hit Wren. Lissa *didn't* have the silvery shine around her. Jimmy did. When Lissa talked about hunting down and dealing with the—what was the murderer's nickname? The CSK. Convenience Store Killer.

*She* didn't kill him.

Jimmy, though…

Wren said as much. "Jimmy's your man, isn't he? He doesn't just shoot birds."

"He aims true," Lissa said, pouring three cups of coffee from the press. The vagueness of her statement hung in the air like a fog. But it was confirmation, right? An admission without an admission? Jimmy, for his part, mostly just stood there looking uncomfortable as Lissa continued. "Cream, sugar? How do you take your coffee?"

"Black."

Lissa nodded, and said, "Mine needs to be sweet. A little honey goes a long way to tame a dark brew." She smiled as she reached for the jar of honey on the table.

# 12. SMOKE ROSE

**Lissa** drove them—just her and Wren—to a strip mall about five miles south of the Kansas City airport. The parking lot was pitted and pocked—the buildings themselves were stripped raw of color, just bone-white against the backdrop of the Kansas flat plain behind.

Smoke rose from its center.

And with it, a smell that made Wren's stomach ache with an old, caveman hunger: slow, heat-plucked, smoke-fucked meat.

The joint was called Selwyn's Smokehouse. That on a simple sign, like something from the fifties. Beneath it someone had painted a slogan in a different font, different color (red versus black): DOWN-HOME MEATS, COMFY SEATS.

The bell jangled as they went in.

"—okay, so, Kansas City barbecue is best in the world," the guy behind the counter, a bony beanpole dude, real Ichabod

Craney, was saying. He was bent over at the waist like a tree broken in a bad storm, leaning over another man at the counter, this one in a rumpled blazer and polo shirt, with a pair of unpressed slacks to match. "Part of the reason is the versatility of it—we're not married to any one *protein* over another. Texas goes ga-ga for beef, in the Carolinas it's all pit pig, but here we eat it all, no one focus on anything, even chicken is a *team player*, yanno. And the sauce, don't get me started on the sauce, it's not sweet, no molasses, no honey, it's *tomato*-based, thick, *real* thick, too—" And as he went on and on, Wren could see the shine of metal along his skin, flashing and oozing like melted silver in hot sun.

A killer.

A Mercury Man.

Was this who they were here for?

Lissa didn't hesitate. She had already sat down at a table. A waitress came over as the bent, bony man—maybe in his late forties, early fifties, Wren didn't know, wasn't a good judge of age, as she was too young to have that perspective—kept talking. Without saying a word, the waitress slid two plastic menus into their hands. "We just opened," the woman said, finally, "might take time to get you what you need. What can I get you two to drink?"

"Water is fine," Lissa said.

"Iced tea," Wren answered. Then to Lissa: "You're paying, right? I have no money. Like, I don't even know if I have two quarters to rub together—"

"I have this, it's fine."

"Iced tea," Wren said again, more confidently.

When the waitress left, Wren leaned across the table.

"—but even there, it doesn't stop," Ichabod Crane kept saying. "So, it's about a lot of meats, one. It's about the sauce, two. But the side plates, that's the trick. French fries are part and parcel of the whole package, pal, and—so, whatever you order, know that it's going to come with French fries that are literally *to die for.*"

"It's him, isn't it," Wren said in a low voice.

Lissa, implacable, blinked. "Maybe. How do you know?"

"The man behind the counter. He has the..." She winced. "He's a Mercury Man."

Ichabod Crane continued: "...so, I'm not taking up too much of your time, right? You said your flight is in a few hours, so you have time to kill—"

"I'm good," the man in the blazer said, chuckling. "Please, like I said, I'm from Connecticut; advise me."

"If I'm telling you to order any one thing, then—" Ichabod drew a deep breath, pressing his hands together under his mouth like he was about to pray. "Then it's the burnt ends. I know! I know. Doesn't sound appealing, but they're the crispy, fatty ends of the brisket, and some people just throw them away, but they are *nuggets* of meaty, salty, smoky joy, and it would be a pleasure if you tried them. Tell you what, I'll go back in the back, get you a few to try. How'd that be?"

"Why, that'd be just fine."

"Hold still, pal. Hold still."

Ichabod bounced into the back, stalking through the kitchen door like a mantis.

"You're sure?" Lissa asked. "You see it clearly?"

"I'm sure. He'll kill someone. Or he already has." A strange question popped up in her head: If someone was a killer already, but had no more kills to commit to the world, would the silvery shine fade? Or was it always there? An irrevocable stain? Shit. She had no idea. Wasn't like this gift-slash-curse of hers came with a fucking instruction manual. Miriam, the real Miriam and the Parasite Miriam, didn't know either—or, if they did, neither one was forthcoming about any of this crap.

"Let's eat. I hear the food's good."

"And then?"

"And then we'll see."

"We'll see what?"

Lissa just smiled at that, and called the waitress over to order.

# 13. BURNT ENDS

The pickup truck hit the back of Lissa's BMW like a giant's fist. *Wham.* Metal crunched. Lissa cried out, spinning the wheel this way and that, fighting the car's desire to now spin wildly on the dirt road upon which they drove. Wren gritted her teeth and braced herself, her eyes fixed like nails on the side mirror—in it she saw the pickup, a new, cherry-red Chevy Silverado, barreling down on them anew. Behind the wheel, a tall man, ropy, with a mask on his face: a mask of dried meat and leather, like jerky and skin, stitched together crudely and stained with smoke.

*The Meat Man*, she thought, grimly.

After eating at the BBQ joint, they found out where the man behind the counter—Ichabod Crane, though soon they discovered his name was Jed Delbert—lived, and for days, they'd been watching his home, a beat-up rancher miles outside of

Kansas City, back across the Kansas border. They staked out his house, Lissa's car parked behind a small copse of oak trees, behind some bushes, so they could watch at a distance. He had no close neighbors. Out there, it was dirt roads and dead ends, a desolate, dust-cloud plane.

They watched and waited.

Watched and waited.

Three days.

Then four.

And on the fifth day—

It happened.

Jed had a schedule, worked eight hours at the BBQ place, open to close, eleven to seven, came home, had a beer, did some grilling outside, or set up the smoker to smoke more meat—as if one could not have enough meat, and Wren decided that the man's colon probably looked like a giant Slim Jim. Didn't seem to eat a single vegetable, this guy. No fiber. Just protein. Not that her diet was much better, once upon a time. Though, since staying with Lissa, she found herself eating a lot more fruits and vegetables. And feeling a lot healthier, too. Energized. Excited. Renewed with a kind of…purpose.

That day, Jed came home, the red Silverado pulling in…

He cut the engine. Got out. Went around back, dropped the back gate of the truck.

And there was a body.

Not dead. Alive. And wriggling like a tree grub.

Jed pulled the man down with a tug, like he was rolling a tire out of the back, and that's just what the man did—his body rolled out and hit the ground in a cloud of dust.

When that dust cleared, Lissa handed Wren the binoculars. That's when they both knew who it was: the man from days before. The man at the counter. Blazer. Rumpled slacks. The traveler, the one receiving the lecture about barbecue.

He looked dried out, chipped, chafed, like he'd been kept somewhere…

But where?

*Freezer*, Lissa suggested.

*Shit*, Wren had responded.

Around the side of the house, Jed got his smoker going. Logs of woods thrown in, each with a bang. A wad of newspaper lit aflame, smoke starting to whirl in whorls. He dragged the other man toward it, and it was then, only then, they realized what was happening, though perhaps it should've been clearer sooner.

Jed was gonna smoke this man's meat.

Kill him. Maybe eat him.

Holy fuck.

Wren had seen some shit in her short life so far, most of it since she'd been on the run after the events at the Caldecott School. Meth-heads. Rapists. Murderers. Bad cops. Good hookers. Not to mention Miriam, who knew how you were going to die. And then there was the Mockingbird Killer, not one monster but a whole a family of them who, in the guise of a single killer, wore a plague doctor mask before binding up young women with barbed wire and chopping them up with an axe. Wren was going to be one of their victims, once upon a time. It was part of the trauma that carved into her, left a ruinous gap in which her accursed power was able to grow, a spider in the dark.

But this: crazy dude planning to smoke and eat another dude—

What the fuck.

What.

The.

*Fuck.*

Lissa said then, *Now we know*, and she told Wren that there was a pistol in the glove compartment, it was hers, go get it, go get it now.

As she did, she watched through the binoculars. Jeb pulled out something from a bag next to the smoker—not one something but several somethings. Tongs. A barbecue fork. Suddenly, Wren realized she had killed a guy with a barbecue fork, once. A tiny voice inside her asked: *Are you that much different than him?* But she didn't have time to ruminate on that, because here the man pulled out the final item:

A mask. Leathery and meaty.

It was then she knew his name, even if he didn't: the Meat Man.

As she stared, Wren moved to the passenger-side door, her heart suddenly pounding so hard, it felt like it was going to come through her breastbone like a chestburster alien. So, when she went to open that door, she didn't think, wasn't smart—when she popped that door, she did it too fast, and the end of it clipped the trunk of one of the oak trees they parked between—

*Ka-thunk!*

The noise it made was loud, and it echoed out across the flat land.

Lissa hissed at her. Stared with wide, panicked eyes.

Wren's heart, suddenly fast in her chest, felt like it stopped dead. Like a clock gone kaput, *tick tick tick* and then nothing.

Jed's head popped up from the smoker like a gopher at its hole, alarmed by the sound of a potential predator. He pivoted his head left, right, looking for the sound—*don't see us, don't see us*—and then he relaxed again, his shoulders slumping—*he didn't see us! he didn't see us!*—

But then he turned right toward them at the last moment.

His body, bristling, snatched something else up from within the bag—

A square-bladed, rusting cleaver—

Then he strode toward the pickup truck.

"The gun," Wren said. She slid past the door, pawing for the glove compartment.

But Lissa was already circumnavigating the car, jumping into the driver's side. She pressed the BMW's start button and the engine revved to life—with a fast hand she yanked Wren into the passenger side. "What are you doing?" Wren barked.

Ahead, the Silverado—high beams on, despite the sun still being up and out—peeled stones behind spinning tires and charged suddenly toward them.

Two hundred yards away was a distance that would shrink fast.

Lissa slapped the glove compartment shut. "Not now. We go."

She ratcheted the car into reverse and slammed the pedal. The BMW did a half-moon circuit around the closest oak, and then she threw it into drive and bounded over a narrow ditch onto the road. Plumes of summer dust grew in their wake, but the truck's headlights cut through the haze—and soon, the truck itself parted the dust as it gained on them. And that's when the truck slammed into them from behind.

The car fishtailed left, then right. Lissa fought to keep it straight but overdid it each time, nearly losing control. Wren again braced herself with one hand while popping the glove compartment with the other. A gun tumbled out. Boxy. Old. A pistol, like a—a pistol you'd see in a war movie, held by a guy in a helmet hunting Nazis in a bunker. She bent to snatch it off the floor—

*Wham.*

That's when it went fuck-all.

As the BMW was drifting right, its ass end sliding one way as the front went the other, the Meat Man came up again, hitting the car in the sweet spot.

Next thing Wren knew, the car was wheeling around and around, a carousel ride in Hell, the world gone smeary as it whipped past—

The flash of something close, near the window—

A dark shape, some immovable object—

Crash. Glass.

And then the car flipped, rolling, end over end. The world went mad, the world went dark, and Wren was sure that if she wasn't dead now, she would be soon.

# 14. THE MEAT MAN COMETH

Cheeks puffed out. A hard breath. Safety glass in her hair.

Wren did a grunting push-up, mewling as she did—her head throbbed with pain. Something wetted the side of her face, her neck, her arm. Blood. She could see it oozing down her arm. Outside, a sound: the revving of an engine.

Lissa, buckled in, hung upside down from the driver's side. Hair inverted, dangling, like they were in outer fucking space.

The other woman moaned. Wren saw no blood. She was alive but knocked out.

*The gun.*

It was right on the floor—well, the *roof* of the car—between Wren's hands. Clumsily, she grabbed at it with numb hands. Picking it up was like trying to dial a cellphone when you're drunk. Wren tried opening her door but it wouldn't move—it was dented in from whatever they hit. A tree, a pole, something. But the window was smashed out, so Wren snake-crawled out from the gap.

The revving engine growled again. Roar, roar.

There. A hundred feet away.

The truck. Its front end dented but not crumpled. It held up under the vehicular assault. Unlike the BMW, which was toast.

Behind the wheel, the Meat Man sat. Bold white eyes behind desiccated meat-skin. Stitches big and bold, like the raw, rough thread keeping a scarecrow's head on its body. Wren stood and staggered one step, then two—

And that was, for the Meat Man, all he needed. Like a shark sensing chum dropped in the water, he pressed the accelerator—

The truck hurtled toward her like a meteor.

Time seemed to slow. Truly. Fingers slid down Wren's right arm, and then under her left—the smell of cigarette smoke tickled her nose. The truck barreled toward her, and she could see the stones and dust kicked up, not flying, but drifting. The seconds oozed forward, pulled like taffy. The gun was heavy in her hand, but she lifted it with the help of the Parasite: Not-Miriam stood behind her, helping her lift her arms.

"Here he comes," Not-Miriam cooed in her ear.

"You aren't supposed to be here."

"Point and shoot, little girl."

"You didn't want me here. Why are you helping me?"

Not-Miriam grinned, open-mouthed, showing teeth clamped around her cigarette. "Honey, I'm a vampire—when there's blood to be spilled, I come hungry whether I like it or not. Now *shoot*."

"I..."

Not-Miriam's fingers became like knives, and they cut into Wren's hands, into the skin and under the bones. The Parasite's bones molded around hers. Her skin lifted as the demon's hands became her own hands, merging, meat to meat.

Her finger squeezed the trigger.

Wren wasn't sure if she did it or the Parasite did.

But the result was the same either way. The gun bucked in her hand. Nearly recoiled back and cracked her in the face. A hole appeared in the windshield of the car, and the Meat Man's head juddered like it had been slapped. The truck bounded forward, time now snapping into its proper speed—Wren cried out even as he slumped forward against the wheel, turning it as he did. The front tires of the truck suddenly cut hard to the left, and the truck jumped in that direction, bounding over the ditch and into a field until it slammed into a tree. Steam rose. Nobody came out.

Not-Miriam was gone. But her words slithered into Wren's ear as a whisper: "Let's see Jimmy beat *that* shot."

And then:

"You did it."

But those were not the Parasite's words.

They were Lissa's.

Lissa, who now was half out of the car, her hands in the dirt. Holding her up. Hair bedraggled, plastered against her face. She was grinning.

"I..." Wren started to say, but didn't know how to finish.

"I knew it," Lissa said. Excitement flashed in her eyes like lightning in the dark. "I knew you were something special, Wren."

# 15. REVELATIONS OF THE MEAT MAN

**Lissa** said to leave her BMW there, as it wasn't registered under her name. Wren said she worried her fingerprints were still on everything, but Lissa had an answer to that, too—a cloth stuffed in the gas tank, lit on fire once fuel soaked it through. In the distance, the car burned. It never exploded, though it did go *whumpf* one time, something inside it going *pop*, but it wasn't dramatic or anything. They had Jimmy come pick them up in an old beater Volvo ("built like a tank," he said, seemingly oblivious to the chaos around them), and they fled the scene.

A scene that, a day later, made the news. It was a big story, too—at first because of how strange it seemed, and later because of what the police and the media found. First thing they found at the Meat Man's house was the victim on his property—the victim they'd rescued. That man was a traveler who had gone missing, name of Kenny Tompkins, a down-on-his-luck salesman of luxury vinyl planking. Divorced. No kids. Easy to take away from the world, with few people missing him. That's what the Meat Man—Jed Delbert—had probably counted on.

That was just a peek into what was to come, though. They found bones. So many bones. Human skeletal remains, some buried in trash bags in the back yard, some left in metal or foil trays. Each one had been cooked, or burned, or smoked, making it clear as anything that what Wren and Lissa suspected was true:

The Meat Man was eating people.

Shit, he was *barbecuing* them.

And it was only once the police began revealing excerpts from the man's half-diary half-cookbook that the one outstanding mystery was answered:

Jed claimed to know exactly what the fat content was of a person just by touching them. And he said he knew how they would taste, too—that touch gave him a little bitty bit of flavor on his tongue, a flavor he could not deny, a hunger he could not refuse. That little taste was both too much and not enough: too much to deny, not enough to satisfy.

That, then, was Delbert's power, such as it was.

They all watched this unfold, and their names never entered the equation, and nobody was able to solve the mystery of the burned BMW. Interviewing Kenny, the victim, made it clear he didn't see anything either. And even if he had, would anyone really suspect Lissa and Wren of orchestrating the Meat Man's end?

And would they even care?

The man was a horror show.

"And we are glad he's dead," Lissa said. Again she heaped plaudits of love and joy on Wren, telling the young woman how special she was, how much good work they would do. Good work, she said, that had to begin immediately, because the world was full of monsters and someone had to stop them. "That's what we are," Lissa answered. "We hunt monsters."

"They're not monsters," Wren said. "They're people."

"Are they, though?" Lissa asked. And then she asked again: "*Are* they?"

# 16. MONSTER MISSION

Time passed, they worked, and death rode with them. Lissa was not interested in resting on their laurels, as she said, but in committing to the work tooth and nail, blood and bone, giving as much of themselves as they could. She had long been prepared, having curated a list of potential monsters that needed Wren's special eye—Lissa knew the people on this list had powers, but what she did not know was if they had the *shine*. The liquid gleam of promised murder. Were they monsters? Would they be killers? That was what Wren could give, but she could also give as Jimmy did, too—Wren was a killer, much as he was, and each time she pulled the trigger, she felt the Parasite's hand guiding her, urging her, the bones of that demon becoming her bones, its muscles becoming her muscles, until they were one, until Wren was lost and all was death. Every morning, they had French press coffee, a hearty breakfast, and then they hit the road—this time in the Volvo, sometimes with Jimmy riding in the back, .22-250 rifle or an over-under twelve gauge in his lap—and they'd hit addresses on Lissa's list, a list that was three pages, single-spaced, a spreadsheet of names and addresses and notes. All collecting potential "monsters" within a hundred-mile radius of Lawrence, Kansas. They drove through blister-hot days. Through wind and tornado sirens. Across open fields and past farms and into Iowa, Nebraska, Missouri.

They hunted.

That's what it was, Wren knew. Just as Lissa had said—they were hunters. Tracking potential prey, as hunters did. Sometimes, the prey wasn't right; most of the names on that list belonged to people with powers who would never kill anyone. Nalla Jacobs, a seventy-year-old black woman sitting on a lawn chair on the front porch of her sagging farmhouse, waving as they went past. Vince Anderson, a thick brick-head of a man, running a pest control company out of Big Lake, Nebraska—Lissa was sure he'd be a killer, considering that in a sense it was his job, but Wren didn't see the silvery shine on him, didn't feel the pull to put a bullet in his temple. He was a family man, too, two kids, a wife, a mother-in-law who lived with them. Marla Staples, motel maid; Dave Timmerman, unemployed asshole and bassist in a Topeka garage band; Abshir Amad, line cook. All of them had powers. None of them were killers.

What their powers were remained a mystery. Lissa could not see that much; her power, like Wren's, was binary. In a time like this, Wren wished her power gave her *more*, like it did Miriam. Miriam saw a whole vision, a story play out around the person's inevitable death, but like Wren, Lissa only received a thumbs-up or thumbs-down. A binary *do they have an ability* or *don't they.* Just as Wren could see if they would be killers, or if they would end no lives in their time on this planet.

That's not to say she didn't imagine what powers they had. How could you not? Nalla Jacobs knew truths about people, she guessed. Marla Staples saw people's dreams, she pretended. Dave Timmerman could pick up an instrument and play it the first time even if he didn't know how, like a marijuana Mozart. Abshir Amad knew just what you wanted to eat. And Vince Anderson, she imagined, was like Lissa—maybe he could control bees or insects. Or maybe he was her opposite: he didn't need chemicals to kill the bees, it just took the snap of his fingers, the blink of his eye, the sheer expressed desire to do it. Then again, who knew. Maybe it had nothing to do with that. Wren didn't know, and neither did Lissa. (Lissa, for her part, was *sure* that Vince Anderson was the real deal, would prove himself a killer. She hated him because he killed bugs like her precious killer bees, and for that, she wanted to him to pay. Wren had to convince her otherwise, said he'd never be a killer. "Not of people," Lissa said, forcefully, angrily, but she did not pursue it, and Vince, for now, was left with his life intact.)

But their hunt found proper prey, too.

*Trophy kills*, Lissa had taken to calling them.

Snapshot: the Mechanic, a mute brute who had hammered an oil pan into a crude mask, the eyes cut out with an acetylene torch, a crass facsimile of a mouth welded from rivets and washers. His power was mercifully simple: He could hear your thoughts, and so, you could never hide from him. He was hard to surprise. He knew they were coming. He clubbed Lissa in the side with an adjustable torque wrench, fractured two of her ribs; Wren fired her pistol at his head, aiming for his eyes with the help of the Parasite guiding her, but he could hear where she wanted to put those bullets, and so he bent his head down, the mask taking the shots, the bullets ricocheting off the fortified steel. He barreled down on Wren, picking her up, slamming her into a work table, the air out of her—Jimmy kicked in the door, fired three times into his back, but it didn't matter. The Mechanic—Herc Nibauer, though Lissa said they shouldn't use their names; it made them people when they weren't people at all—didn't go down, though, and flung Wren toward Jimmy like she was a fucking baseball and he was a stack of bottles in a carnival game. She slammed into him. He went down. Her on top of him. They were dead, she knew, dead fucking meat, but then Lissa had other ideas. Like with Pigface, the Mechanic loomed over them, but then began to twitch and shudder, swatting at himself, squealing and bleating—harvester ants. They swarmed up from his feet, streaming in diligent, dutiful lines up his dungarees, under his shirt, to his neck, his hands, stinging and biting. Anaphylaxis seized him like a crushing fist. He swelled up, a balloon of blood and antihistamines, until he choked on his own soft, closing esophagus.

Then, two weeks later: the Midland Vampire. John Avalon Gordon, a wormy slip of a man, skin a kind of gray-green, a nose that looked to have been broken again and again and again, so fucked-up was this nose that it looked like a caterpillar smashed against the bark of a diseased birch tree. Lissa said she *knew* he was a monster, and Wren confirmed her suspicions—Gordon's ability was that none could refuse him entry. This is why he believed himself a vampire, and so he bought into the role completely, wearing no mask but his own wretched face. Though he did not choose to drink *all* the blood in the bodies of his victims, he always took a *taste*. He'd kill his victims with a knife and then lap at one of the wounds like a little bat, its eager tongue playing in the blood. He was hungry to be caught, and hungry to die. He knew what he was doing was wrong. He said he expected that one day, "vampire hunters" would come for him, and in a sense, he was right. The Vampire demanded that he be slain in the "way of my forebears," which was a wooden stake through the heart. Lissa simply nodded to Wren, and Wren shot him in the chest. They left evidence of his killings on the floor of his double-wide trailer—knives used in killings, locks of hair he kept.

Finally: the Maize Witch. Crazy bitch lived in a shack out in a Nebraska cornfield. Bone-thin, the skin hanging on her bones no different from the rags that hung upon her frame. That one, *that one* was the toughest of the three, wasn't she? For her power was as sinister as any Wren had faced—she knew what would hurt you the most. Not physically, oh no. But mentally. Emotionally. She knew where to stick the metaphorical knife and how best to twist, turn, and lever the pain to its maximum. Strangest still, it was private pain, whispered only to you, on the wind, like a song only one person can hear—a song of lamentation and sorrow, a song of the most miserable regret. Wren's song was an endless replay of the gun going off, bucking in her hand, the crack of bone as the bullet went through Louis's head, the splash of blood on the ground, the one last sound he made before he died, a mumbled whimper that could've been Miriam's name—it was that moment, those sounds, replayed again and again and again. It brought Wren to her knees. Weak and soft, ready to die. Lissa, too, was on the ground of the woman's shack, curled up there in the dust of old corn silage as the witch—ageless in that she could've been young or old—stood over her with a sickle, her weapon of choice. Raised up, ready to *whish* through the air and slice through throat—

It was the bark of a gun, a bullet that couldn't miss, that saved them. James—Jimmy—stepped in, aimed his rifle, and got her dead-bang. Later, when Wren asked him why her "spell" didn't work on him, why he did not crumple under her siren's song of endless regret, he said quite simply:

"I don't have any pain like that."

And that's when Wren fell in love with him.

# 17. MISTAKES WERE MADE

**They** did it under the moon at the edges of the meadow of wildflowers, while the bees slumbered. He, eighteen, she, sixteen. She gave her heart to him first, then the rest of her after. She hesitated, at first. He had the glow, after all, the silver shine, but she felt in her heart she knew why it was: he was killing for Lissa, just as she was, and they were bonded together in that role, that act. Therefore, it felt perfect when she gave herself to him, her own little snow-globe moment. Moon and stars. Flowers and flesh. She felt a feeling she hadn't felt in a while: *happy*. So alien was this concept, it took her time to even remember what it was, or that it had a name. And so guilty was she that she was sure she did not deserve it—the Maize Witch's whispers stayed with her, like nicotine staining the walls in a smoker's house. But she pushed it aside, praying that it would never come to bear, that this happiness would not be found out, that she would be allowed this one good (no, *perfect*) thing. As they drifted off to sleep, she heard the bug-wing buzz of a bee overhead, in the dark, hovering there. And then it was gone again.

# 18. JANE COLEMAN

**Then** came Jane Coleman, who fucked it all up.

# 19. ESCHATOLOGY

"Well, Lauren, we're almost at the end," Lissa said. Of her list, she meant, which she had in front of her, on the table, pinned by a cup of steaming tea. A single bee crawled around the rim of the teacup, supping at the sweetness it found there.

Wren gave a look back to Jimmy, who stood by the doorway, eating a carrot with big, bone-breaking crunches. He risked a small smile to Wren, and she gave one back. A blush rose to her cheeks. A blush that grew from happy embarrassment to sudden shame as she wondered, *Is this how Miriam felt about Louis...*

Which itself was absurd because surely, Miriam and Louis, who had spent years together on and off, had a real relationship. Wren and Jimmy were just two fools.

Weren't they?

Lissa watched them both carefully. With the indifference of a spider.

"Who's, uhh, who's next?" Wren asked.

"Here." Lissa touched a name. Her finger lingered over it before sliding aside and revealing: *Jane Coleman*.

"What do we know about her?"

"She works at one of the big craft stores. Jo-Ann Fabrics. She lives in KCK—Kansas City, Kansas, not Missouri—in a neighborhood. A development, Whisper Ridge. The house is a Cape Cod at the end of a cul-de-sac. Two children, one husband, a dog, a cat. She has powers. I can't say what they are, yet—that is for us to find out."

"Doesn't sound like this one will be a monster," Wren said, dismissing it. "I mean, she's a mom, with a family. She works at a fucking craft store."

"Your own mother—was she a good person?" Lissa asked.

It punched through Wren like a piece of pipe. Sucking the air right out of her. "I... My mother..."

"Parents can be monsters, too, Wren. Husbands kill their wives. Wives kill mistresses or drown their own children. Monsters wear masks for a reason. Sometimes, they're real masks, like our killers: they want to hide who they are behind a countenance of their own creation. Sometimes, they are horrible, deformed masks—their own flesh and bone, twisted and made awful. Many times, they are the masks of human beings. Normal, everyday people. The humanity is the mask; the monster is the truth. You see?"

Wren nodded. "Yeah." She forced a smile, tried to make a joke: "Maybe Jane knits her masks out of alpaca wool or something. Stabs people with crochet hooks."

"It's almost evening," Lissa said, ignoring the joke. "She's on shift for another hour. Let's go meet Jane Coleman, shall we?"

# 20. THUNDER RUMBLES AND THE CRAFT STORE LOOMS

**Wren** couldn't remember the last time she'd been in a big department store. Walmart, probably, months ago. It was jarring, in a way: the big bright lights, the white floor, the colors everywhere. And the people. Handcarts of colorful yarn here, a birdhouse kit there, some fabric, some paints, a cheap plastic frame under someone's arm. Mostly women shopped here, it seemed, which she guessed didn't surprise her. Were men afraid of crafting? Took more work and creativity to make a sweater than to fix a flat tire. Maybe that was the problem with most men. All that anger, pent up, because they were too afraid to learn how to cross-stitch or put puffy paint on some shit.

Then again, Wren knew she shouldn't be too judgey when it came to pent-up anger, since she wanted to punch half these shoppers just for the sin of being in her way and smelling like cheap Midwest perfume.

Lissa and Jimmy were back out in the car. In the rain now—soon as Wren set foot in this place, thunder tumbled like a drum announcing the coming deluge, and then rain began to hammer the asphalt, the windows, the roof of the store. Once, the lights flickered, and Wren thought, *Shit, please don't go out, I need to see this woman.*

She decided she'd buy something, get in the woman's line. Hard to see past the shoppers there. So, Wren took the five-dollar bill Lissa had given her and she grabbed the nearest stupid thing—a magazine about beadwork, of all the stupid shit—and hopped in line. Impatiently she waited, three shoppers left, then two, then one—

Then she was face to face with Jane Coleman.

Blond hair, but the kind of blond where it's almost brown. Dirty blond, is that what they called it? She was boyish, a bit rough in that Midwest farmer way, but she was pretty enough, and put together enough, to be on public display the way retail employees were. In the nostril of her long nose was a little puckered hole, the ghost of a more rebellious past, maybe.

But Wren cared about little of that.

What she cared about was the silver shine crawling all around Jane Coleman. Sometimes like liquid, other times like ants of mercury. Sliding and shifting.

"You're—" *A killer,* Wren nearly said. But instead, she just let the sentence die on her lips, and she put the magazine down in front of her, on the conveyor. It landed aggressively, like she was trying to swat a bug. She flinched at her own overeagerness.

"You okay?" Jane asked her, holding the magazine for a moment above the retail laser scanner. "Miss?"

"Yeah. Fine. Fucking fine." Wren wrinkled her brow. "Shut up."

Jane, to her credit, didn't seem taken aback. "I have a daughter. Not quite your age but…close enough." As she booped the magazine across the scanner, she leaned forward and in a low voice said, "It's hard. I know. Being a girl, a woman. Especially out here, middle of the country. But you'll be okay. Okay? I promise."

Wren blinked.

She felt hot tears at the edges of her eyes. She tried to blink them away, but they kept coming, those traitorous tears, and all she could do was throw down her five-dollar bill and then run out of the store. Jane called after her, telling her she forgot her magazine, but Wren couldn't stand to go back. She ran into the rain, into the thunder.

# 21. THE NATURE OF MASKS

**Back** in the Volvo, under the hammering rain, Wren peered out through the frame of dark, stringy, soggy hair at Lissa. She stammered, yammering, "I… I don't know that she's a killer. Okay. I mean—*okay*. She *has* the shine." And immediately, right there, for reasons she couldn't quite figure out, she regretted telling Lissa that. *I could've lied*, she thought. But lying to Lissa felt wrong. After the last six weeks, they'd grown so close. "Lissa, she told me—she was nice to me, okay? Really nice. She told me that everything was going to be okay, and I just st-started crying—"

"Maybe that's her power."

"Wh-what?"

"Maybe she said something you needed to hear. Maybe she can bring her victims to tears. Incapacitate them. Draw them down low, and then she kills them."

"I… I don't think she's the kind."

"That's exactly the kind you need to worry about." Lissa reached out and put her hand over Wren's. "Let's watch her. We'll find the monster in Jane Coleman. You'll see." And then, echoing the other woman, Lissa said, "It'll all be okay."

From the backseat, Jimmy nodded to her and touched her shoulder gently.

# 22. SHOUTING AT THE DEAD

A week they sat, they watched, they waited. A *week*. Not long in the grand scheme of things, Wren knew, but at no point did Jane Coleman do anything untoward. Home to work, work to home. Sometimes to the grocery store. Walked the dogs. Helped her husband—a portly man, crispy dressed in polo shirts and khaki shorts—grill out while her kids either threw a Frisbee or stared into their phones and tablet devices.

She didn't deviate.

She didn't yell or scream.

Didn't throw anything.

Didn't have bodies corded like firewood in their backyard. No strange furnace. No secret pit. No mask. No axe.

And then, on the eighth day, a deviation.

Home to work, work to—

No, not home. A cemetery. She pulled off suddenly, down a long road, to a flat span of land marked with the broken teeth of old gravestones. No trees there: all of the dead lay exposed under the acid-wash sky and hot Kansas sun.

Jane went into that graveyard, found a grave, and yelled at it for an hour. Just *yelled*, worked herself into a froth and let the storm out—she pointed and paced, she kicked at a headstone, she throttled her fists in the air like an angry child. And then, at the end of that hour, she composed herself, blew her nose, and headed back to her minivan.

Then she went home, and the routine continued apace.

They saw all of this through the binoculars. Later, they went to the graveyard, to the grave in question: It was a plot for two people, an Alfred and Janice Hamilton.

"Jane Coleman's parents," Lissa explained. A breeze kicked up, whistled through the headstones like a summoning from Death itself.

"Maybe she hated them," Jimmy said.

"She definitely did," Wren said. "Way she carried on like that."

"That anger unleashed—it might be deadly someday."

Wren shook her head. She stood in between Lissa and the headstone. "I don't think so. We have to take a pass on this one." She threw a pleading glance to Jimmy. "I mean, right? We can keep a watch but…I don't think she's a monster."

A shadow passed in front of Lissa's face—that from a cloud overhead moving in front of the sky, but it met her darkening countenance. "She's a killer, Lauren."

"I know. But that doesn't mean—"

"It means she's going to murder someone."

"But I didn't get that *feeling* about her—yeah, I know, I saw the silver—"

"Which means she's a monster."

"Not a monster. Not a monster! You can't—we can't just *say* that." Miriam's warnings arose anew inside Wren like vengeful ghosts. She started giving voice to these things, to Miriam's counsel, speaking them out loud: "Just because someone's a killer doesn't mean they're bad, or, or, or that they're evil. People kill for reasons good and bad. A wife might kill an abusive husband or someone who wants to steal their kid in a fucking van. Maybe it's an accident—a car accident, or something at work. Maybe it's an act of mercy, right? Like, an old-ass parent on, uhh, on whaddyacallit? Hospice. They give them morphine, a dose too big and..."

"Stop."

"Lissa—"

"*Stop.* We don't need to think this through anymore. People who kill are monsters. That's not arguable."

"But...I kill."

Lissa smiled, coldly. "Of course, dear. You're my little monster."

"And you kill too."

"Not me." Lissa held up both hands, as if to demonstrate how sparkling clean they were—no blood on her palms, fingertips, under her nails. "I'm without sin."

"You fucking cunt."

"We kill Jane Coleman tonight."

"No. *No.* I won't be a part of it."

"Then go home. We'll handle it."

"I..." Again tears pried at Wren's eyelids.

"Go! Home!"

Wren swallowed hard and ran.

# 23. MILES TO GO

It was a three-mile trip back to the house. Wren made the journey on foot, in the fading sun as afternoon gave way to evening. Evening would soon be shot in the gut, the light bleeding out and yielding to night. For now, by the time she made it back to Lissa's house, the sun was still up, but already she could hear the crickets getting an early jump on the end of day.

She was alone.

Or she thought she was.

Someone waited on the porch for her.

Miriam.

No. The *Parasite*. Not-Miriam. For a moment, though, her heart fluttered in her chest like a moth captured in a jar... both excited to see the real Miriam again and also recognizing that maybe, *probably*, the real Miriam would kill her. And let her sleep.

But it was just the phantasm. The spectral facsimile.

"Psy-cho," Wren said, clomping up onto the porch.

"Aw, widdle baby wooks sad," Not-Miriam said.

"Eat shit and choke on it." Wren sat down on the porch, on a squeaky rocking chair. "You don't understand anything."

"You had a conscience. They sent you packing. Now they're going to do the job for you, but you're not sure they should. And now a woman is going to die and you're not really sure that she should. It's not your idea of making good on your promise to me—the real me, not this crass, ghostly photocopy of me—and it's driving you nuts."

Wren's mouth formed a hardened line. "I…trust Lissa."

"Do you? Do you really? She's just some strange-ass bee-controlling bitch; you don't know anything about her. But you're too young and too dumb to ask questions."

"I know enough."

"Oh." Not-Miriam manifested a cigarette, suddenly, then sucked on it so hard, it went from just-lit to a limp twig of ash in a few seconds. A plume of impossible smoke blew from her puckered lips. "Then I guess you won't want to see what's upstairs."

"What?"

"What what? You're unswerving in your trust, so we shall not speak of it again, no sir, no ma'am."

Wren stood suddenly. "Show me."

The Parasite's black eyes twinkled.

"Are you sure?"

"Sure as anything."

"Then let's go, little girl."

# 24. THE DRAWER

**Not-Miriam** was gone—like that, she was no longer there. But Wren could still hear her. Upstairs, the floorboards in the old farmhouse groaned. And she could follow the sulfurous hell-stink of her otherworldly cigarettes, which should have been unpleasant but which only gave Wren the desire to smoke one herself. She followed the sounds, and that smell, until she found herself standing in front of Lissa's office: a bedroom upstairs converted into an austere space, like something out of a magazine. She'd been in there before but it never felt comfortable to her—and Lissa did not spend much time in there, either, only using it for a short time to gather her list or to collect a book to read from the repurposed bookshelves that stood against the right wall. The desk in the center of the room was practically just a table, though it had three shallow drawers hanging underneath it. Not-Miriam sat at the desk, in the simple wooden chair there. The bleached, dying light of day framing her from the window just behind.

The Parasite gently tapped an unsmoked cigarette against the leftmost drawer.

Tap, tap, tap.

Then she screwed it into her mouth and lit it with a fire that popped from the tip of her middle finger. And then, like that, Not-Miriam was gone again. Gone to vapor.

Wren hesitated.

This was not her space.

Lissa would consider this a betrayal.

But…

What did she really know about the woman who invited her there? She was cagey about her past. Said it didn't matter, and Wren agreed with that implicitly—though perhaps more as an act of wishful thinking, where she got to live in a world where the past genuinely didn't matter, where the only thing that was important was the things you said and did in the here and the now. But even there, that was bullshit, wasn't it? Wren was there, doing this work with Lissa, *precisely* because of the past. Her own past mattered, and it's why she was trying to do better, to *be* better.

So, didn't Lissa's past matter, too?

Was that even what this was? A mining of Lissa's days before this one?

Wren stepped into the room. A ginger, uncertain step. But then she saw in her mind's eye Jane Coleman, dead after dark, and suddenly her steps came in a flurrying rush—Wren raced to the desk, ripped open the left-side drawer, and began going through what seemed like a small stack of papers. Receipts. Business cards. Invoices and bills. It gave her nothing. It was just...the remnants of a normal, adult life. Boring and grotesquely necessary. Electricity bill. A handyman invoice. Business card for someone selling natural gas. She shoved it back in the drawer and then—

Wait.

The drawer was shallow, but not *this* shallow.

She opened the right-hand drawer, found it deeper than this one.

And yet, from the outside, they were the same size.

She again slid the left-side drawer open, and felt along the bottom of it—

*There.*

A small half-moon indentation where her fingernail could fit, and pluck, and pull—and with that, the bottom of the drawer drew away, revealing a second, shallower compartment. Shallow enough for a stack of ten, twenty pieces of paper at most.

Atop it was a single business card. A thick card, heavy stock, nearly unbendable.

It had no information on it—just a woodcut-style icon of a honeybee, its wings and legs out, forming symmetry.

And underneath it...

A document. Confirming a name change.

Lissa Larson was once—

*No.*

Eliza Caldecott.

Caldecott.

Like Eleanor Caldecott, like Edwin Caldecott. Two of the scions of that Caldecott legacy—a school used to farm and kill young women, women who were believed to be *bad girls* that needed purging from this mortal coil. Wren was one of those girls once, and now, *now* she was helping another Caldecott—Eliza!—do it all over again. But her mind warred with itself because those they killed *were* horrible. The Meat Man, the Maize Witch, the Midland Vampire—all genuine monsters, *real-deal* demons out in the world, using their traumatic powers to inflict more trauma and terror on the world…

Until Jane Coleman.

Maybe Lissa—Eliza—was right, that Jane had to go. But maybe she wasn't.

The cherry of a cigarette bobbed in the shadows of the office doorway. There the Parasite stood again, smirking. "Once more, you find yourself as the tool in an untrustworthy hand, Wren. That's fucked up. Seems to be your destiny, doesn't it?"

"I need to see Lissa. I need to…stop her from hurting Jane Coleman. Until we sort all of this out. I need answers and—" She drew the .45 pistol from the back of her jeans. "I'm going to get them."

"One more thing," Not-Miriam said, tongue dancing around the unfiltered cigarette. "You're gonna wanna check that drawer. There's, ahhh, there's one more piece of paper I think you should see, little girl. Go on. Have a peek."

Wren hesitated.

And then she looked.

# 25. A LIFE OF REPARATION AND REPENTANCE

**Her** legs burned with the strain. She ran like hell, the gun tucked behind her, the evening giving way to night all around her. It was three miles to the graveyard, and another two to Jane Coleman's house—*You're going to be too late*, she told herself, too late to stop Lissa and Jimmy, too late to save Jane Coleman. Acid flushed into her throat—the remnants of having forgotten to eat today. As her blood sugar dropped, Wren's brain felt light as a feather, like it could blow away on the lightest breeze, off into the darkness, lost. But still she kept on, because she had to.

Into the neighborhood. Into Whisper Ridge. Down one avenue, then another—then a curse as she realized she had gone the wrong way, *fuck fuck fuck*, back again toward the other road, toward Oak Tree Lane, toward Chestnut Drive, and there, ahead, she saw the Volvo parked at the mouth of the cul-de-sac. She saw two shapes sitting in the car, and her heart felt suddenly buoyant with hope—

They hadn't gone into the house yet.

Jane Coleman was still alive.

*Jane Coleman was still alive.*

She pulled the pistol and stormed up to the driver's side window—she tapped the glass with the barrel of the .45, and the window rolled down. Lissa sat in the driver's seat, her hands at ten and two. The engine was off. The keys in the ignition.

"Get out," Wren said.

"Lauren. You're making a mistake."

"*You* made a mistake, *Eliza*."

The other woman blinked. She swallowed hard and nodded gently. "I'm coming. Step back and I'll join you outside."

"Don't try to pull any shit."

Lissa nodded and eased open the door, hands up the whole way. "I'm going slowly. No need for any drastic action, Lauren."

"Wren. *Wren*. My name is Wren. Just like *his* name is Jimmy, not James—" Wren thrust the barrel of the gun toward the back window. "Tell him to get out too."

Lissa stepped out, stood up, and offered a quizzical glance. "You think..." She sighed and smiled. "Lauren—Wren. That's just his backpack hanging off the headrest. Jimmy isn't in the car, honey; I'm so sorry."

"Then where—"

But she heard the faint rattle of the rifle behind her as someone—Jimmy—put it to his shoulder. He said, "Wren, you need to put that gun down."

Wren took a step sideways, turning herself so that she was perpendicular to the two of them. Sure enough, there stood Jimmy, his rifle held low, near his hip. He didn't need to aim it. Such was his talent.

"Did you know?" Wren asked him.

He didn't answer, so she kept going.

"That she wasn't Lissa Larson, but Eliza Caldecott? *Did you know?*"

"Wren, put that gun down."

"So, you did know."

Lissa said, "Wren, this isn't what you think. I changed my name for a reason. I'm not like them. I'm not part of their family anymore. They…they wanted to reinforce the pattern, to shore up fate," and as she spoke, her words came out faster, more agitated, gilded with raw, red anger. "All that *nona decima morta* garbage. I want the opposite. I want to break the pattern. I want to give life back to the unloved and the vulnerable. Victims are victims because nobody is there to help them, but I'm there to help them—my other family members are the spider, preying on the weak, but I am the honeybee, don't you see? Together, we're the *hive*, the weak made strong by our numbers, by banding together and—"

"Shut up," Wren said. "Shut up with the crazy talk! I don't care about any of this. You're part of a bad family. A family that tried to kill me."

Lissa's face lit up in the half-dark. "I know. And how glorious is that? We found each other in this mess, Wren. And we're doing good work. Don't you see that?"

"I..." She tried to calm herself, to still her heart, to push the vomit bulge back down into her belly where it could dissipate. "Let's go. We can talk about this somewhere else. Tonight, Jane Coleman gets to live."

Jimmy and Lissa remained silent. They surreptitiously cast looks toward one another. Oh. Oh, no.

"She's already dead," Wren said in a small voice.

"The whole family," Jimmy said. "We had to."

Lissa fired off another look at him—this one scathing and retributive. She did not want him to say that, but he said it.

Wren turned toward him now. The gun leveled at his head.

And his gun tilted upward at his hip, pointed at her head.

"I don't miss," he said.

"I don't either," she said.

And then she shot him through the eye.

He never got off a shot. Why he didn't shoot, she'd never know, because he was gone. But it would be a question that would haunt her until the end of her days. Was it because he loved her? And couldn't bring himself to do it? And if that were the case, why could *she* shoot *him?* Was he the monster, or was she?

Or maybe, just maybe, he was too damn slow.

Wren, blinking back tears, turned the pistol again toward Lissa. Now, in the distance, the sound of sirens arose, banshee-like.

"Wren—"

"Eleanor Caldecott is dead. So are her children, Edwin, Beck, the cop, Earl. And now I find out about you. And I find out about your other brother."

Lissa smiled sadly. "Emerson."

"Is he it? Is he the last?"

"Him and I, yes. That's right. Listen, that was my plan. You and I would work our way toward him—he's in California—"

"I have the address."

"He's a monster too. He's the head of a *network* of monsters. A host of killers reinforcing the pattern, making new victims in the wake of their torment and torture. We can do it, Wren. You just have to come with me, now. Before the police arrive…"

Wren sniffed, and sneered, and then said, "No. I'm not coming with you. I won't be your tool anymore. I should've listened to my fuckin' gut and left your house."

"Then we wouldn't have met. Then we wouldn't have this mission."

"We don't have a mission. I do."

Lissa, her face sagging with sorrow, said, "I'm so sorry to hear that."

A sound reached Wren's ears. A sound competing with the coming sirens.

A *buzzing* sound.

She felt the air vibrate and boil, and the first sting landed on her hand, and then it was like blacking out—except it wasn't her consciousness that was fading, it was the real world hidden suddenly behind a curtain of buzzing bees, and another sting hit her neck, a third on the inside of her ribs, and again and again the stingers fell, and she cried out—

And then the gun bucked in her hand—

A shell *tinged* against the ground—

It was like the world clicked *pause*.

The swarming cacophony suddenly went *bzzz* to *vzzt* and then—

Like the bees held their collective breath—

Before falling to the ground, dead. As sure as the empty .45 shell fell.

Lissa leaned against the Volvo, propped up by the side mirror tucked under her armpit. A drizzle of blood oozed down from a hole in her head, dripping down her nose like a rivulet of slow honey. Her mouth hung open, slack.

Dead.

Wren, thrumming with adrenaline—

And fear—

And grief—

Tucked the pistol back into her pants and she ran, again, away from it all.

# 26. THE LEFT COAST

**But** this time, she did not run away from it all.

Rather, she ran toward something.

Destiny. Destiny was a stupid idea, she thought. Silly. Fate felt like a dumb idea for a dumb girl, but fuck it, she decided it was true anyway. As she sat on the bus cutting a line through the wheat and the corn of the heartland, headed west, she knew that she had a role to play yet, a job to do, and that job was to end the Caldecott bloodline for good. However she could, however she must. Eleanor and her children were gone, as was the monster, Carl Keener. Now Eliza Caldecott—Lissa, the liar—was gone, too. One last one remained. Eliza and Eleanor's brother, Emerson.

Her time with Eliza was regrettable, but now she knew: it was necessary.

Necessary to kill her.

And necessary to find the last brother.

And then, after that, Wren would be free. Though what that meant remained woefully unclear. She would blow that bridge up when she got to it.

Not-Miriam, the Parasite, sat next to her. Tongue in cheek, literally. She twirled a cigarette like it was a drumstick.

"Is there smoking on this bus?" the Parasite asked Wren, cheekily.

"Fuck off, Psy-cho."

"That's my girl. That's. My. Girl."

# ACKNOWLEDGMENTS

Delilah, Chuck, and Kevin would like to thank Tricia Narwani for her insightful edits, Richard Shealy for rigorous copy policing, and the inimitable Galen Dara for awesome cover art that strikes the perfect balance between deadly and sticky sweet. Power high five to Yanni Kuznia at Subterranean Press for shepherding the amazing print edition to fruition. And turbo mega thanks to our readers: You deserve all the royal jelly. Peace and tacos and fine whiskey unto thee.